I0579267

JUMPING JUDE

A MADE MARIAN NOVEL

LUCY LENNOX

Copyright © 2016 by Lucy Lennox

All rights reserved.

No part of this book may be reproduced in any form or by any electronic or mechanical means, including information storage and retrieval systems, without written permission from the author, except for the use of brief quotations in a book review.

Cover Designer: Angstyg - www.AngstyG.com

Editor: Hollie Westring - www.HollieTheEditor.com

✿ Created with Vellum

KEEP IN TOUCH WITH LUCY!

Join Lucy's Lair
Get Lucy's New Release Alerts
Like Lucy on Facebook
Follow Lucy on BookBub
Follow Lucy on Amazon
Follow Lucy on Instagram
Follow Lucy on Pinterest

Other books by Lucy:
Made Marian Series
Forever Wilde Series
Twist of Fate Series with Sloane Kennedy
After Oscar Series with Molly Maddox
Licking Thicket Series with May Archer
Virgin Flyer
Say You'll Be Nine

Visit Lucy's website at www.LucyLennox.com for a comprehensive list of titles, audio samples, freebies, suggested reading order, and more!

ABOUT JUMPING JUDE

Jude: Reaching the top of the country music charts brings out the crazy, and there's no one crazier than my ex. Unfortunately, his threats to out me are escalating. Enter the bodyguard of my dreams.

I'd probably chafe under his constant presence if his attention to my body wasn't so... ah... thorough. Now I have to worry about outing myself to millions of fans if I can't keep my hands off him in public.

Derek: Now I'm an ex-Marine turned babysitter. If I have to hear Jude sing his mega-hit Bluebells one more time, I might murder him myself, and after 6 years in special ops, I know my way around a weapon. Unfortunately, so does he. Except his arsenal includes washboard abs and a killer set of pipes.

I've faced guns, knives, explosives and yet it's Jude Marian who may end up bringing me to my knees.

Jumping Jude is dedicated to
Leslie Copeland
who made the revision process more fun than it should have been.
Jude and Derek's story is better because of you.

PROLOGUE - JUDE

I should have known the man guarding me that night was an idiot by his nickname alone. *Brick.* As in, "Dumb as a." He was just the latest in a long string of celebrity babysitters whose main job was to look intimidating to any overzealous fan who wanted a piece of me.

We left the dance club that night through the back entrance. Normally, my bodyguard would alert the driver before we walked out of the building so the car was waiting for us. In this case, Brick hadn't bothered. He was too busy trying to make up with his multiple girlfriends over the phone to be able to use the device for something as mundane as keeping me safe.

Once we exited into the dark alley and found no town car waiting, I took matters into my own hands, texting Carl to bring the car to the rear door of the club. Brick gave me a slight chin tilt of appreciation and wandered farther away to get some privacy while he kissed some ass over the phone.

That's when the three guys jumped me. They came out of nowhere. One minute I was standing there waiting for the car and the next I was knocked to the ground, greedy fingers reaching into pockets and meaty hands shoving my face into the pavement. A sharp knee drove into my back and a booted foot caught me in the hip. Motherfucking assholes.

It was over almost as quickly as it began. Three figures running into the night, past a shocked Brick who stood there gaping like an idiot.

Just then, Carl brought the car around. Would arriving one minute sooner have killed him? Jesus. I struggled to stand up, but my body rejected the idea. Never mind. I'd just lay there instead.

Once Brick had come to his senses, he'd admitted noticing those three guys eyeing me in the club earlier but had thought they were harmless. It was like the man had the instincts of a jellyfish.

A couple of days later, when I was patched up and over my initial shock, I paid a visit to my security company. The owner of On Your Six, Joel Healy, had the rare opportunity to be on the receiving end of my anger.

I never got angry. Ever. But I'd also never been jumped in an alley. Since the attack, I was easily spooked. If anyone walked into a room unexpectedly, I jumped or squeaked like a child. The fear left me feeling fragile and vulnerable which pissed me the hell off.

After screaming at Joel for assigning Brick in the first place, I demanded he get serious about assigning me someone permanent I could rely on to watch my back.

"Joel, he saw the guys watching me, and it didn't occur to him something was up. What the fuck? I'm paying you to protect me and I end up getting jumped by three men in an alley right in front of my own goddamned bodyguard?" I yelled. "Get me someone reliable and preferably not currently involved in a threesome relationship with the goddamned 49ers cheerleading squad!"

At this point several of the men who worked for Joel had found excuses to walk past the conference room. I'm sure seeing Jude Marian lose his ever-loving shit was something to write home about.

"I hear you, Jude, and I'm on it. I've already assigned Brick's replacement. He's here right now if you want to meet him. His name is Derek Wolfe and we served in the Marines together. He's the best.

The guy was special ops and has a knack for reading faces and body language," Joel said.

I let out a breath. Special ops. Good. That was reassuring. Not some regular club bouncer type, but a serious soldier who had combat training. Maybe I could go back to getting a full night's sleep again under the protection of someone like that.

"Okay. Let's meet him," I said, standing up.

Joel led me to the gym in the back of the warehouse office. Several men and women were there working out on the equipment and music pumped from somewhere in the room.

"Hey, guys," Joel called into the space. "Has anyone seen Wolfe?"

"Locker room," one man called back.

We headed to the locker room to find him. And boy did we find him.

The man was standing at a bench in front of his locker. Imagine the picture-perfect example of a Marine - towering height, muscles bulging everywhere, covered in tattoos and combat scars. This man was all of those things with one exception. His skin was pristine. There wasn't a single mark or scar that I could see. And I could see a lot. Miles and miles of lightly tanned skin, still wet from the shower and barely covered by the tiny towel at his hips.

Derek Wolfe was six and a half feet of pure delicious sex appeal. His body was a chiseled rock face and I wanted nothing more than to climb to the top.

Oh *shit*.

This was going to be a problem.

"Derek Wolfe, this is Jude Marian," Joel said. "Jude, this is Derek."

The man's face lit up in a sexy smirk as he reached out a hand to shake. This wasn't happening.

Get a grip, Jude. Jesus.

"Nice to meet you," he said. "I hear your new tour starts in a few days. Don't worry. I'm not going to let you out of my sight for the next six months."

1

———

DEREK - SIX MONTHS LATER

If I had to hear the song "Bluebells" one more fucking time, I thought I was going to vomit backstage before Jude even finished the first chord of the intro. I wanted someone to shoot me in the face. Give me a good old rendition of "Born to Be Wild" and I'd be a happy man. But I wasn't Steppenwolf's bodyguard. I was Jude's. Yes, *the* Jude of Jude and the Saints, three-time Grammy-winning country music superstar and total pain in my ass.

My head pounded, and I was ready to be done for the day. Unfortunately, the last song of the encore was usually when my night really heated up. As soon as the star himself stepped off the stage, it would be balls-to-the wall security threats until I practically tucked the little guy into his bed around 2 a.m.

This concert was a taste of freedom, landing us in our hometown for one night before the tour took us on the road again the following day. In three days' time, Jude and the Saints were going to be performing their final concert of the tour at the Hollywood Bowl. Finally. The tour had lasted six months, and I was so sick of the same damned songs. At least we'd have four or five months off before his manager, Clint, pressured him to go out on tour again.

Jude's personal assistant, Ollie, stood next to me with a small towel and an ice-cold bottle of water ready for Jude the minute he finished performing. She was one of my favorite people to hang out with during downtime because she was batshit crazy. Six feet tall and sporting hot-pink spiky hair, she was about as sassy as they came. Half of Jude's fans thought she was his girlfriend, but the two of them were really best friends from grade school. No, Jude's actual girlfriend was a piece of work, and not the good kind.

I could never remember the woman's name because it was something made up and stupid. Bentley? Barkley? Dandelion? Anyway, she was a wannabe country singer herself, and those of us paying attention could see she was one hundred percent using Jude as a stepping-stone to get into the business. Her singing skills were equivalent to Jim Carrey trying to sing *Evita*. It was pretty rough. Even money-hungry Clint wouldn't take her on as a client. And he was a sucker for a hot piece of ass.

The woman was what my dad would call a whole lotta nothin' wrapped up with a pretty bow. She was never there for Jude when he seemed to really need a friend, but she magically showed up if he needed someone to accompany him on a red carpet. His family despised her and pretty much pretended she didn't exist. The feeling was mutual.

When the man himself came jogging offstage, he was electrified. If I had just danced, played guitar, and sung under the hot stage lights for two hours, I'd be about ready for a cold beer and a recliner. Not this guy. Performing cranked all of Jude's switches to maximum. If I didn't know better, I'd think he was on drugs like so many other famous musicians. But he wasn't. He was a vegetarian health nut. The kind of weirdo who'd much rather have a green smoothie than a nice juicy burger.

Ollie handed Jude the towel and water as the three of us hustled back to the dressing room.

"How was it?" Jude asked Ollie. He knew better than to ask me. First of all, I was usually quiet and tried to be invisible. Second of all, I hated country music and he knew it.

"Great, baby cakes. How did it feel?" Ollie humored him.

"Amazing. I was exhausted before going out there, but they were a good crowd." He wiped the sweat off his face with the towel as we entered the room. I quickly closed the door behind us and stood in front of it to go over our plan for greeting the crowd after he showered and changed.

I began to speak as Jude pulled off his black boots, and I tried not to roll my eyes. Granted they were more like motorcycle boots than cowboy boots, but they still made him look like a poser. Jude was way more himself when he was wearing his red Converse sneakers. He was significantly shorter than I was and had the lean muscles of a runner. I'd heard people refer to him as petite, but that may have been due to the fact he was always seen standing next to me or someone my size. His long brown hair was thick and wavy and did rude things to the fit of my pants. I really thought he should get it cut off so I could concentrate on my fucking job.

"Jude, Clint has arranged for you to spend half an hour shaking hands in the lobby with a couple hundred select VIPs. They are allowed to ask for autographs and photos, but Clint wanted me to remind you to keep moving. Don't get stuck in a conversation with one person."

One of the things that drove me crazy about being Jude's personal bodyguard was his over-the-top friendliness with his fans. No one could be that nice in real life. He was all smiles and bubbly chitchat until he was alone. And then he was a quiet, sometimes brooding, artist.

I had never been able to reconcile the two Judes, and it frustrated me.

I continued, "After that, we will exit through the backstage loading door where the cars will be waiting. You have dinner with Lawrence Hammond and his family at El Manjar. Clint will meet you there with... what's her name," I finished.

Jude stripped off his sweaty T-shirt and I tried not to look at his bare upper body. *Eyes on the ceiling, Wolfe. Nothing to see here. You've seen his ripped chest and abs enough to reproduce them in your dreams every fucking night, so there is absolutely no need to look at them again. I* looked down at the very interesting hangnail on my index finger instead.

"Wolfe, I've been seeing her for months and you still don't know her name?" Jude asked. "Really?"

"Paisley?" I guessed.

Jude snorted as he began undoing the fly of his jeans. Holy mother of god, how was I going to continue talking to him while he was wrestling off tight pants? Things were jiggling, for god's sake. *Think of something else, Wolfe. Weeping sores, naked grandmas, anything. You can do this.*

"Not Paisley." Jude chuckled in his melodic voice. "But close. It's Jae."

"Like hell," I muttered under my breath.

Jude turned around and finished pulling his jeans off as he walked into the small bathroom, leaving on only a thin pair of royal blue boxer briefs. Not that I noticed, because I was totally doing triage on my fingernail problem.

"Wolfe, I'm counting on you to bust me out of that dinner as soon as humanly possible," he called back over his shoulder. "You know that guy always tries to set me up with his daughter even if Jae is there."

"Sure thing, boss," I called back to him, letting out a sigh of relief as he turned out of sight before revealing his perfect freaking ass. Jesus, I needed a shot of vodka.

I turned to look for a bottle of water instead and caught Ollie staring at me. "What?" I snapped.

She burst out laughing. "Oh, Wolfe. You don't fool me one single bit."

I looked at her with narrowed eyes. "What's that supposed to mean?" I asked, feeling my blood run cold and my stomach begin to knot. No way could she tell how much I was lusting after Judy's body. Could she?

"You know exactly what Jae's name is. No way in hell would you let someone that close to Jude without knowing every single thing about her." I felt my insides relax and I prayed it didn't include bowels loosening. The last thing I was expecting that night was a sudden outing after thirty-one years of being nice and cozy in the closet. "You just don't like her and you delight in reminding Jude every chance you get, don't you?"

I smiled a shit-eating grin at her. "Don't *you*?"

She laughed. "Hell yeah, you know I do. I hate that skank. But I also know better than to believe everything I see, Derek. Sometimes people aren't what you think they are. Be careful you don't fall into the trap of judging an apple by its skin."

I was just getting ready to tell her I thought she got that saying wrong when Jude came out of the bathroom dripping wet with only a small towel slung low around his hips. Goddammit. I needed hazard pay for this crap. If I wanted to pretend to ignore sexy men roaming around in their skivvies, I'd re-up in the damned Marines. Ollie handed me something out of her big bag.

"What's this for?" I asked, holding the fingernail clipper.

"Didn't you want to go back to fixing that pesky invisible hang-nail?" she asked. Shit.

"Never mind," I muttered, chucking it back in her bag.

I looked at my watch and turned back to Jude. "Put a spring in your step, Bluebell," I told him. "Time's a-wasting."

He finished buttoning his fresh blue jeans and slipped a crisp charcoal-gray button-down shirt over a faded Clint Black concert tee.

"Coming. Jesus, you'd think I work for you the way you boss me around sometimes," he muttered. "Let me just grab a banana. I'm starving."

I tossed him a banana from the bunch in the bowl on the coffee table and stuck a pack of peanuts in my pocket to tide me over through Jude's dinner meeting. I'd eaten something a few hours before, but I still had several more hours before I'd get a chance to sit down again and relax long enough to eat another meal.

Jude left the shirt unbuttoned and rolled up his cuffs before slipping the boots back on. I caught a whiff of his clean, soapy smell and hid a smile. I loved the way he smelled after he'd gotten out of the shower. It didn't matter what kind of soap he used, he always smelled like soapy Jude.

He peeled the banana and put his full lips around it to break off a piece. Anndd hell. I turned and put my hand on the doorknob to wait for the signal he was ready to go meet his fans. After months of lusting over the body of a person I didn't much care for, I was over it. Maybe I needed to request a new assignment. What danger was this guy really in anyway? Rabid teen fan tries to maul him with a permanent marker? Middle-aged woman tries to hug him to death? Not likely.

I felt a warm hand on my lower back, and the hairs prickled on the back of my neck.

"What's the holdup, He-Man? Let's go," Jude's teasing voice said from behind me.

2

JUDE

Derek Wolfe smelled good enough to lick. I stood close to him so I could smell the unique spicy scent of aftershave or deodorant that always surrounded him. He was six feet four inches of solid muscle mass waiting to pounce on anyone intending to do me harm. That thought took my breath away. Sometimes late at night I imagined his hot, taut body protecting me, fending off danger and gathering me up in his arms. It was my deepest fantasy, one whose bubble always seemed to burst as soon as the asshole opened his mouth.

So, fine, he was handsome in a military hero kind of way. He'd been a Navy SEAL or something like that before they put him on my detail. But Derek hated country music like it consisted of a cat in heat singing him to death one screeching cry at a time. Maybe I was exaggerating, but I had a feeling he would've liked me better had I been Mick Jagger or Bruce Springsteen singing about something red, white, and manly while women threw themselves at the stage.

None of this bullshit mattered because he was obviously G.I. Joe, all-American, boy-next-door straight, and, as far as almost everyone in the universe knew, so was I.

I silently gave myself hell for lusting after the bodyguard in the first place. I'd been celibate way too long if this big oaf was lighting my fire. He wasn't my type. Not sensitive and sweet. The brute's main goal in life was probably to bench-press a pickup truck. Clearly the only explanation for being attracted to this alpha male was my out-of-control libido after years of self-imposed celibacy. My horniness was off the charts. I needed to consider finding a way to get laid, but it always came back to one thing. I couldn't trust anyone not to out me to the press.

So I stopped peeking through the crack and silently slid my figurative closet door back to the closed and locked position before exiting the dressing room to meet the fans awaiting me. When I arrived in the lobby, I saw my bandmates already mingling. Our keyboardist, Sutter, was taking a photograph with a gaggle of teenaged girls. Beck, the percussionist and a guy who grew up next door to me, spoke animatedly to a group of people by the bar. Finally, I saw Joey, our bass guitarist, and Fiona, our other vocalist and strings player, walking my way from the direction of their dressing rooms behind me.

A PR handler came out of nowhere to lead me to the spot where fans had formed a line to meet me. As I signed autographs and took photos, I ended up speaking to a few fans longer than others.

There was one man in particular who tried to keep my attention a little too long. He was in his thirties and gushed about how I was his favorite singer. I was as friendly chatting with him as with anyone, but something about him put me on alert. He stood a little too close, and I kept backing off, keeping the smile on my face and trying not to look uncomfortable.

The slightest movement brushed my elbow, a touch I'd felt a hundred times before. Derek was reminding me to keep the line moving. We would never get out of there if I didn't speak to as many people as I could. Even though I'd felt it many times before, the light touch still gave me goose bumps.

"I'm sorry to do this, but I have to move the line along before people get too antsy. It was nice meeting you." I smiled and started to turn away before the man caught my hand in another shake and started to pull me toward him. Before he had a chance to put his other hand on me, Derek stepped quickly between us, pushing me behind him with one arm and putting his other hand gently against the man's chest.

"Sorry, sir. Handshakes only," he said in a calm, low voice.

The man grinned and put both of his hands up in an apologetic gesture, causing Derek to drop his arms and allow me to move back around him.

Before I could stop him, the man lunged at me, attempting to smack a kiss on my lips. It happened so quickly and unexpectedly, Derek barely got the guy off me before his mouth landed on mine. When he returned from dragging the guy to the exit, I could feel Derek's residual tension as if he wanted to go after the man again and teach him a lesson. I gave him a look that said, *Stand down, Marine.*

The fan had seemed sweet and sincere, if a little bit awkward. He'd laughed and apologized profusely as Derek dragged him away. Obviously he was just an overzealous fan. Stuff like that happened often enough. Still, the attempted kiss had left me with the heebie-jeebies.

A few minutes later I saw a familiar face in the crowd looking determined.

"Aunt Tilly?" I called out in surprise.

Her head swiveled, looking through the group of people around me until singling me out with her steely gaze.

"There you are," she said with a smile, nudging a few fans out of her way with her elbows and hips before moving to the front of the line. It was hard for them to complain about being taken advantage of by an eighty-year-old woman.

She caught sight of Derek behind me and her entire face turned predatory. "Well hello, there, hot stuff. Where have you been all my life?"

"Tilly, it's good to see you again," Derek answered.

I gave Aunt Tilly a big hug and kiss on the cheek. "This is a nice surprise. What are you doing here?"

"Your mom wanted me to bring you some food. Said she was worried about you. You know how she gets when she's stressed. I think Simone's wedding plans have pushed her over the edge," she said.

I looked at her empty hands. "Uh, where's the food?"

Tilly blinked at me and then looked at her own empty hands. "Well, fuck."

I heard Wolfe chuckle behind me.

"It's fine. I'm headed out to dinner next anyway. Do you want to come with us?" I asked.

"That depends. Who's going to be there?"

"Lawrence Hammond and his family. We're just discussing the charity event I'm helping him with."

"Larry? Hell no. That man's an insufferable bore. I might as well head down to my friend Janet's place. She said her seniors group is doing strip poker tonight. The game goes fast in summertime, but I planned ahead. Got all kinds of layers on under this," she said, pulling her sheer blouse out from her chest, revealing a sliver of a lace camisole underneath. "Gonna make those horny old bastards work for it."

I noticed the crowd getting antsy behind her and knew I needed to wrap it up.

"Aunt Tilly, I have to keep working here but you have fun, okay? Be safe, and I'll see you at the wedding. Is your driver around here somewhere?" I asked.

"Oh crap. He's in the red zone. I should probably go. You got a hundred bucks I can borrow?"

I couldn't help but bark out a laugh before reaching back to pull out my wallet. I fished out two large bills and handed them to her. "Don't spend it all in one place, crazy girl."

"Thanks, sweetie," she said before turning to the man behind me. "Wolfe, always a pleasure."

"Keep your pants on out there Tilly," he said through a grin.

"That's the plan, gorgeous."

The rest of the reception went by quickly. I shook hands, gave hugs, and took selfies with people despite my shaking hands. Derek did his usual ignoring trick when people asked him if he could take a picture. He pretended to be deaf, blind, and stupid until they gave up with a shrug. I kept telling him one of these days I was going to get him a selfie stick so he could at least offer the poor fans another option when he refused them.

The band exited the facility without incident before making our way to the Spanish restaurant for dinner. On the way there, Clint told me that someone named Ari Crowe kept trying to get in touch with me through my publicist's office, insisting he was an old friend whom I would want to speak with. He asked if Ari was someone I wanted to contact directly. I cringed at the thought of talking to an ex after all these years, but I ultimately told Clint Ari wasn't anyone important.

Once inside, a hostess led us to a private room with a large dining table. Lawrence Hammond, the CEO of CleoTech, was already standing with a cocktail in his hand when we entered. He reintroduced us to his wife, Debbie, and twenty-five-year-old daughter, Chelsea, whom I had met several times. That night was the first time, however, Chelsea's brother Adam was with them. He worked for Doctors Without Borders and was always out of the country when I ran into his family at charity events. Clint was the one to introduce me to Adam before we were seated.

When I reached out to shake his hand, I noticed he was attractive in a boy-next-door way. Friendly, open face and a genuine smile when he met me.

"I've heard so much about you from my family, Jude. It's nice to finally meet you. I know you do lots of good work for the charities my parents are involved in," Adam said.

"Finally I get to meet the elusive Hammond son who is always off saving the world," I said with a smile.

"Nah, more like saving myself from attending so many of my parents' charity galas. I had to go to med school to get out of wearing a tux every weekend and making small talk over hors d'oeuvres." He laughed. "Don't get me wrong, I fully support the organizations. I just don't like the monkey suits."

"I don't blame you. I'm not even their son, yet your parents manage to wrangle me to most of them. Maybe I've been taking your place all this time, and you need to come back and save me," I teased. Adam winked at me, and suddenly we were flirting with each other. Not okay. I gave him a polite smile and turned to include the rest of the family in our conversation.

Once we sat down, I realized, once again, Chelsea was seated next to me. I wondered where the hell Jae was. Ollie had decided to hang out in the limo with her laptop instead of suffering through the small talk of one of these dinners. She would watch *Game of Thrones* or catch up on some social media posting on my accounts while the driver no doubt catered to her every whim. Ollie had a tendency to wrap everyone she met around her little finger, including me.

Chelsea was in the middle of telling me a particularly non-riveting story about clubbing several nights before with Miley Cyrus when I discreetly made eye contact with Derek where he stood by the door to the private dining room. I tugged my earlobe. He carefully looked from my hand gesture to my salad plate and rolled his eyes. That was Derek-speak for, *You dumbass, you can't leave before the entree.*

I opened my eyes wider and tugged my ear again. *Jesus, do something or I'll surely die.*

Derek twisted his tongue in his mouth and clamped down, his signature look for trying to hold in a laugh. I ground my back teeth together in frustration, which egged him into a cough-covered laugh. He made as if to excuse himself from the room to get his coughing under control and two minutes later I heard my phone ring.

"I'm so sorry," I said, standing up and reaching for my pocket. "Maybe this is my girlfriend calling to let me know where she is. Please excuse me."

I made my way out of the room and down the restroom corridor behind Derek. He stopped and turned around to face me, finally letting himself have a few open laughs at my expense. "Fuck you," I told him. "Do you hear the made-up shit she's spinning about clubbing with random-ass celebrities? Jesus. Doesn't she realize those are people I know? Miley has been on tour in Asia for a month."

Derek quirked an eyebrow at me. "And?"

I wanted to lay my forehead against his chest and be still for a minute, but of course I couldn't. "And I'm tired. I want to go home and get into my own bed. I've been waiting months, Wolfe. Can't you do something?"

Derek put his hands on my shoulders and leaned his head down to look into my eyes. "One more hour, Bluebell, and I'll get you out of here, okay? You can do it. Chin up. Only a couple more nights of this tour and then we're off to your sister's wedding in Napa."

"Ugh." I sighed. I made my way to the men's room, letting Derek go in ahead of me and check it out before leaving to wait in the hallway. After I finished washing my hands and was walking back to the dining room, I heard Derek say something. I turned to look at him.

"What?" I asked.

"Paisley was spotted at a club with her girlfriends a few minutes ago. Ollie texted to tell me. I guess that means she's not coming. Sorry, Jude."

I cursed. "Why did Ollie text you instead of me?" I didn't care about Jae more than my wish to have someone there to take some of the attention off me with the Hammond family. Nothing she did surprised me anymore. Her ability to maximize selfishness and minimize inconvenience was truly impressive. She had agreed to act as a girlfriend for me in exchange for help meeting people in the industry and being seen around town on my arm. I guess that only lasted until she found the newest rising star.

Thank god she didn't know the truth behind our little arrangement. She thought I needed her in order to keep my real girlfriend's identity a secret from the media. There was one thing Jae was not, and that was bright.

"I guess Ollie was worried about your reaction in mixed company."

"Great," I muttered before walking back into the dining room. "Goddamned Jae."

When I returned to the table, Lawrence finally brought up the charity project I'd agreed to participate in, and the reason for our dinner meeting. The auction was in Nashville the following night, and he wanted to personally thank me for helping draw attendance to the event. Most people in my position were auctioned off as dates, but I had known that was a recipe for disaster in my case. It had taken some negotiating, but in the end I had agreed to be auctioned off for a two-hour private guitar lesson. The lesson would take place the day after the auction, before we left Nashville for our final concert in LA.

3

———

DEREK

Immediately after dessert I announced Jude and the band had to leave because they had a fan event the following morning. Joey and Fiona looked at me like I was a god while Beckett looked like he was ready to contradict me. He knew better, but I made serious eyes at him anyway to get him to zip it.

Jude said goodbye to everyone in the family, politely thanking the Hammonds for including him in their charity plans. When he got to Chelsea, I could see a potential problem so I bumped Jude's shoulder "accidentally" just before Chelsea's arms were set to go around him. When he stumbled, I steadied him, discreetly placing him a good foot and a half farther away from Chelsea's reach. It was just enough to make trying to embrace him again awkward.

That was a move I'd done for Jude many times over the months. It seemed so blatant, I was shocked no one ever called me on it. Jude said it was because I did a good job impersonating a bumbling oaf. I didn't appreciate his opinions.

What I didn't expect was the exact same embrace attempt coming from Adam. It came out of left field and caught me unaware. Jude was used to being hugged, but when it happened unexpectedly, I could sense him tense up in fear for the briefest of moments. I kicked myself for not anticipating the move, especially after what had happened earlier that night. I hadn't been expecting it because Adam was the son of one of Jude's philanthropist friends. And a guy. Jesus, how stupid was that logic?

After Adam's awkward hug, we walked out of the restaurant, Jude giving quick goodbyes to the band members he'd see the following day. We settled into the limo with Ollie, and I was finally able to sit and relax. I took the pack of peanuts out of my pocket and began eating them, glancing out the window at the lights of San Francisco all around us.

Ollie talked softly to Jude, but I noticed Jude watching me instead of her. I raised an eyebrow at him wondering if he needed something.

"You're hungry? Why didn't you say something at the restaurant?" he asked me.

"Uh, because you're not my mom," I replied, more rudely than I'd intended.

"You could have ordered something to go," he said.

"I brought the peanuts from the dressing room so I wouldn't have to. In case you didn't notice, entrees at that restaurant started at sixty bucks, Jude. The peanuts were free. Big difference. The frozen dinner waiting for me at home is practically free too. If I steal one from your place before going home, then it really is free," I teased.

"I would have paid for your dinner. You were on the clock anyway."

"Yes, I was on the clock. Exactly why I didn't stop to indulge in a little paella. Instead I was protecting your paella-eating ass, remember?" I smiled to let him know I was joking. He still looked concerned. "Jude, it's my job. It's what you pay me to do. Would you eat dinner while you were singing on stage?"

"Of course not," he replied. "But you've been on the clock for over twelve hours. I'm never on stage for more than three."

"Please let it go. We're almost back to your place. I'm fine."

He turned back to Ollie to continue discussing something about the event the following day. I finished the peanuts and put the wrapper in my pocket. When we pulled through the gatehouse onto

Jude's property, Ollie disappeared into her apartment over the garage and I headed to my car for the drive back to my place.

Before I got into the car I looked back to where Jude was standing by the door from his driveway into his kitchen.

"Jude?" I asked.

He turned to me, long hair following in an arc. "Yeah?"

"I'm sorry about tonight. About earlier, I mean."

His forehead crinkled in confusion. "What do you mean, Wolfe?"

"That crazy fan at the VIP thing. I should have seen it coming and stopped it sooner," I said.

Jude let out a laugh. "Oh, you mean that guy who tried to kiss me? Don't be sorry, that's the closest I've come to getting any action in years. Night, Wolfe."

He turned and entered his house, leaving me to wonder what in the hell that meant when he'd been seeing his girlfriend for months.

THE FOLLOWING day Jude's driver delivered him to the airport and I met them at the drop-off. We had a VIP escort through the airport to the boarding door of the plane. Because it was just the two of us traveling to Nashville, we flew commercial. Jude wore his long hair tied back under a worn baseball cap, and he had on sunglasses in an effort to be inconspicuous. When we got on board the airplane and found our seats in first class, I had Jude take the window seat. He looked down at his phone to keep prying eyes from recognizing him. He was a nervous flyer, and takeoffs scared him the worst.

He wore a plain white T-shirt and an old faded pair of blue jeans. I could smell the soap scent coming off him and fought the urge to lean a little closer to smell it.

"You didn't bring your guitar," I said. "How are you going to give the lesson without it?"

"Gibson is headquartered in Nashville so they're donating some guitars. I'll sign one for the winner of the lesson. Since I usually play on a vintage Fender, I didn't want to step on Gibson's toes by bringing it while they're being so generous to the charity this week."

"I guess the winner will be thrilled to get a signed Gibson in addition to the lesson. What's the charity?"

"The auction is primarily benefitting a pediatric cancer organization, but Lawrence Hammond has pledged to match each donation for an equivalent one to the charity of the celebrity's choice. So if my lesson goes for a thousand dollars, a thousand goes to the children's cancer group and another thousand goes to my charity. It's a great way to get celebrities on board for the auction."

"What charity did you choose?" I asked, expecting him to rattle off something expected, like a children's hospital or the animal shelter he normally donated to in San Francisco.

"Wounded Warriors," Jude said before looking back down at his phone.

I looked at him in surprise. "Really? Why them?"

Jude's knee began bouncing up and down. I wanted to put a hand on it to stop the nervous gesture but didn't. He stopped what he was doing and looked at me.

"You," he said.

I sat there frozen for a minute in disbelief before finally speaking. "Me? What do you mean me?"

"Don't you volunteer for them?" Jude asked.

"Well, yes, but I didn't realize you knew that," I said, stunned.

"You received the Bronze Star and were seriously injured on a mission. I assumed that's why you supported them so actively."

"How the hell do you know all that?"

"Wolfe, do you really think I'm going to have someone working this close to me every day without learning a little bit about them? I know about your time in Afghanistan."

I was temporarily speechless. We'd never spoken of my time in the military or what I'd been through before working for Joel as a bodyguard. I turned in my seat to make eye contact with him.

"Thanks, Jude," I said. "That means a lot to me. And you donating to the organization does too. There are so many men and women who need their help."

"I sent them a check already too, but I'd love for my guitar lesson to bring in some good visibility. We'll see what happens. Maybe no one will want to buy a lesson with me, and it'll all be for nothing." He chuckled.

"Want to place a bet on that?" I asked with a snicker.

"Shut up. Don't think I don't know what you're doing." Jude reached down to his bag to pull out a hoodie. He was always cold, especially on airplanes, and had about a million hoodies.

"What am I doing?" I asked.

"You're trying to distract me from getting freaked out about take-off. You do it every time we fly." Jude offered me a genuine smile. "It's very nice of you, actually."

I laughed. "Well if you don't need me to distract you then, I might as well go back to listening to my music."

"What are you listening to?" he asked.

"Guns 'n Roses," I said.

He let out a laugh as the plane began its acceleration down the runway. "I should have known," he said, clutching the armrests on either side of him. I knew in a minute he'd squeeze his eyes closed and make whatever deal with whatever god he believed in to keep the plane safe in the air.

LATER THAT EVENING we made our way to the charity auction in downtown Nashville with Jude dressed in a tuxedo and me in a dark suit. I stood against the ballroom wall near wherever he happened to be mingling and kept a general eye on him. The crowd at an event like this one was usually well behaved and didn't include crazy fans who would mob Jude for attention.

In general, my job was to protect Jude from being mobbed, embarrassed, hassled, or otherwise impeded. I was always on my toes in public, constantly sweeping for threats. But at these smaller functions, I had more time to appreciate just how easily and confidently Jude interacted with people.

He was heavily involved in charity work and had attended many of these highbrow fundraisers in the past. In several of the tour stop cities, there had been a charity event like this that would beg Jude's participation. He was usually ready and willing with a tux and a large donation. Until our conversation on the plane, I'd always wondered if it was for show or if he really cared about the groups he was helping.

As he worked the crowd, Jude seemed to shine. I overheard several conversations where he described both the research the pediatric cancer group was doing with their funding as well as the Combat Stress Recovery Program Wounded Warriors provided. Instead of the exhausted, burned-out singer who was at the end of a six-month tour, he appeared to be an enthusiastic evangelist for the evening's charities. My respect for him grew as I overheard him speaking with conviction.

The organizer for the auction came to give Jude a five-minute warning to head to the backstage area, and I saw him smile his thanks to her. As he began to excuse himself from the group of people he'd been speaking to, his eyes swept the crowd. Before his head came all the way around to where I stood, he must have seen something or someone he recognized because his entire body froze in a tense rigor.

My senses went on high alert and I pushed myself off the wall to stride over to him.

"Jude?" I asked quietly from over his shoulder. He jumped at the sound of my voice and he turned to me, white as a sheet.

Lines creased his forehead and he looked almost... scared or nervous.

"What is it? What's happening?" I asked.

"Wha—? Uh, nothing. It's fine," he said, looking around again.

I put my hand on his elbow and began to lead him to the gathering area for the auction celebrities.

"Bullshit," I said into his ear. "What did you see that spooked you?"

He didn't answer me, his head swiveling behind us in search of whatever or whoever it was.

"Dammit, Jude, talk to me. Do we need to leave? You look like you just saw an escaped python heading right toward you."

He finally looked at me as we arrived at the event organizer checking in celebrities with a clipboard.

"No, it's fine. I thought I saw someone I knew a long time ago when I lived here. It's nothing. Just took me by surprise, that's all."

Like hell that was all, but it wasn't my place to argue with him. He checked in and waited for his turn on stage.

Because Jude was one of the more famous celebrities at the event, his guitar lesson was close to the end of the auction. While we waited, he mingled with others waiting for their turn on stage. The man knew almost everyone and seemed to relax after talking to them for a while. By the time he was called to the stage, he appeared to have forgotten the python in the ballroom.

4

JUDE

Ari fucking Crowe. I knew it was him. As I looked around the ball-room for Derek, my eyes landed on Ari and I felt like I'd been zapped with a stun gun. Seeing his face in that room was like feeling a sharp claw take a swipe at my heart. Six years of healing erased in the blink of an eye. There I was back again in the dingy roadhouse with peanut shells scattered on the floor, hearing the man I thought I'd be with forever tell me I wasn't ever going to amount to anything and sure as shit wasn't worth coming out of the closet for. He'd decided our two-year relationship had all been a big waste of his time.

Within a couple of months he was engaged to his high school sweetheart, the daughter of one of the richest, most conservative politicians in Nashville. They'd been married in a big society wedding while I was recording the song I'd written after our breakup. "Bluebells" went on to debut at number one on the charts and stayed in that spot for months. The band catapulted overnight from a Nashville club favorite to the Grammy-award-winning group it was today.

The six years since I last saw Ari had been quick and wildly successful for me. On the outside I'd looked like a man whose dreams and hard work had finally come to fruition, but on the inside I'd been shattered, feeling like I would never again feel the touch of loving hands on my body. I'd thrown everything I had into becoming the best at what I did, and I'd hoped like hell the stardom would somehow mitigate my broken inner confidence.

While we were together, Ari and I had stayed in the closet for several reasons, mainly his family and my career. When he'd dumped me, he'd made it clear our relationship would forever stay locked away in that closet for both of our sakes. His Nashville high society could never know, and the world wasn't going to fully accept a gay country music singer anyway. Our shared history seemed to evaporate, disappearing like a morning mist. One minute we were thinking about engagement rings and the next I was staring at a half-empty apartment.

I heard Derek calling my name, but I couldn't move or speak. Was I imagining Ari there in that ballroom? Had it been real? Why hadn't it occurred to me he would be at a black-tie event in Nashville? How could I have been so stupid?

Derek's hand guided me somewhere and I blindly accompanied him, my brain clicking through years of memories, feelings, and ultimately, the same old questions. How could you up and leave someone like that? Why did he walk away from me?

I rubbed my hands over my face and tried to focus on what I needed to do next. Luckily I was distracted with many familiar faces backstage and I did my best to fake it through some small talk.

By the time my name was called, I'd had enough of a distraction to put on my game face. I wasn't there as Jude Marian, starving artist mooning over Ari Crowe six years ago. I was there as Jude of Jude and the Saints, multimillionaire and Grammy-winning superstar. If there was one thing I'd perfected since I'd seen Ari last, it was performing for strangers—putting on a mask and becoming someone else on stage. I tucked my heart back into its familiar lockbox and strode confidently up onto the stage.

"Next up we have a VIP private guitar lesson given by none other than Jude of Jude and the Saints." The announcer introduced me and gave the rah-rah about my success and how I started playing guitar when I was a toddler. It was a bit of an exaggeration but true to some extent. Instruments had come easy to me from a very early age, and guitar was no exception.

The crowd in the room was rapt with attention, and I gave them my best heart-stopping smile. I picked up one of the Gibson guitars displayed behind me and tuned it. Momentarily catching sight of Derek behind the stage, I found myself idly strumming the acoustic intro to "Sweet Child o' Mine" by Guns N' Roses before realizing what I was doing and transitioning into the popular riff from our song "Startin' From Scratch." As people began bidding, I lightly plucked out little recognizable acoustic riffs and country licks from popular songs, trying to encourage people to keep bidding.

I looked up from the strings to smile at the audience and saw Ari lift up his paddle to bid. My fingers tripped over the chords and quickly fell back on the most familiar muscle memory of all, "Blue-bells." *Goddammit*. Of all songs, that was the one I never wanted to play in his presence. But I was on autopilot. I knew my smile had faltered and I tried desperately to put my public mask back on.

The bidding finally winnowed down to two bidders. Ari was bidding against a familiar looking man, maybe a fan or bigwig I'd met before. Every time the man raised his bid, Ari upped it. Finally the man gave up with a frustrated grumble, and Ari won with a bid of $32,000. I was stunned, both at the value of my guitar lesson and at the fact Ari had just donated money for the opportunity to see me for two hours the following day. I was going to have to spend time with Ari Crowe.

My stomach planned a revolt, and I couldn't feel my fingers. I felt like everyone in the ballroom knew my secret. Ari's eyes were laser-focused on me from across the room. I tried to remain neutral, not giving away my recognition of him.

After I exited the stage, Derek approached me to lead me to the table where I would meet with the winning bidder to arrange the details of our meeting the following day. I shook and thought I might vomit.

"Wolfe, where's the men's room?" I asked quietly. He looked at me with concern.

"You okay?" Derek asked, gesturing to the coordinator we'd be back in a minute. He led me out of the room and down the hall to the bathroom.

"No," I breathed. "Not okay."

He swept the bathroom quickly, and I entered behind him to splash some cold water over my face. Derek's hand came down warm and strong on my back while he held some paper towels ready for me with his other hand.

"You going to tell me what's going on, Bluebell?" he asked.

I thought about confiding in him but realized this wasn't something he should have to deal with. If I was going to succumb to my own feelings of worthlessness, wouldn't it be better to go it alone instead of having a witness?

"Maybe I'm coming down with something," I lied.

5

DEREK

No doubt about it, something had gotten to Jude.

"I'll be fine," he mumbled as he straightened his tux jacket and combed his hair with his fingers.

"Let's just go make the arrangements and then head back to the hotel. Do you think it's a good idea to go to Puckett's?" I asked. He'd made plans with some of his old friends to meet up at the popular bar in Leiper's Fork to play for a bit after the auction.

He'd lost his sparkle again and looked exhausted. "No, probably not."

"Come on," I said, opening the men's room door and peering out into the hallway before waving him through ahead of me.

When we arrived back at the coordinator's table, the man who'd won the auction was waiting. The small hairs on the back of my neck stood up when I saw the way the man looked at Jude.

"Jude," the man said with a giant smile before stepping forward to hug Jude. Jude's entire body went rigid, so I put a hand out to stop the man before he embraced Jude. The unofficial rule about hugging a celebrity was it was acceptable if the star wanted to hug someone but not the other way around. Usually people were polite and asked permission first. Jude almost always said yes.

When the man looked up at me in surprise, I gave him my usual calm face and low voice. "Sorry, sir. Handshakes only."

"It's okay. Jude and I are old friends. Right, Bubba?" he asked with a genuine smile.

Jude said quietly to the man, "Ari, let's make arrangements for tomorrow, then we can talk in the hallway."

I wondered who this guy was. Jude obviously knew him, but it seemed to be throwing him. The way he was reacting to the man made it clear there was a history between them.

As the man gave his contact information to the woman at the table, I committed it to memory so I could get a background check before morning. He was a local named Ari Crowe. I quickly shot off a text to my office, requesting as much information as they could dig up on him.

After the coordinator told Ari when and where to meet with Jude the following day, the man acted like he was going to step forward and hug Jude again, and everything in my gut told me to stop him. I stepped forward again and the man stopped and put his hands up in a conciliatory gesture. "Okay. I'll meet you out in the hall."

"You going to tell me who this guy is, Jude?" I asked quietly after he walked away. Jude looked everywhere but at my face.

"Just an old friend from when I lived in Nashville years ago. I'm going to find somewhere to have a private conversation with him. He's fine, Wolfe."

"If he's fine, then why are you acting strangely?" I asked.

His eyes narrowed as he finally made eye contact with me. The warm brown eyes I knew so well were glinty with steel. "None of your business, He-Man. I said I'm fine. You can leave me alone while I talk to an old friend, all right?"

Without waiting for my response, he strode over to the guy and led him to the corridor where we'd entered. I followed at a distance, trying to balance respecting his privacy with keeping him safe. I certainly wasn't going let him out of my sight.

When they entered the hallway, I stayed by the ballroom doors to make sure no one interrupted them. They continued far enough down the hallway so they were out of earshot. Not that it mattered, because they were speaking at low volume to keep their conversation private even from me.

As they spoke, I realized how well I had come to learn Jude's body language since I'd been guarding him. He was wound up tight in addition to the exhaustion plaguing him. I could picture him finally reaching his limit and collapsing right there on the carpeted floor.

Every time the man reached for him, Jude's body tensed further until I wanted nothing more than to make up an urgent excuse and hustle him out of there. It was so obvious to me that he didn't like this, and it was making me crazy just standing there doing nothing. I could feel my back teeth grinding against each other.

Jude shook his head emphatically. The man leered at him like he was a slice of cake. The look was almost feral. Finally Jude threw up his hands at the guy in frustration and started to turn back toward me to return to the ballroom. The man grabbed him and pulled him into a tight hug.

Suddenly I was the one uncomfortable, and as I felt bile rise up my throat, I recognized it as jealousy. That was *my* Jude. As ridiculous as it sounded even to myself, I had been practically living with him all day every day for months. I was in charge of watching over his very body. Nobody got to touch him without my permission. Did that sound overly possessive and Neanderthal of me? Sure. But it was an actual logistical fact. Usually. Not today, apparently. I tried to respect Jude's request for some space to talk to this old "friend." But he sure didn't look like just a friend anymore.

He looked like something more than that. The way he held on to Jude was equally possessive as the way I felt about Jude. More than friends. Sexual possession, or at the very least attraction.

Jude began to relax into the embrace, and I felt like I was intruding. My gut was sour and I felt like I should turn away. Next, the guy lowered his hands to Jude's ass. Just as I was about to freak out on Jude's behalf, Jude straightened and pushed the guy away. Thank god.

Realization dawned. It wasn't the shove of a straight guy fending off advances from a gay guy. It was the resistance of something familiar, comfortable. Like an old lover.

Jesusfuckingchrist.

Was it possible Jude Marian was gay?

6

JUDE

I felt blindsided. Ari acted like we'd never been apart. Like he'd never told me I was nothing.

"Bubba, can we go somewhere private to talk?" he asked.

"Don't call me that. And we are someplace private, so talk," I said.

"I mean someplace truly private. Like your hotel room." His eyes held a sparkle of desire and my desperate dick started responding against my will out of sheer habit from being near Ari after all this time.

"No. That's not happening. I'll see you tomorrow for the guitar lesson, Ari," I ground out, trying my best to remain neutral and not show him how affected I was by his physical presence.

"Please, Bubba, I really just want to talk. I've missed you. Haven't you missed me too?"

"No, I haven't. And I don't believe you really have either. What's going on?"

"I've been thinking about you and wanted to reconnect. Plus, my company is pressuring me to sign you as a new investment client so I was hoping to set up a meeting with you while you were in town. I heard you were going to be here so I thought it would be good timing.

Not that I wouldn't mind sleeping together for old times' sake," he winked. "You look hot as shit and I'd love back in that ass."

"Jesus, Ari. You want me to hire you as my investment manager?" I said, starting to lose my patience over the blatant flirting. I could only hold off the temptation to give in to him for so long. The aforementioned ass had spent a lonely six years without him.

"Yes, but I really do want to sleep with you too. I can't even think standing here in front of you like this. Brings back dirty memories." Ari looked at me like I was in his lusty crosshairs, and I worried that anyone who saw him would know immediately there was sexual history between us.

"No. I don't want that," I lied. "Any of it. I'll see you tomorrow."

"Your body is saying otherwise," he teased with a laugh. "Seriously, though, Jude, my firm just spent thirty grand to get your attention. At least give us a meeting."

"Not a chance," I replied. "Thank you for the donation, but that's all it is."

Ari gave me a tender smile, reminding me of the better times we'd had. Not the last time, when his words were like needle pricks to my self-esteem. "Tomorrow then?" he asked, alluding to our guitar lesson.

Damn it.

I threw up my arms and turned around to leave. Before I had a chance to escape, he was holding me in an embrace. I tried to resist, but then my body recognized the feel of his, and I was flooded with memories of lazy days naked against him, hours spent memorizing every inch of his body. My own body betrayed me by relaxing in his arms for a moment. I felt Ari's hands move to my ass. Remembering we were in public, I shoved him off and turned to walk away.

That's when I saw the look on Derek's face.

Oh shit.

Hold it together, Jude. Don't lose your composure until you get into your hotel room alone. I could feel myself trembling, so I overcompensated by putting on a fake cheerful facade.

"You ready, Wolfe?"

His eyes searched mine and I could see the concern in them. I tried to fill my own with a pleading to leave me alone. Derek must have gotten the message because he nodded and led me to the exit. Before stepping into the town car, I felt his hand land on my back. The warm feeling of physical touch made my eyes sting, and I began subconsciously counting down the seconds until I could be alone.

In the car I closed my eyes and leaned my head back against the seat. I felt the heat of Derek's powerful thigh next to mine, and his spicy scent drifted through the backseat with us. The desire to lean over and put my head on his shoulder was unbearable.

By the time we pulled up in front of the hotel, I had my arms crossed in front of my stomach and gripped my opposite forearms to keep them to myself. My teeth hurt from clamping my mouth closed, and my head was beginning to pound. Derek was even quieter than usual as we made our way up to the suite.

As soon as I entered the suite, I made my way to my bedroom and closed the door for the night. Derek stood looking after me, but I couldn't bear to meet his eyes and see concern, pity, or any other supportive look on his face.

After a long shower, I fell into my bed. My mind raced with speculation and dread. What did Ari want? He couldn't really want to get together for a quick fuck, could he? Was this just about managing my money? I had deliberately avoided seeking any information about him over the years, because there was no reason to pour salt into old wounds. Maybe I should do an Internet search on his name and see what I could find out.

I typed into the browser on my phone to see what I could find on Ari Crowe. All I learned besides his connection to the wealthy and powerful Crawford family he'd married into was his role as a senior investment manager for a financial company. No doubt a company primarily tasked with babysitting his father-in-law's poultry fortune. There were photographs of Ari and his wife, Britta, at Nashville society galas and a ribbon-cutting ceremony for a community center. If Ari had been involved in charity work before tonight's auction, it was a surprise to me. He'd never really been the type to focus on helping others.

I finally crashed around midnight but only stayed asleep for a couple of hours. I woke up and threw on a sweatshirt over my pajama bottoms before putting my earbuds in to listen to the instrumentals for a new song I'd written. I wandered through my room out into the common area of the suite, singing the lyrics softly.

I wasn't looking up when I came around the corner to the kitchen area and ran right into Derek's massive body. I screamed and ripped off my headphones, scrambling backward until I hit a wall.

"Jesus *Christ*," I shouted, in complete freak-out mode. My breathing hitched from the adrenaline spike.

Derek held out his hands to keep me from tumbling to the floor, his fingers grabbing my biceps. "Shit, Jude. I'm so sorry. I didn't mean to scare you."

My chest heaved and I struggled to catch my breath. "The fuck are you doing?" Derek was dressed in his T-shirt and boxers. His muscular legs were bare, and my heart began to hammer even harder.

"Uh, just getting some water," he said. "Are you okay?"

Derek looked so stricken I wanted to reassure him. "I'm fine. I just didn't know you were up."

"I'm sorry," Derek said again, looking down at his bare feet. "Want me to leave you in peace?"

"No. Not at all." I tried to give him a reassuring smile.

"What were you singing?" he asked. "One of the new ones?"

I took a few breaths to calm down before answering. "Yeah. It's called "Broken-Down Bus." I'm still working on getting it right," I told him, proceeding to the refrigerator to grab a bottle of juice now that I'd regained control of myself.

"What's it about?" Derek asked, rubbing his hands over his face as if to wake up.

"You remember my brother Jamie was left at the altar a few months ago?"

"Yes, I also remember trying to stop a million Marian men from going on a revenge quest," he replied.

"Right, well, I was more worried about what poor Jamie must have been going through. Can you imagine that feeling of rejection and betrayal? It would kill me."

"I can't imagine someone leaving you like that, Jude. They'd have to be crazy."

A blush heated my face. I knew he was referring to my wealth and fame, but it still felt nice to hear. If only he knew. "Thanks. Anyway, on my flight to the next tour city after that, I started hearing this tune in my head. I imagined Jamie on an old bus heading home to Alaska by himself to hide out in his cabin and maybe find someone else to help him heal.

"But heartbreak is a solitary pain," I continued. "In my imagination, the bus broke down before he could get into someone's comforting arms, leaving him feeling let down all over again. Like hitting rock bottom, you know?"

I felt Derek's eyes on me like he was looking right into my soul as he spoke. "The broken-down bus is a metaphor for the heart. When it breaks down, you can't just leave it on the side of the road. You have to fix it before you can move on."

My heart raced as I heard my innermost thoughts come out of his mouth. "Exactly," I said.

Derek looked at me for a few beats. "And do you listen to your own lyrics?"

I couldn't sit still under that searing gaze. It was as though he knew everything about me and could see every weakness I had. I didn't *want* him to see my weaknesses.

I shrugged and stood up, depositing the empty juice bottle into the trash under Derek's watchful gaze.

I looked at him before leaning against the counter. "Some busses can't be fixed, Wolfe. They're just fucking broken, and they'll never be able to get anyone anywhere ever again."

Silence thrummed like the beat of a bass guitar until Derek broke it.

"Bullshit. Sometimes you just have a shitty passenger and need to kick them out for good. Tell me who Ari is, Jude."

7

———

DEREK

Jude had always been jumpy, so it killed me when I was the one who accidentally spooked him in the kitchenette. If there was anyone besides his family who he should never have to fear, it was me.

Before he'd seen me in the suite's common area, he'd been singing a song that was heartbreaking. The silky sound of his voice turned the lyrics into roots that grew around my very soul. There was no accompanying music, just his voice drifting throughout the suite. I would have tried to alert him to my presence had I not wanted so desperately to hear him continue singing.

I'd never really admitted to myself there were times I liked Jude's songs, but when I heard him singing that night in his pajamas, I finally did. I loved the singing he did when he was alone, not realizing anyone was listening. There was something raw about the way he sang when he was by himself. I'd overheard him many times in the months I'd known him. Times when he'd forgotten I was in the background or didn't realize I was around the corner.

I wasn't a fan of country music necessarily, but the man himself had a stunning set of pipes. Sometimes I'd catch him singing other kinds of songs. Once, I overheard him singing the Leonard Cohen song "Hallelujah" and it blew me away. He was alone in his hotel room with his acoustic guitar, and I was in the common area just outside his door. I stood stock-still and felt that song all the way into the very marrow of my bones. His voice was haunting and raised goose bumps all over my skin. I caught myself looking around, stunned there wasn't anyone else there to witness that incredible moment besides me.

Another time I was waiting in his dressing room after a concert, and he was in the shower singing "Ruby Tuesday" by the Stones. He was still pumped up from the concert and I could hear the energy in his voice. I imagined him dancing around the shower with the beaming smile he usually had when he came off stage.

Jude Marian was a pretty quiet man behind closed doors. I wouldn't necessarily call him shy, but he was quieter than you'd imagine. At first I had assumed it was a result of giving all his energy to his fans, but then I learned it was actually a complete difference between his private and public personas. Had he known I could hear him singing in private any of those times, he would have blushed deep red and hidden his face. Yet, put him on stage in front of tens of thousands of fans and the man was a star performer.

As we stood in the little kitchen space in the suite's large common area, I confronted him about who Ari was. He seemed to waver in his decision to open up to me. I wanted to shake him and scream, *Just spill it already!* But I stayed patient and calm.

"I'm gay," Jude eventually said.

I stood there blinking. Even though I'd had the thought earlier at the auction, I'd talked myself out of it while trying to fall asleep that night. On the one hand, it was too good to be true. On the other, he had a girlfriend. Tilting my head to look at him, I blinked some more. Could he really have just said...?

"I'm gay," he said again, this time much louder. "Fucking get your head out of your ass and say something."

"You can't be," I decided. "You have a girlfriend."

He looked at me like I was an idiot. "Right. Paisley? Come on."

"Her name is Jae," I snapped, feeling angry for no reason.

"Oh, now her name is Jae? That's cute," he barked, and then pushed me in the chest. "Come on, damn it. Out with it, He-Man."

"Why are you yelling at me?" I shouted back, grabbing his wrists before he could try shoving me again.

"I know you've got judgy shit stacking up in that big head of yours, so open your goddamned mouth."

So I did. I opened my mouth and brought it down on his before I even knew what I was doing. He scrambled back at the same time my brain caught up with my mouth, causing me to do the same. We ended up about ten feet away from each other in the large room.

"*Shit*," I said, raking my fingers through my hair.

"Jesus, Wolfe. What the hell?" he gasped, bringing his hand up to his lips.

"I'm so sorry, Jude. *Damn it*. I'm so sorry. I don't know what the hell came over me," I stammered while my brain screamed for me to run. Just get in the hotel elevator and leave. But years of experience told me to stay, that it would only be harder to come back here if I ran.

"Just forget about it. I shouldn't have shoved you," Jude said. "Clearly you find me irresistible." The joke fell flat, and I heard a thread of self-loathing in it.

"Actually, I think resisting you for this long should win me some kind of award," I admitted under my breath. "You're hot as shit."

"Shut up. Just because I told you I'm gay doesn't mean you get to make fun of me," he said, angry fire blazing in his brown eyes.

"Make fun of you?" I asked. "I was complimenting you."

He looked at me funny. "What?"

"You're sexy, Jude. It's not like you don't already know that. Why would you think I was joking about you being hot?"

"Because guys like you would never call another man hot," he said.

"Guys like me? What, you mean tall guys?" I baited him.

"Fuck you. No, I mean Navy SEAL guys. Macho commando guys."

"I was a Marine Raider. Don't insult me with that Navy shit," I warned.

Jude rolled his eyes. "My bad. Marine Raider then. Those guys don't call other men hot and live to tell the tale. They get their parachute cords cut early on."

"Well, then, it's a good thing I never told them I was gay. Taking a splat onto a cement landing pad would not have been as nice a send-off as the Bronze Star ceremony I had," I said, watching him for his response. I expected relief at hearing me say I was gay, but instead I was surprised to find suspicion.

"You're not gay," he informed me.

I snorted. "You're right. Maybe I have the word wrong. What do you call it when a man is attracted to other men instead of women?"

"Now you're seriously messing with me. Maybe you should go back to bed." Jude looked at me with narrowed eyes.

I wandered back to the more comfortable seating area by the television and sat on the couch. "Sit down, Jude, and talk to me. Whether you want to believe it or not, I'm gay. You can trust me to understand how sensitive this is."

He must have heard something in my voice that let him know I was being sincere.

"Really?" he asked as he came to sit on the other end of the couch, curling up and wrapping his arms around his knees. "You're seriously gay?"

"I seriously am. Obviously I'm not out. My family is beyond traditional southern conservative, and my job still revolves around ex-military personnel who aren't very accepting. It's getting better, but I've never really felt the need to talk to people about it."

Jude sighed. "I've lived in the closet my whole life, and just when I thought I might have found someone worth coming out for, he dropped me like a hot potato. Ari Crowe."

He shifted in his seat, pulling his knees in even closer and taking a deep breath before continuing.

"We met in Nashville around seven years ago. It was just after I'd arrived here to try the music scene. The band and I were playing clubs and bars and trying to get some traction when Ari chatted me up one night after our set.

"I was in my early twenties and finally considering living openly. At that point I had two brothers who were already out, and my parents were heavily involved with the LGBTQ youth program. Fear of my family's rejection was never the reason I was in the closet. This is going to sound silly, but by the time I realized I was gay, Blue and Jamie had been out for several years. I felt like everyone was going to assume I was a copycat, or outsiders would tease me for having been 'made gay' by my queer family," he explained.

I gave him a reassuring smile. This was all beginning to make more sense. "Does your family know?"

"Just my brother Blue. The rest of them can't keep a secret to save their lives. Anyway, Ari and I were together for two years. His family was very conservative and wealthy, and Ari went to snobby Nashville prep schools before graduating from Duke and moving back home. His family would have flipped. So we decided to stay in the closet. Between his family and my country music career, it seemed safe to take things slowly and not come out until there was a damned good reason for it.

"Then one night we were out to dinner at a restaurant, and Ari just dumped me out of the blue. Told me I was never going to be the successful musician I wanted to be and that hanging around in seedy bars with someone so worthless was not the life he'd worked so hard to achieve. I think it was his way of trying to convince himself I wasn't worth coming out for. A couple of months later he was engaged to his high school girlfriend."

Jude ran slender fingers through his hair before picking at a spot on the pajama pants he was wearing above his knee. I couldn't take my eyes off of his fingers as they toyed nervously with the loose thread.

"Blue knew how crushed I was by the breakup so he told me to channel that energy into my songwriting. He made me promise I would use the hurt to prove to myself and the world that his words weren't true. Even though 'Bluebells' is about my breakup, I wrote that song for Blue. To fulfill the promise of using my pain to kick-start my future success. It's a song of strength, like my very own fight song, and its success makes me incredibly proud. When the song hit the top of the charts, we were on our way. When 'Heavy Chevy' came out and did almost as well, the rest was history."

He dropped his feet to the floor and leaned forward, resting his elbows on his knees. I wanted to reach out and reassure him. Somehow show him that he was better off without someone who didn't support his music career. But I didn't dare touch him. Instead I moved my hands under my thighs to keep them from reaching out to him.

"Sometimes I'd wonder why Ari never contacted me to reconnect. Even just to say he was friends with me before I hit it big. He was the kind of guy who got off on bragging about big-name people he knew. You know from your job how common it is for old friends to show up out of the woodwork when someone becomes famous. But he never did. I assumed it was because of his need to stay in the closet. His wife's family had a shit ton of money, so I didn't ever think he'd be after mine."

"He calls you Bubba?" I asked.

"Like an endearment. He thought it was cute, but it drove me fucking crazy. It was his way of poking fun at the fact I was a California boy singing country music. He'd always been a preppy guy. To him, only rednecks liked country music. So he called me Bubba."

I suppressed a wince. "So you've been gay this whole time I've known you, and I've never caught wind of it. When do you hook up? You're never alone."

"I don't," Jude said. "It's not worth it. I haven't been with anyone in six years. Being alone is easier than being hurt again."

That might have been the moment when looking out for Jude Marian became personal.

8

———

JUDE

Derek's dark eyes bore a hole through me. "If that asshole dropped you years ago, why was he acting like he wanted to eat you for dinner tonight?"

"He seemed to be up for a quickie," I confessed. "I told him I wasn't interested."

"Why is he approaching you now? Because of your fame? Is he still married?"

I shrugged. "I think so. It was a request for a fuck, not a relationship. But what he really wanted was my money to manage. He is a partner for his father-in-law's investment firm."

Derek looked at me like I was insane. "What did you tell him?"

"I told him to go to hell," I snapped. "But now I have to spend two hours with him in the morning."

"Maybe he's not going to take no for an answer. Or maybe he wants to open the closet door and rip you out of it for the whole world to see. This is a major problem, Jude. Can't you see that?" Derek railed at me.

I felt myself start to shake and ducked my face down into my chest before Derek could see me lose it, curling my hands over my head and feeling my hair come down around my face. It was overwhelming. My exhaustion from the tour was making me unusually sensitive. This shit had come at me out of the blue, and now I was going to have to deal with it. I wasn't ready.

"I'm sorry," Derek said softly. "I didn't mean to upset you."

"You didn't," I said into my knees. "I know you're just concerned because it's your job."

Derek didn't respond, so I looked up at him. His piercing green eyes sparked at me. "I'm concerned because I care what happens to you, Jude. Yes, it's my job. But you're also a man I've practically been living with twenty-four seven for months."

"Right, so that begs the question. When do *you* find time to date or hook up?" I asked him, trying to change the topic off Ari Crowe.

He looked everywhere but at me as he clearly contemplated how to answer. "Sometimes I go to clubs when I have time off. I don't do relationships because I travel too much for work. And when I was in the military, I kept myself to myself for the most part. There was a stint of a few months when I was on a mission with a guy I messed around with. That was nice." He shrugged.

God, that sounded lonely. He sounded like he was stuck in a similar hell to mine.

"Why don't you just come out now and live openly? I mean, you live in San Francisco and you're an adult. What's holding you back?" I asked.

"My father is a general in the Marines. He's at the level where he could be nominated by the president to become commandant. I have two brothers, both in the service. I grew up in the South on a military base. My family goes hunting, fishing, and rides ATVs in the mud for fun. My mother is in charge of the ladies' guild at the local Southern Baptist church. Have you heard enough yet? Because I could keep going." He laughed.

"I get it. How in the hell did you ever admit to *yourself* you were gay if you were raised like that?" I smiled at him.

"It's hard to deny getting a hard-on in middle school wrestling practice," Derek admitted with a shrug. "I quit the team when I realized I was enjoying my sweaty opponents just a little too much. Then

I started playing baseball where the guys were less tempting. Spitting and scratching. Plus, it helped when I switched to a sport where the players wore plenty of clothes and didn't touch each other. Did you play sports?"

"Soccer. And I was a big rock climber until it became too much of a pain in the ass to go to the climbing gym without being recognized. You already know I run since we run together sometimes," I said, thinking about how much I enjoyed his quiet company on my runs. His legs were so much longer than mine that my runs were easy jogs for him. Derek was in amazing shape. He ran and lifted weights religiously, even if we were traveling. When we had downtime I often caught him doing martial arts moves or pushups and crunches when he thought no one was looking.

I hadn't seen him bare-chested since the day I met him. The most I'd ever seen since then were his bare arms and legs when we were running. His upper body was fucking glorious. Back muscles rippled under his shirts. Shoulders filled out his jackets. Biceps popped and stretched shirtsleeves. And then there was his ass. I had definitely noticed his ass. And his muscled thighs and shapely calves. Damn, the man was a specimen of human perfection. I didn't realize I was staring at him.

Green eyes smoldered back at me as the air seemed to thicken between us. "What's going on in that head of yours, Bluebell?"

"Nothing. Never mind," I said, turning my head to face away from him. "Just thinking."

I heard a low chuckle. "Just thinking, my ass," he muttered. "You were looking at me like you wanted to see me naked."

My head whipped back around to face him. "Fuck you, I was not."

I totally was.

"All right. Whatever you say." He grinned. "For what it's worth, I meant what I said before about you being gorgeous. I know it's not appropriate, but there it is."

After a six-year hibernation, my libido uncoiled and struck like a viper. Before I knew what was happening, I was in his lap crushing my lips to his. My hands snaked behind his neck to hold him tight against me. My knees straddled his hips on the couch, and I felt his arms come around my back, splayed fingers pulling me toward him. We devoured each other's mouths, and I couldn't get my fill.

Derek tasted amazing, like toothpaste and man. His sleepy, warm scent washed over me, going straight to my extremely overwhelmed cock. My pajama pants resembled a Barnum and Bailey tent as I rocked my hips, seeking friction.

I felt a moan escape Derek's mouth, and I responded in kind. My hands started moving down to his throat, his collarbone, his chest. I felt the convex arcs of his pec muscles and the dip between them. God, I wanted to sink my teeth into those muscles.

Warm, strong hands pushed underneath the hem of my sweatshirt and onto the bare skin of my back, causing ripples of goosebumps everywhere they brushed. They came up to cup my shoulders, and I had this overwhelming need to be owned by this man. Just held down and fucked until I couldn't question a thing he wanted to do to my body. I needed to surrender, and he was a man I trusted enough to surrender myself to.

"Fuck me, Derek, *please*," I said against his mouth.

9

———

DEREK

Jude almost never called me Derek. He called me Wolfe, He-Man, Oaf, Jackass, or Hulk. So when he asked me to fuck him and called me Derek? I was a goner. I pulled back and looked at his blazing brown eyes. I was a goner but not an idiot. "Are you sure this is what you want, Jude? It'll change things."

"It doesn't have to. We're both adults. Why can't we enjoy each other's bodies without things having to get weird?" Jude said between rapid breaths.

"I agree with you in theory, but you need to be sure. It's been a long time for you, and I don't want you to regr—"

Jude's mouth was on mine again and this time his hand landed on the bulge in my boxers as well. Talking time was finished, and that was A-okay with me. I gripped his ass and stood up, carrying him toward his bedroom as he continued kissing me all over. Face, neck, ears. His fingers explored the hair on my head and snuck their way down the collar of my shirt.

When we finally got to Jude's bed, I laid him down gently on the soft white sheets, still rumpled from his earlier sleep. I pulled his hoodie off and then leaned in to kiss him on the mouth again once he was free of it. My hands stroked every inch of that glorious exposed skin. His body composition was like that of a featherweight fighter, small but built. That's why every time I saw him come out of a post-concert shower, I could barely stand it.

"God, I've wanted to touch you for so long," I admitted, pushing him onto his back and leaning over him to kiss my way across all those little muscles. "Your body is amazing."

Jude snorted. "This coming from you," he said before I clamped down on a nipple, and he sucked in a breath.

"What's that supposed to mean?" I asked between nibbles.

"You're built, you're beautiful, and also, you hate my guts, oh *Jesus* that feels good."

I made my way down his abdomen and had moved my hand down to press against the outline of his hard cock through his lounge pants. "I don't hate you," I said before untying the string of his pants with my teeth. Jude saw me and squeezed his eyes shut, throwing his head back with a groan.

"Maybe less talking and more dick sucking," he choked out as I pushed down the waistband with my scruffy chin, drawing a scratchy trail across the tender skin of his cock.

When I slid the pants off all the way, I sat back on my heels and let my eyes feast on the body before me. Jude Marian was stunning. Lean muscle, smooth skin, long, thick wavy brown hair that seriously fucked with my equilibrium, and dazzling brown eyes that seemed to pull people into an abyss. The media called them soulful eyes, but I knew better. They were lonely eyes. Right now, they were fuck-me eyes.

I slowly peeled off my shirt and shucked down my boxers. Jude watched me, mesmerized. I crawled just far enough up his body to settle between his legs and feast on his straining erection. A long strand of precum stretched from his tip to the happy trail on his belly, and I went right to it, licking it off like the first taste of an ice cream cone. Jude hissed and his stomach muscles contracted. I slid my hand over those muscles as I went for it again, this time taking his whole cock deep into my mouth and sucking in.

"Oh god, *fuck*," he cried. His hands came down on my head and his hips bucked. Clearly he wasn't going to last long, so I decided not to fight it. I'd suck him off fast and dirty to get the first orgasm out of the way so we could move on to the second round.

My mouth swirled and sucked its way back up to the crown where I licked and kissed the tip again. I made a show of wetting my finger before lowering my mouth again. He bit out another curse.

His hands scrabbled for purchase on the bed as I worked his cock up, down and around without mercy before sliding a wet finger inside him. Jude writhed under my hands and cried out. I swiveled my finger around to find his prostate. *Bingo.* Soon after, come shot down my throat and Jude found religion, screaming to god, Jesus, archangels, and any other deity who might be on call to help a guy brought down in his prime by the simple crook of a finger.

I moved up the bed to cradle him against my chest as he came down from his high. He turned in to me, tucking his face into my side and plastering his body against mine. His arm rested across my stomach and my hand came up to stroke it softly, my other hand around his back, holding him close. My mouth found the top of his head and kissed it. I felt his lips push into the skin on my side in response, the tiny tip of a tongue sneaking out to swipe at me.

After several minutes, the arm Jude had resting on my stomach began moving up my chest, his hand seeking the contours of my muscles and the tight buds of my sensitive nipples. He looked up at me, his grin turning devilish. "Your body is a masterpiece," he said.

His mouth found my nipples and his hand moved farther south, along my stomach to my inner thigh. After nudging my thighs apart, he shifted over me until he was straddling one of my thighs and his arms hooked under my shoulders. Jude's soft lips came down on mine in a caress, tongue sweeping across my bottom lip before slipping inside. I was hungry for his tongue, and he fed it to me slowly. My hands moved up into his hair and brushed it away from his face, tucking it behind his ears so I could see his face better.

It seemed like my mouth tangled with his for hours before he finally broke away, gasping and moving down my neck to my chest and beyond. He traced my happy trail toward my cock so slowly I was mesmerized. My breath hitched and I caught Jude grinning in satisfaction. My erection jumped under his light touches; he seemed to enjoy teasing me.

When Jude finally put his mouth on me, the sound I made was feral. Desperation clawed at me and I wanted my cock inside his body more than I wanted my next breath. My self-control faltered and I considered tossing him over and fucking him face-first into the mattress. I remembered how long it had been for him though, and restrained myself. Closed my eyes and took slow breaths.

His tongue moved up and down my shaft and I felt the promise of his hot, wet mouth. I couldn't take it anymore and begged in a strangled voice, "Please, Jude."

He sucked me down, and I bit out a curse. His mouth was magical and it began to work my cock over and over again until taking it deep into his throat. I hissed and pulled him off me. "I'm going to come if you keep going like that," I ground out. "What do you want, Bluebell?"

Brown eyes peered up at me, pupils blown. "I want you to fuck me until I can't remember my own name."

His words thrummed through my body, causing my dick to throb almost painfully. I lifted Jude off me and strode quickly back to my room, pulling a condom and lube packet from my wallet. When I returned and knelt back on the bed, Jude was lying on his side following me with his gaze. He was so sexy in that moment, I was struck with the knowledge I was the only human being who was allowed to touch Jude Marian's naked body. There were tens of thousands of fans who would give anything to be where I was, naked in Jude's bed. People who had his poster on their walls, his photographs on their computers, and his image on their brains when they touched themselves.

Out of all the people who'd fantasized about it since he became famous, I was the only one lucky enough to be invited into Jude's body.

10

JUDE

Derek was looking at me as if he wanted to feast on me. His eyes were hungry and his lips swollen. As he crawled toward me on the bed, his entire body language was predatory. "Wolfe," I whispered.

When he reached me, I expected to be mauled, but Derek touched me with the gentleness of goddamned butterfly wings, soft and delicate and so very careful. His hands fluttered along my skin and his lips barely brushed mine. The effect was striking. Every nerve ending thrummed in anticipation.

He was so much bigger than I was that his body came down over mine like a protective shell, curling around and encircling me. His arms slid under me to pull me closer, deepening the kisses until I was dizzy. One of his hands snuck down to jack me for several strokes before he licked a finger and brought it down to my hole again. I moaned and arched, relishing the feel of any part of him entering me.

His mouth landed beside my ear and his low growl slithered between us. "I want to stick my tongue into this tight ass of yours."

My eyes rolled back in my head. "Oh *god*."

He pushed my knees practically over my head and landed his hot, wet mouth on my crease. His tongue trailed from my ass to my balls and then pressed inside before pulling back again. He spit into my hole and rubbed it in with quick, teasing licks. If I had ever been rimmed before, the memory was wiped clean away with the feel of Derek Wolfe's expert attentions. His beard stubble sanded my tender skin as he sucked and licked his way inside my body.

"Oh *fuck*." I moaned before reaching behind me to pull a pillow over my face to bite down on. "Mfphhhh, ggnhh."

I could hear the wet smacking sounds his mouth made between grunts. Periodically he'd mumble something like "gorgeous" or "tight" or "fuck." My cock was pressed against my own stomach and hard as a rock again. I tried to reach down to grab it but Derek grabbed my wrist. "No way," he mumbled before licking into me again.

He wet his fingers with his mouth and slid them inside me, stretching and probing, making me blubber stupid begging sounds. Finally when I didn't think I could take it anymore, he slid the condom on and tore open the lube with his teeth. As I felt his tip nudge my entrance, I had a moment of fear it wouldn't work. That his big cock and my smaller body wouldn't be able to come together.

Maybe he had the same concern because he approached me slowly and carefully, leaning back up to kiss me senseless while he breached me. I felt the delicious stretch and burn as he entered me. Sucking in a breath, I tried to relax through it, but it had been so long. Derek stopped his progress and stayed still, waiting. "Want me to pull out?" he whispered. I shook my head.

"Just wait," I hissed, meeting his gaze and seeing in it more emotion than I wanted to. He was worried about me, but it was more than that. He looked like he cared about me too. I didn't want that. I didn't want a man to pretend to care about me the way Ari had. Was it wrong of me to just want a good fuck after all this time without the sticky mess of emotions? I had a hot, naked alpha male in my bed, on top of me, and the sex was going to be out of this world. That's all I needed. Nothing more.

"Do it," I said between clenched teeth. "Just slowly."

His forehead creased, but he did as I said, hips moving slowly but surely until he was all the way in. I felt sweat beading up on my skin, but I also felt the sweet release of my body's stretch around him. I let out a big sigh and groaned in relieved pleasure. "Okay," I said.

Derek began thrusting in and out, starting off slowly as I moaned my approval through every move he made. God, it felt so damned good to be filled up again. To feel the stretch and fullness of a cock inside my ass. The smooth glide in and out as the scent of sex fogged around me and the strong body weighing me down as he held my ankles over his shoulders. God, how I'd missed this feeling.

The gorgeous man above me looked at me like I was a delicacy at a banquet. But I didn't want to be a delicacy. I wanted to be a piece of ice that got crushed and pulverized until it melted and disappeared. I wanted him to wreck me.

My hands wrapped around the backs of his thighs, squeezing him hard against me as he continued to thrust. I vaguely registered the uneven feeling of scar tissue under my hands, but I was too drunk with lust to dwell on it. I lifted my ass closer to him in the silent demand for more. His eyes narrowed as he increased the intensity and began to pound me harder. I wanted to feel this ache for days, to stand on the stage during the LA show remembering this one glorious night after years of going without.

I reached for my cock again to stroke it, my heart thundering and breaths heaving. Derek knocked my hand away again, and I whim-pered a complaint. Our coupling became frantic and chaotic, desperate and grabbing. My hands reached for his face, pulling it down to mine as I devoured his mouth. His hand landed on my throat, caging it against the sheets. I bit his bottom lip and sucked on it hard. When I let go, he flipped me over and lightly smacked my ass all in one smooth move.

Yes.

I scrabbled to my hands and knees, ass in the air as an offering to the man. He grabbed it with both hands and slammed back in, his cock feeling like it was going to rip me in half but in the very best way. "*Ohfuckyes*," I gasped. He pressed one giant palm down between my shoulder blades and began to pound me, grabbing my hip with his other hand so hard that I thought there might be bruises later. I still wanted more.

My face and chest were pressed against the sheets and I felt Derek grab both my hands and stretch them up over my head, lacing his fingers through mine. His sweat-slicked body was pressed against my back; the feel of him was driving me out of my fucking mind. I tried again to reach down and grab my cock to stroke off, and he finally let me before I lost my shit.

"Derek, *Derek*, god, I can't..." I whimpered as I felt myself reaching the peak.

"Go." His low growl blew into my ear.

My climax hit, hot and wet streams of come jetting out as I cried out and convulsed. My body squeezed Derek's from the inside and I heard him gasp and curse before coming deep inside me. Our bodies shook, our skin was slick with sweat, and our hearts pounded. It was without a doubt the hottest sex I'd ever had.

After several beats of nothing but the sounds of our breathing slowing down, Derek asked, "What's your middle name?"

"Huh, what?" I asked him.

"Your middle name. I don't know what it is." He pulled out, leaving me with a feeling of loss.

"Wha—? I don't... what?" I said, turning my face back to look at him but not having enough energy to sit up and try to figure out what the hell he wanted from me.

He burst out laughing. "Mission accomplished." With that, he climbed off me and strode into the bathroom.

"Cocky bastard," I called after him. "And for the record, my name is Jude. Jude Allgood Marian. So there. You're not as great at sex as you think, jackass." I couldn't help but laugh at the end. Because, come on, the man was a goddamned hero in bed.

11

DEREK

Allgood. You fucking got that right. Sex with Jude had been like trying a tiny taste of something amazing and realizing one taste would never satisfy the craving of a lifetime. Not only was the man gorgeous with a perfect body, but he'd wanted it hard and fast. I had the feeling he liked being manhandled, and if there was one thing I'd been fantasizing about for a long time, it was manhandling the country music star in bed.

When I entered Jude's bathroom, I quickly shucked the condom and turned on the tap before letting out the breath I'd been holding back. My eyes slid closed as I considered what had just happened. I'd basically had sex with my boss. Not cool. But I didn't regret it for a minute. That wasn't it; it was more the fear about what was supposed to happen next. Because I wanted to do it again. As soon as possible.

The truth was, I'd enjoyed my time naked with Jude way more than I should have. Was it great sex? Yes. Had I been lusting after his good looks and fit body for a while? Yes. Did I feel noticeably more than just lust while inside him? Hell yes. I knew that was a recipe for disaster, so I had to remind myself why entertaining thoughts of Jude as more than a fuck buddy was a big problem.

Jude was in no position to have a relationship with a man. And even if he was, would I want to be that person? In a perfect world, maybe. But in this world? No freaking way. If Jude was discovered in a gay relationship, his partner would be stripped bare by the media, his privacy obliterated. I didn't want that, and I knew Jude didn't want that. I also felt the only reason Jude had broken his celibacy was because he was handed a trustworthy single gay man on a silver platter. I'd have done the same thing he did. Clearly he was desperate enough to pick the only safe option that had presented itself in years. That wasn't the same thing as being interested in me specifically.

I washed myself and then readied a warm washcloth for Jude. When I returned to the bedroom I found him dozing where I'd left him, buck naked and facedown in bed, probably lying on his own wet spot. I rolled him over gently to wash him off and move him. He opened one eye to peer up at me.

"Thanks," he mumbled with a sleepy smile. Before I had a chance to tell him it was my pleasure, he seemed to drift off again. I wanted nothing more than to climb back into his bed and hold him in my arms all night, feel his warm, lithe body against mine. We'd had sex, but we weren't dating.

I didn't want things to be awkward between us. As it was, I felt like we were going to have to talk about it. To be on the safe side, I turned to walk back to my own room after cleaning him up. Just before I passed through the doorway, I heard him speak.

"Wolfe?"

I turned back to face him, feeling my heartbeat thump harder in my chest. "Yeah?"

"Stay with me?"

"You sure?" I asked.

"Mm-hm."

I walked back to where he lay curled up on his side. After I slid between the sheets, Jude snuggled up next to me, pressing as much of his bare skin against mine as he could. I wrapped my arms around him and pulled him even closer.

~

THE SQUAWKING of Jude's phone alarm woke us the next morning. I felt him lean across me to grab it off the table, his morning wood pressing into my hip. Instinctively I pressed into it and heard a hum.

I peeked between my eyelids and saw Jude Marian above me, long, tangled hair falling down to brush against my cheek. He had a mischievous grin on his face I couldn't help but return.

"Uh-oh," I mumbled, reaching a hand up to brush the hair back behind an ear. "You look like trouble this morning."

"Can you blame me? I have a goddamned Green Beret in my bed and—"

"*Marines,* not Army," I corrected him.

His grin grew wider and I realized he was baiting me. "You sure you weren't Delta Force?"

"Fuck you," I said with an eye roll and my own grin. "You sure you don't sing hip-hop?"

Jude laughed and I was grateful he was still lying across my body. My hands came around him to explore the smooth naked skin of his back and his perfect ass. I felt our erections graze each other, and I let out a groan. That only encouraged Jude to start wiggling, which elicited more groans from me.

I wanted to be inside him again, but I'd only brought the one condom. It had been that "wishful thinking" condom men keep in their wallets.

"Take a shower with me," I commanded, sitting up and slinging him over my shoulder without waiting for his response. He yelped his approval before latching his mouth on to my shoulder blade. I carried him into the bathroom, enjoying the hands all over my ass and lower back.

As soon as I had Jude under the warm spray I placed his hands on the tile wall and nudged his feet apart with my own. My mouth trailed wet kisses down his back until I nibbled on his perky ass cheeks.

Finally I turned him around and took his hard cock into my mouth, relishing the feel of the warm water on my tongue and his stiffness against my lips. Hearing Jude Marian beg me to finish him off made me hornier than I'd ever been in my life. His stomach muscles rippled and his hands clutched my hair and my shoulders.

"Wolfe, *fuck*. Oh god," he gasped as he got closer to his relief. "*Please*."

My sucking intensified, drawing in my cheeks with every strong pass down his length.

"Mphf... Derek, gonna come, *Derek*," he said, fingers gripping my hair tighter. When he came I clasped my lips tighter around him to swallow and then sucked gently before releasing him. Before he had a chance to slump against the wall, I stood up and grabbed him around the waist, pulling him against me for support.

"Don't pass out on me, superstar." I laughed.

"Just leave me here. If I drown, at least I'll go out happy," he admitted.

I wrapped his arms around me and then found the hotel shampoo to wash his hair, followed by a thorough soaping of his entire body. Touching him all over had me so hard I was going to have to stroke myself if I couldn't find any volunteers. My hand roamed down to palm my erection.

"What's the matter, He-Man? Is someone feeling a bit neglected?" he teased.

"You're the one who made it this hard. It's only fair you're the one to tame it."

His hand covered the one I had wrapped around my cock, but his eyes locked onto mine with a saucy glint.

"Challenge accepted."

And damn it if that man wasn't a beast at giving head. By the time I came, I was a pile of quivering goo. That little powerhouse had me screaming his name so loudly I had to bite down on my knuckles to keep from alerting the people in the next room.

By the time I could see straight again, he had bathed me and dried me with a hotel towel. Every time I looked over at him, I caught his smile. Smug bastard.

Jude took his time staring at my naked body as if he wanted to start all over again. If he did that, I wouldn't let him up for days. One of us needed to be responsible.

"Okay, slowpoke, shake a tail feather. I'm starving," I said.

We dressed in our own rooms before packing up and heading down to hand our bags off to the driver. The town car dropped us at a small café for breakfast. We sat at a booth near the kitchen with Jude's back to the door so no one saw him, and I could keep my eye on anyone approaching us.

I noticed Jude wore his eyeglasses instead of his contacts and I wondered about it. It was pretty rare for him to wear his glasses in public.

"I assume you're wearing your glasses today to ensure you can see all the details of my manly perfection," I said with a straight face before opening the menu.

Jude had just taken a sip of coffee and almost spit it out. "Shit, don't make me laugh. No, I have all the details of your manly perfection memorized already. I'm wearing my glasses because of the long flights coupled with the lack of sleep last night. My eyeballs would revolt later if I didn't give them a break. I don't want to play my last concert wearing my glasses tomorrow night."

"Mm. Makes sense," I said before sipping my own coffee. "I just don't see you wearing them when you're out and about."

"They make me look nerdy, so I avoid wearing them in public."

I looked up at him. "Actually, they make you look hotter than ever. Like sexy accountant hot."

He narrowed his eyes at me. "Sexy accountant isn't a thing."

"It is now," I said, gesturing to his face.

As a blush filled his face I couldn't help but keep staring at him. "Oh my god, Jude Marian is blushing," I said with a laugh.

"Shut up and figure out what you want to eat," he said, putting his hands on his pink cheeks.

My eyes never left his as I grinned. "I already know what I want to eat."

12

JUDE

That man needed to stop flirting with me before we ended up on the cover of a magazine with the headline "Famous Musician Humps Bodyguard in Nashville Eatery."

"Stop," I told Derek. "Unless you want to become famous right fucking now, you'll stop trying to rile me up."

"Okay, okay. Sorry. You're just easy to rile, that's all."

"No shit," I muttered under my breath, lifting up the menu to make my final selection.

After we ordered, I asked Derek something that had been on my mind.

"The scars on your hip. Are those from Afghanistan?"

His eyebrows furrowed, cutting lines into his forehead.

"Yes. There's still shrapnel in there they couldn't remove. That's why I couldn't continue to serve. If I stayed on active duty, they were afraid it would increase the chance of the shrapnel moving and causing serious problems."

"Does it bother you? Hurt, I mean?" I asked, sipping coffee.

"Not usually. Sometimes there's a faint ache, but I'm so used to it, it doesn't really slow me down."

"You seem to run on it just fine. That's not bad for it?"

"No. Jogging is fine. I don't think they'd want me to be a marathoner or sprinter, but jogging for exercise isn't enough to worry them."

"Especially at my pace," I added.

"You said it, not me." He winked.

We flirted a little more throughout breakfast until I began to feel the meeting with Ari looming ahead of us. I wasn't sure why I was so nervous to see him, but I was. I guessed it was because he still held power over me. The power to out me to the media.

Ollie called to check in with me before we left the café.

"Hey, baby doll, how'd the auction go last night?" she asked in her usual perky morning voice.

"Fine. My lesson brought in over thirty grand, so I guess you could call it a success."

"Whoa. That's some serious dough. Maybe you should consider going into the music teacher business." She laughed. "I was just calling to remind you there is going to be press at the lesson. Be sure you're on your best behavior."

"What? What press?" I asked, feeling my stomach knot as I looked over at Derek with my eyebrows up. I saw his jaw tighten.

"Just a handful. It was part of the deal. They had to make donations to get access. No biggie."

Shit. Biggie. Very biggie. Photos of me sitting close to Ari. Possible media exposure of me with him. Would he keep his hands to himself? I felt my frustration build and my stomach tie itself in knots.

"Gotta go, Ollie. Call you after," I said before hanging up. I didn't even wait for her to say goodbye.

We made it out to the town car and began the drive to the recording studio hosting our lesson. I looked over to Derek.

"There's going to be media there," I said.

He huffed out a breath. "Do you think he'll behave?" he asked. It was a safe way of asking if I thought he'd try to do something inappropriate in front of the reporters and photographers that would wind up making headlines the following day.

"How the hell should I know? I haven't seen him in six years.

Should I talk to him alone first? Feel him out before the media comes in?"

"What if you tell him that if all goes smoothly in front of the media, you'll give him a private audience afterward?" Derek suggested. "I get the feeling he wants to talk to you, so dangle that in front of him."

"Okay. I'll do that. If I don't vomit first," I admitted.

"Why does this guy make you so nervous? Is it the fear of exposure or something else?"

"Not sure. For sure the exposure fear, but also... I don't know. My gut is telling me there's something up with him. It just doesn't make sense. Why now? Why all of a sudden?" I let out a breath. "Maybe I'm overreacting."

When we entered the recording studio, the receptionist showed us to the room we'd be using for the lesson. Ari arrived, but he wasn't alone. I was surprised to meet his wife Britta. I'd heard all about her when we were together but had never met her. Had he seriously brought his wife to meet me after coming on to me the night before? I did my best to smile and greet her sincerely, trying to read Ari's body language to determine how he was going to play this.

He was all smiles. "Britta, this is Jude."

"Nice to meet you, Britta," I said, forcing a smile. She seemed genuinely friendly and extremely happy to meet me.

"Oh my gosh, I can't believe you're really here right in front of me. I've heard so much about you from Ari," she gushed. "I'm a huge fan of yours! I have all your songs and sing them around the house, right Ari?"

Ari turned to me and winked. As if we were together. "That's right. She does. And her favorite is 'Bluebells,' if you can believe it," he added, giving me significant eyeballs.

Damn. I didn't think I could survive the next two hours. I looked over to Derek and, if it was possible, he looked even more pained than I felt. Clearly this was stressing him out, too, for some reason. I decided to be the bigger person and stop being such a baby.

"All right, so who's taking the lesson?" I asked.

"Britta is going to take the lesson. She's learned the basics but would love a chance to learn from the best," Ari said. Why the hell was he acting like such a kiss-ass?

I felt my nostrils flare. "Let's get started then."

After an hour of showing Britta how to play two of the band's easiest songs, it was time for a break. Thankfully, Ari had kept his comments to a minimum. As long as I didn't look in his direction, I could try to tune him out. The media was outside of the studio room and could only take photos at the moment. I caught Derek's eye and noticed him tug his earlobe.

"If you'll excuse me. I need to make a call while we take a quick break. Feel free to grab a drink or snack in the lounge out there," I offered.

I followed Derek down the hall to an empty conference room. After he closed the door, I let out a breath.

"You're doing great in there," he said in his signature calm voice.

"Thank god it's his wife I'm teaching," I said.

"No shit. What's that about?" Derek returned.

I shrugged. "I'm hoping her presence means he won't want to speak to me alone after. Maybe you can rush me out of there somehow?"

"I can certainly try," he said. "You realize she's flirting shamelessly with you, though, right?"

"What?" I asked. "No, she isn't."

Derek gave me a look that called bullshit.

The rest of the lesson was straightforward although I discovered Derek might have been right about the flirting. I taught Britta some country licks and she seemed very excited to go home and practice them. The representative from Gibson was there to present her with the guitar. After I signed it, we posed for photos with the photographers and answered a few questions. Thank god the press didn't know Ari and I knew each other.

Finally, Ari pulled me aside and asked if he could have my phone number.

"Sorry," I said. "Only my family have that number. If you need to reach me, feel free to contact my manager, Clint." I pulled out one of Clint's cards, which was my usual schtick when asked for my number.

Ari held it between thumb and forefinger like it was a piece of trash. "Really?" He grinned. "You won't even give me your phone number, Bubba? We were together for over two years. I'm not some random member of your fan club."

"I'm not getting into this with you again, Ari. And stop calling me that."

"Jude, I really just want to talk to you about the investment opportunity, nothing more. I didn't mean to make you feel uncomfortable last night." he said with a smile. He seemed to be sincere.

"Ari, even if I felt comfortable working with you, which I don't, it's never a good idea to hire a friend to manage your money."

"I'll come out to San Francisco with a couple of my business partners. Call me to set it up, okay?"

Ari took out his own card and handed it to me. I slipped it into my pocket to avoid further confrontation and turned to walk away. As we walked into the lobby, I said a final farewell to Britta and the people who hosted us, before offering my hand to Ari. He shook and then yanked it, pulling me in for a bro hug. The kind you'd give your friend who just got drafted first in the NFL. A giant bear hug with strong hands clapping me on the back.

"Call me."

Knowing we were headed to the airport and then Los Angeles for the final concert of our tour, I tried to shake it off. We would be miles away from Ari by dinner time.

Once we boarded the plane, I turned to look at my seat mate. He had his eyes closed and his earbuds in. I wanted to talk to him about the situation. Ask him if he thought I should worry about it or if maybe my gut was sensing something that wasn't there. But he hadn't gotten any more sleep the night before than I had. I decided to leave him alone in case he was able to doze off. I put my own headphones on and turned on the instrumentals for my new song again, mentally singing the lyrics.

I didn't realize until I woke up that my head had fallen onto

Derek's shoulder. It wasn't the first time I'd done that. There had been plenty of late nights when I'd fallen asleep in a car or on a plane next to him and woken up to find myself using him as a pillow. But this time was different because I would have given my last cent to keep my head planted solidly against his warm body.

I slowly shifted off him, carefully keeping my face neutral and mumbling a "sorry" as I moved my head over to the window instead.

"S'okay," he said in a low voice.

13

———

DEREK

Jude was silent on the drive from the studio to the airport. I was impressed with how well he'd handled the whole thing, and I left him alone to give him some space.

Halfway through our flight, he fell asleep and slid over to land on my shoulder. As usual, I pretended to be asleep so I could let him rest there. Only one more concert left and then he'd be with his family through the rest of the week and weekend. Hopefully he could catch up on sleep and get some love and support from the people who cared about him the most.

When we landed, we made our way through LAX to the hotel where we would meet the band for a late dinner. There was a morning visit to a local radio station the following day, so everyone needed to be in town the night before.

After checking in to our suite, I sat on the sofa to wait while Jude showered and dressed for dinner. I had on my earphones and wouldn't have noticed him approach if it hadn't been for the tiny hairs on the back of my neck prickling. Pulling out the earphones, I asked if he was ready.

"Yes. What music were you listening to?" Jude asked as we exited the suite to walk downstairs.

"Nothing," I said, hoping like hell he wouldn't push me on it.

"Oh, it's for sure something," Jude said with a grin. "Gimme." He reached out his hand for my phone. I pulled it behind my back to hide it from him.

"No. Never mind," I insisted.

"You're listening to my songs, aren't you?" He gasped.

"No way. Jesus, I might be crazy, but at least I have taste," I teased, not able to hold back a laugh.

"Liar, you are so listening to your favorite Jude songs." He laughed, still reaching for my phone. I smelled the Jude soap smell and my cock stirred against my jeans.

"Ugh," I moaned. "Here, have it." Handing him the phone, I tried discreetly adjusting myself before the elevator arrived.

He looked at the screen. "Lynyrd Skynyrd?" Jude laughed. "That's your dirty little secret?"

"Shut up," I said, walking into the elevator and silently thanking god it was empty.

"You really are a southern boy, aren't you? Are you sure you're even gay?" he whispered the last word with a grin.

"Not sure. Maybe I'm not. Wanna find out?" I said with a raised eyebrow.

"I definitely do. But right now, I have a six-foot-tall pink-haired lady waiting to boss me around for a few hours. Later?"

"Mmm. Promises, promises."

Once we arrived downstairs, we met up with the other members of the band and crew who were all headed to a group dinner at a nearby Mexican restaurant. We greeted everyone and began to walk toward the hotel doors. I heard someone squeal Jude's name and assumed it was a fan who recognized him. As I looked around to see where the voice came from, I instinctively stepped in front of Jude.

"Fucking Paisley," I muttered under my breath when I saw who it was.

"What?" Jude asked, placing a hand on my elbow. "She's not supposed to be here is she?"

"Jude!" she crooned. "There you are. You forgot to tell me what time you were landing, so I've been here since noon waiting for you."

She had bags from expensive boutiques draped over her arms, so she didn't appear to have been waiting for him idly. Clearly the sales people in the shops had kept her company.

Jude was engulfed in a perfume cloud and smothered against a pair of fake boobs encased in a thin tank top. Now that I knew he was gay, I caught little tells I hadn't been able to put my finger on in the past. His hands never strayed lower than her waist when he hugged her. He never turned his face into her hair or neck. If he kissed her, it was only ever on the cheek. The full Jude smile was never unleashed on her.

Maybe I had noticed those things before but chalked them up to his avoidance of PDA in general. Now, even knowing she was nothing more than a beard, I was uneasy in her presence. A jangly feeling of jealousy wavered through me, which pissed me off. I had no right to feel that way about Jude Marian. Not only did I have absolutely no claim on him, but I also knew there wasn't anything to be jealous of. If he was to be believed, the only person he'd had sex with in years was me. I was the person who even had a chance of going to bed with him that night. And fuck if that thought didn't rev my cock up again.

I took several deep breaths and looked around to focus on the job I was there to do. While accompanying Jude to the restaurant down the street, I tried not to think about the possibility of Jae sleeping in our hotel suite. It occurred to me she had shared Jude's hotel room many times. Were they seriously only sharing a room platonically? Shit. Regardless, that meant she would expect to share his room again, and I'd be stuck sleeping alone. The suite we were in had two bedrooms, one for me and one for Jude. There was no way he and I could share without Jae noticing.

My jaw began to ache from clenching my teeth. After everyone was seated in the private room of the restaurant, I felt my phone buzz with a text.

Jude: *Can you step out and book Jae her own room at the hotel? I completely forgot she was coming.*

Derek: *You sure?*

Jude: *Uh. YES.*

Derek: *Thank god.*

I looked over at Jude and saw him smirk when he read my last text. He didn't look up at me, so I ducked out of the room and made the call. The hotel was booked solid due to a conference in town. I begged them to release a room to us and even dropped Jude's name. They apologized profusely and offered to call a sister hotel twenty miles away. I slunk back into the dining room.

Derek: *Bad news. Hotel sold out.*

Jude: *Don't mess with me.*

Derek: *I wish I was.*

Jude: *Fuck.*

Derek: *Nope.*

I looked over at him in time to catch his furrowed eyebrows looking down at his phone. Stress lines carved into his face and his exhaustion showed again. It had been a really long day for him.

The band members talked about their schedule after they returned to their normal routines at home. Their plan was to record another album as quickly as they could in hopes of beginning the next tour in February. It was late August, so they would have to move fast. I saw Jude take off his glasses to rub his eyes. He looked over at me, and his face lit up into a full smile. God, he was beautiful. I returned his smile quickly before looking down at my feet. What if someone could tell from the look on my face how badly I wanted him?

The dinner seemed to take forever, but it finally ended. On the walk back to the hotel, Jae linked her arm through Jude's and began whispering in his ear. Thankfully Ollie interrupted them to talk to Jude about the following day's schedule.

After entering the lobby, we made our way up to the suite with Jae.

I'd had enough for the day and was going to wallow in my own lonely horniness. Maybe treat myself to a little stroking action in the shower as a pathetic consolation prize for not getting to sleep with Jude.

I was under the hot spray with my eyes closed, just standing there feeling sorry for myself, when I felt a slight draft. Opening my eyes, I saw Jude standing in my bathroom. Steam swirled in the air between us, and I felt my body react to his presence.

"Hey," he said quietly.

I stuck my head out of the glass door. "You want to join me?"

"More than anything, but I'm not sure I could explain the wet hair to Jae." He smiled. Goddamned Jae.

"Tie it up and get your ass in here," I urged. "Hurry up." He turned around and left. *So much for that. Worth a shot anyway.*

I went back to washing myself when I felt the draft again, but this time it was stronger. My eyes opened to see Jude standing naked in the shower with me, hair tied in a messy knot on his head and miles of naked Jude skin displayed in its glorious perfection within striking distance.

Careful not to get his hair wet, I grabbed him and kissed him fiercely, leaning myself out of the spray rather than pulling him toward it. His tongue joined mine in a wet tangle before I moved down his body with wet kisses.

I got a kick out of seeing how quickly I could suck him off, and as soon as his cries began to ring out in the tiny room, I reached a hand up to cover his mouth.

As he came down from the high, I straightened up. He started to kneel to reciprocate and I shook my head. "Next time," I said with a smile. "You need some sleep, Jude."

My hands reached for the little bar of soap and I began washing his lower body carefully. We didn't speak, just made eye contact periodically and enjoyed the easy silence between us.

Once we were finished drying off, Jude put his clothes back on and followed me out of the bathroom.

"I'm sorry," he said quietly. "I wish I could stay in here with you."

"Me too," I said through a smile. "But you really need to sleep. And if you stayed in here, I'm not sure how much rest you'd get."

"Night, Wolfe," he said before standing on tiptoes to kiss me. God, I loved the taste of him. My hands went to his hair and pulled out the tie. I ran my fingers through the long strands, smoothing it down. He pulled back and looked at me. Tender brown eyes with amber gold specks.

"Night, Bluebell," I said.

14

———

JUDE

My phone woke me up the following morning.

"Hullo?" I answered.

"Hey, it's me," my brother Blue said. "Sorry to wake you. Want to go back to sleep?"

"No. S'fine. What's up, Bee?"

"I met someone," he blurted. I sat up in bed, hearing something different in his voice.

"Tell me."

So he did. He told me everything about a man he'd met at the vineyard where our sister was going to be married that weekend. I envied him the ability to live in the open, flirting with a new guy and not worrying about it showing up on TMZ an hour later.

When we ended the call, part of me felt guilty for not telling him about the Ari thing. Blue was the only one who knew about my past with him. But it wasn't something I wanted to share over the phone. And if Blue was busy flirting with some new guy, I wasn't sure I'd feel like telling him at all. I just needed time to think about it first.

I quickly dressed for the radio show appearance and walked out of my bedroom. Derek was talking on the phone while looking out of the window to the view of the city below. It sounded like a call with the concert venue confirming security details for that evening. When he was finished, we made our way out of the suite to meet the others in the lobby.

"Sleep well?" Derek asked me with a smirk on his face.

"Better than you did, probably," I returned, feeling guilty for leaving him hard the night before.

"Nah, I helped myself after you left. Slept like a baby."

The mental image of Derek Wolfe handling his own pleasure made my mouth water. "Oh, fuck you," I grumbled.

He laughed and the look of relaxed pleasure on his face made me chuckle too. When the elevator stopped at one of the floors below us, Ollie stepped on. She was immediately suspicious of the two of us laughing and asked what was up.

"Jude just told a really funny joke," Derek said.

"Really? I want to hear it." She smiled at me with expectation. I glared at Derek, who smirked back at me.

"Uh... what kind of music are balloons afraid of?" I tried.

"Dunno. What kind?" Ollie said.

"Pop music," I answered pathetically. Derek snorted and shook his head.

Ollie looked at me like she was still waiting for the punch line.

"Okay, what were you two *really* laughing about?" she asked.

"Wolfe just did a really funny impression of you. He probably didn't want to embarrass you, but you should totally ask him to repeat it," I suggested. Now it was Derek's turn to glare at me.

"Derek?" Ollie asked.

"It, ah, wouldn't be as funny the second time around," he stammered. Ollie narrowed her eyes at him.

"Why do I not believe either of you?" she said.

"Okay, fine," Derek said. "We were making fun of Jae. She snores really loudly. And farts. It's pretty bad."

I snorted before I could stop myself. "Oh my god, you're so mean."

He pretended to look innocent. "What? Are you saying she doesn't?"

"I'm not saying a single word," I replied, still laughing.

The elevator arrived at the lobby and we found everyone waiting for us by a coffee cart.

The radio station visit went off without a hitch and before I knew it, it was time for our final concert. As we made our way to the Hollywood Bowl, I began to get excited about seeing my family the following day in Napa. After that, I would have several months of downtime to recuperate at home, write new material, record the next album, and make time for my family.

The concert that night was amazing. More than fifteen thousand people were there and they all seemed to share the energy of our final performance, reflecting it back to us in their screams and chants. Bon Jovi showed up and joined us on stage for a song. The entire night couldn't have gone any better for our final show.

When we got called back for our last encore, I sat on my stool, idly strumming the intro to "Sweet Home Alabama" as I waited for everyone to settle into their places. I could see Derek waiting for me in the wings and I winked at him. Anyone watching would have thought I was winking to Jae or Ollie or even fans in the wings. But that one was just for him. Under the lights, I wasn't able to see his reaction, but I imagined him twisting his tongue in his teeth to keep from laughing.

When the band was settled and ready, I began singing "Bluebells" with more intention than I had in a long time. I sang it for Blue, who had encouraged me to fight through my heartbreak and prove to myself and the world I could succeed. I sang it for me, to remind myself that my heartbreak had made me stronger and left me better off than before. And a small part of me sang it that night for Derek. In six years of performing that song, it was the first time I sang of those memories in the past tense.

15

———

DEREK

After the concert Jude was sucked into a vortex of fandom unlike we'd seen for a while. It started off with an unbelievable backstage visit from Jon Bon Jovi himself. I was a big fan of his and enjoyed seeing him up close, but when he put his arm around Jude for pictures, I felt faint curls of jealousy winding around my gut. Suddenly, Bon Jovi didn't look quite so tempting.

Because it was Los Angeles and the final show of the tour, Jude's manager, Clint, had arranged too many meet-and-greets after the show. There was dinner with the recording company executives excitedly talking about the next album already, and then drinks afterward with some VIPs Clint said were critical to setting up the success of the next tour.

As the night wore on, I could see Jude flagging. He looked like a cheap latex balloon deflating before our very eyes. It was one in the morning before he was finally released from his responsibilities and escorted back to the hotel.

When we entered the suite, Jude was still explaining to Jae that she had her own hotel room that night across the hall. I sat on the sofa in the common room while he waited for her to gather her things.

After she left, Jude crawled into my lap and buried his face in my shoulder. My hands instinctively went around him to hold him close, lips finding his temple and pressing a kiss there. "You okay?" I asked.

I felt Jude nod his head against my shoulder and then say in a muffled voice, "Is this okay? Want me to move?"

"Hell no," I replied. "Honestly, I've wanted to touch you all day."

"When I saw you sitting on the couch in my dressing room after the concert, all I could think about was wishing I could straddle your lap and just fall asleep against you."

I let out a breath and relaxed into him. "That would have been nice."

"I miss being touched, Wolfe. Maybe I didn't realize it before because I was just so used to going without. But today all I could think about was touching you and feeling your hands on me. Is there...? Is there any way we could...?" He let out a deep sigh.

I pulled his face back to look into his eyes. "Is there any way we could...?" I asked.

Jude was blushing. "Never mind." He tried to lay his head back down on my shoulder but I stopped him, holding his face in my hands.

"I hope to god you were getting ready to ask if there's any way we could have sex again." I smiled at him and he grinned.

"That was certainly part of it." Jude let out a breath. "It's just awkward because you kind of work for me, and I don't want to put you in a bad position."

"Trying not to make a joke about positions you could put me in." I laughed. "I know how to say no, and I know you're not the kind of person to use my job against me."

"Good, because I wouldn't. I promise. And I know you would speak up if I ever made you uncomfortable," he said.

"I would indeed. Now, am I going to have to pull out my advanced interrogation techniques on you or are you going to ask me what else you want to ask me?"

"Fine. Is there any way we could just enjoy having regular sex with each other without the drama of a relationship? I mean, clearly you're not out, I'm not out. You said you're not really the relationship type, and I certainly don't feel like traveling through that quicksand again. But I love touching you and feeling you touch me, and I would love to share a bed with you and I trust y—"

I stopped him with a kiss before he could continue his nervous rambling. "Yes, perfect. Now stop talking." As I gathered him up, I returned to kissing him. Halfway to my bedroom we were already panting and hard, Jude's hands roaming all through my hair and behind my neck. I dropped him down onto the big bed and took a minute to lock up both the suite and my bedroom properly. When I returned to my bed, I stood back to appreciate his flushed face and swollen red lips. He looked so sexy that I felt the anticipation of being back inside of his body rocket through me. Just as I reached for the hem of my shirt, I heard a knocking on the outer door.

My eyes shot to Jude's and I saw the same guilty fear race through his as I felt in mine. Luckily the fear deflated my cock almost immediately, and I held back a groan.

It was just Jae retrieving a few shopping bags she'd left by the door to the suite. Once she was gone, I hustled back into my room to find Jude dead asleep, still fully dressed in the center of the bed. I carefully stripped him down to his boxers and then did the same to myself.

Sliding under the covers, I gathered Jude in my arms and sighed with relief. Holding him while he slept was like getting into my own bed after months of being on the road, and I fell asleep almost as quickly as he had.

Several hours later I awoke to knocking on the outer door of the suite. I untangled myself from Jude's sleeping form and made my way to my bedroom door. Stumbling out, still half-asleep, I assumed it was Jae needing something else or just being generally high-maintenance.

It wasn't Jae.

16
———

JUDE

I came awake to the sound of Derek's voice in my ear.

"Wake up Jude. We have a little situation," he said in a low voice.

"What? Where are we?" I asked.

"The hotel. Los Angeles. I don't know how he found our suite, but a really drunk-ass fan just showed up. I'm pretty sure it's that guy who tried to kiss you after the San Francisco show the other night. The cops are on their way."

I sat up and tried to grasp what he was saying. A fan from home? Here?

Derek threw his clothes on before tossing me mine.

"Where is he?" I asked, slipping them on.

"Hotel security is taking him to their office. I want you to come tell me if you agree it's the same man so we can file a report."

"Jesus," I muttered.

I rubbed my eyes and ran my hands through my hair. It was after five in the morning and I felt like ass. After grabbing my glasses, I slipped on some shoes.

"Okay, Wolfe. Lead the way."

As I stood next to Derek in the elevator, I felt myself falling back to sleep on my feet. His hand clamped down on my shoulder as he laughed softly.

"You still with me, Bluebell? Should I go back and get you a blankie?"

"Shut up," I mumbled, removing my glasses to rub my eyes again.

It was, indeed, the same man. And Derek was right. He was loaded. Slurring and proclaiming his love for me at the top of his lungs as the cops marched him through the lobby to the street, he insisted that night's show had been the best concert ever, and he just had to tell me himself.

The LAPD officers who responded agreed to take the guy in on a drunk and disorderly charge but said that was all they could do since he didn't really commit a crime. There was no history of stalking or harassment, but they cautioned Wolfe to keep an eye out. Having been involved in many celebrity stalker cases, the LAPD was aware of how quickly they can escalate from a drunken door knock to an obsession.

As they led him out of the hotel, the drunk man squinted back at me one more time, "But Juuuuude, I neeeed you to loooove meee! You're my special sweetieeeee." Then he broke out into a fit of giggles that ended in a fit of dry-heaving in front of the door. After he calmed down, he looked at the officer to the right of him and stage-whispered, "Isn't he just as cute as a *pug*?"

Great. Just great. Now Derek was going to call me a pug.

By the time we returned to the suite, it was after seven in the morning and I felt like I'd been hit by a bus. We were due at the airport in just a couple of hours to fly to my sister's wedding.

Derek joined me on the sofa, and I leaned against him.

"Not a word about this to my family," I warned.

"No problem, pug."

I sighed and ran a hand through my hair. Derek chuckled and pulled me into his arms, laying a kiss on my forehead. "I'm sorry. Your fans can be crazy sometimes. Does it worry you?"

"Kind of. But at the same time, I'm getting used to it. Not sure if that's a good thing or not."

"I'll need to make some calls to Joel at the office and have them double-check the security on your house. We won't go back there Sunday night until we're sure this guy isn't planning on coming around," he said, rubbing his warm hands up and down my back in a soothing rhythm.

"Damn it," I said. "At least they have several days to do their thing before we get back. I'm not going to be threatened into staying somewhere besides my own damned house."

"Let's just wait and see. In the meantime, we're heading to Napa and don't have to worry about him right away. Thankfully that vineyard is private and pretty small. It should be easy to notice anyone out of the ordinary."

"Jesus, I hope so. That's all we need at Simone's wedding." I leaned my head against his chest and rested for a minute before speaking again. "I can't decide if I want to try to sleep for another hour or if that will just make me feel worse," I said.

"No, let's go ahead and head to the airport. We'll catch an earlier flight and get settled at the hotel so you can sleep longer than an hour." Derek patted me on the knee before pushing me onto my feet. "Hustle up, Bluebell. Places to go, people to see. How about we shower together to save water?" He winked before grabbing my hand.

"I think you secretly enjoy rushing me," I grumbled as I got up and followed him to the bathroom.

ONCE I WAS at the vineyard, I got a second wind. Greeting all my family members was energizing because I hadn't seen most of them since Jamie's aborted attempt to get married several months before.

Blue asked me to take a walk with him so he could catch me up on the saga involving the fake boyfriend. Derek followed behind, never letting me leave his sight after what had happened the night before. Blue seemed to spark with energy over the man named Tristan who owned the vineyard. I listened while he spoke and was surprised by how jealous I was.

As it was, I felt like I had only a tenuous hold on my ability to keep Derek at a distance. I craved personal connection. Keeping everyone at arm's length was exhausting. I needed to remember to enjoy the physical without wishing for more. As Ari's visit had reminded me, it would just be easier that way.

When we finished our walk, Derek caught up to us and quietly pointed out I was about to keel over from sleep deprivation. I agreed to take a rest and specifically didn't invite him to join me. We had rooms side by side. Entering my room alone, I forced myself not to look back to see if he was bothered I hadn't invited him in. He had a key to my room for security reasons, but I knew he wouldn't use it unless it was an emergency.

Throughout the time at the vineyard with my family, I managed to keep Derek at a distance. Maybe he sensed I wasn't comfortable hooking up with him that close to my family, or maybe he wasn't that interested in me to begin with.

The only time things really got personal between us at the vineyard was when Derek thought he couldn't find me on Friday evening. We were hanging out on the back patio of the lodge before the rehearsal dinner when he got a phone call. After he stepped away to take it, I went back to my room to take a shower and get ready.

I was standing under the spray of the shower when Derek burst through my bathroom door with an angry growl, scaring me half to death and causing me to almost pull the shower curtain off its hooks. In the blink of an eye, he had my naked, dripping wet body up against the shower wall pressed into the cool tiles by his very large, very dry, fully dressed self. Before I could even wonder what the hell was happening, his hungry mouth landed on mine like a heat-seeking missile.

17

DEREK

When I'd ended the phone call with my main office after hearing about a break-in at Jude's house, I felt frustrated and helpless, which in turn made me feel angry. How could this be happening when he had a team of security professionals specifically hired for the purpose of keeping him safe? I knew I was going to have to tell Jude about the break-in, so I turned to find him on the patio. He wasn't there.

I asked his brothers where he'd gone, assuming it was to the men's room, but they were in the middle of some argument about what they were supposed to wear to the rehearsal dinner.

"Where's Jude?" I asked again, only this time I used my military command voice. The voice that meant business. Four pairs of wide eyes turned to stare at me.

Maverick was the first to make a sentence. "I, uh, think he went back inside."

I stormed into the lodge, feeling an irrational sense of nerves about the coincidence of finding out about a second security incident at the same time I lost track of Jude in person. There was hardly ever a time when I didn't know exactly where Jude Marian was. Even if I wasn't in the same room with him, I knew where he was. This may have seemed like a silly thing to civilians, but to a security specialist, losing track of the body you're supposed to be protecting was kind of a big deal.

He wasn't in the lobby or the lobby men's room. I strode down the hotel room hallway, rifling through my wallet for Jude's room key. When I found it, I was surprised to see my hand shaking. I was known in the Marines for being unflappable. Nerves were not something I did.

When I entered Jude's hotel room, it was empty. For a split second my stomach dropped at the realization he might actually be missing, but then I heard the shower running.

Thank god.

I barged into the bathroom, pissed he'd left without telling me where he was going. I fully intended to bark my frustration at him. That is, until I saw his perfect fucking body flushed and wet from the shower.

The energy of my relief came barreling out in a rush of pure greedy lust. Jude was there. Jude was safe. Jude was *naked.*

Before I could stop myself, I had that sexy man up against the shower wall whimpering into my mouth. My hands were all over him, and I felt his cock stiffen quickly enough to stab me in the gut. His legs came up to wrap around my waist and his hips rolled into me.

"Wolfe, not that I'm complaining, but what the hell?" he gasped.

"Want you," I replied between hungry nibbles on his neck.

"Take me," he said before starting to work on separating me from my wet clothes. I helped remove them, trying not to dwell on the ridiculous instinct that resulted in soaking my leather shoes.

Before shucking my pants, I grabbed my wallet to retrieve the condom and lube I'd restocked several days before. If I'd thought my hands were shaking before, they were downright uncontrollable now. I wanted Jude Marian frantically. No, I *needed* him. Needed to crawl inside him and just feel him all around me. Anchor myself in his body. Hold the man still and safe and connected to me for a moment in time.

I flipped him around until he was facing the shower wall before pressing into him with a slick finger. My lips grazed his earlobe as I fingered him and rasped out dirty promises into his ear. Jude quaked at my words and pleaded for me to fuck him. Whatever this was between us was raw and frenzied, breathless and hot.

As soon as I could, I withdrew my fingers and bent my knees down enough to slide my stiff cock inside his tight passage. My relief came out in a loud groan, and blood pounded in my ears. I took a moment to curl around Jude's body and just hold him. My front was slick against his back and my arms wrapped around his front in a possessive embrace. I nuzzled my nose against the nape of his neck, the top of his spine, the angled blades of his shoulders. My throat was packed full of sappy words that wanted to spill out, but I pressed my teeth together as hard as I could to keep them in.

There was no room between us for those words.

When I felt him begin to wiggle, I answered him with a thrust. Out, in, stroke after stroke. I pulled back to watch my cock disappear into his body and teased a thumb along the top of his ass crack to feel his muscles clench around my erection. God, that was hot. My other palm slid up and down his back before grabbing his hip and changing the angle.

Jude cursed, and I stayed at that angle, stroking in and out of him until my head was buzzing and my nerves sparked like live wires. I felt more than saw Jude grab his own cock to jack himself. His noises were incoherent, and I could barely process any sounds over the rush of the water and the blood in my ears.

"Jude," I breathed. "*Jude.*"

His body pulsed, intensifying into a full orgasmic spasm around my cock. I felt like I was splintering apart, flying into a million pieces of jagged, shimmering pleasure.

When we were able think again, I peeled myself off him, leaned outside the curtain, and tossed the condom into the trash. For some reason I felt sheepish and a little bit stalkery myself. For god's sake, I'd come into a man's shower unannounced and basically jumped him.

"Jude, I—" I began.

He started laughing.

"What?" I asked defensively.

"You look like you just accidentally wrecked my new car," he said.

"I shouldn't ha—"

"So help me god, if you say you shouldn't have done that, I'm going to have to knee you in the groin. I'd threaten to punch you, but we all know how that would end."

I smirked. "You with a broken hand and me with a great story to tell?"

"Fuck you." Jude laughed. "But yeah."

"I just didn't mean to go all caveman on you like that."

"What did you mean to do?" Jude asked, picking up the shampoo.

"I was all set to yell at you actually."

His lip curled up in amusement. "Coulda fooled me."

"No shit. Then I saw you all... like that. And I couldn't think anymore," I admitted.

His laugh was a lovely sound and his eyes were clear and bright as they shined at me.

"What were you going to yell at me about?" he asked in a more serious tone as he massaged shampoo into his scalp.

"I couldn't find you, and I may have freaked out a little bit. Next time, a heads-up before you leave the area would be appreciated."

"My brothers were supposed to tell you where I went," Jude said.

"Apparently they were distracted. But I overreacted anyway," I admitted. "That was Joel on the phone, giving me an update about something that happened at home."

Jude's hands were now shampooing my own hair and I was having trouble concentrating on putting words together.

"Something happened," I said.

"What do you mean?"

"Your house was broken into."

I felt Jude's body stiffen in my arms and his hands still on my scalp.

"What?" he asked. "When? How do you know?"

"That call was from the office. The intruder entered through the

French doors of the sunroom some time this afternoon. The police and security team are pursuing it aggressively, but there doesn't seem to be much to go on."

I could see the surprise in Jude's face and wished like hell I could assure him everything would be fine.

"Was there anything missing? Or a note?" Jude asked.

"Not that they could tell."

"Should we assume it was the drunk guy?" he asked.

"It seems unlikely. He would have had to get there awfully fast, but we can't make any assumptions at this point. Nothing obvious was taken, but who knows? There will be a guard on site around the clock until you get home."

"Oh shit, Wolfe. What about Ollie?"

Ollie lived in an apartment over Jude's garage. "The office called her as soon as the alarms went off, and she confirmed she was away at her parents' house. She's fine. I think she'll stay there for a little while, but you can call her to be sure."

We finished washing and dried off quickly, realizing we might be late for the rehearsal dinner. After he dressed, Jude took my room key so he could gather my clothes for me. My own were dripping wet in his bathroom, and if there was one thing I couldn't do, it was go into the hallway where Jude's entire family was staying, wrapped in nothing but a towel.

The rehearsal dinner was the typical elegant but emotional affair, and I could see Jude's pride in his beautiful sister, Simone. He stood and gave a toast that made his parents cry and Simone rush over for a hug. More than a few guests in the room seemed to look at Jude with cartoon hearts in their eyes, and the sight gave me a strange sense of possession. Almost like I wanted to mark the man so that everyone would know he was mine.

Of course it was silly. Not only was he *not* mine, but I wasn't even supposed to want him to be. What I should really want was some-one's body to enjoy. I needed that wedding weekend to be over so I could stop thinking relationship thoughts and return to thinking plain old sex thoughts.

After the rehearsal dinner, the Marian siblings proceeded to get wasted in the lodge bar. Jude started giggling and didn't stop for the rest of the night. I had never in my life seen Jude Marian relaxed to the point of nonstop laughter. First of all, he rarely drank much on tour. Second of all, he never allowed himself to lose control and give over to the moment. Maybe I just hadn't seen him around his family very much.

I loved watching this side of him. The baby brother. The goofball who tried to give his brothers hell but ended up getting his hair ruffled by them instead. They adored Jude and treated him with the gentle affection you'd give to a beloved but familiar treasure.

Later that night he invited me into his room. I wanted nothing more than to hold him while he slept, but I knew I couldn't. If I ended up in his bed I would say the things I shouldn't. Words about maybe wanting more than his body. Just the thought of it had me twisted up inside. I couldn't allow myself to want anything more than sex with Jude Marian.

I would soon learn that keeping my distance from him would become impossible. Two days later, I moved in with him.

18

JUDE

On the drive home to the city Sunday morning, Derek received a phone call from his office alerting him to another trespassing situation at my house. This time it was someone setting off the perimeter alarms on the property, but it still increased the security concerns enough to mandate a live-in bodyguard. And that bodyguard would be Derek.

When Derek hung up the phone and updated me, the awkward silence in the hired limo was excruciating.

"What do you think?" I asked him. The privacy glass was up, and it was taking all my self-control not to climb into Derek's lap.

"From a purely professional standpoint, I agree with them completely."

"And from a non-professional standpoint?" I asked.

Derek sighed. "I feel like it's putting you in a weird situation because we've slept together."

"I feel the same way, but you're the one between a rock and a hard place," I told him. "Honestly, it's your choice. I think it's a good idea for someone to be around, but it doesn't have to be you if you don't want to do it. Just to be clear, having you sleeping at my house would be pretty flipping fantastic for me. Just saying."

He laughed. "Yeah. Okay then. That's sort of what I was thinking. And it's not like it'll last forever. Just until we figure out who's messing with you."

"Right," I agreed. "And in the meantime, we can fuck like bunnies while you're on the clock, and I'll try not to think of you as a prostitute."

Derek's hand shot out and pushed me in the shoulder. "Asshole." He laughed. "What does that make you then?"

"Lucky as hell?" I suggested.

"Damned straight."

The rest of the ride back to the city was uneventful. I told Derek I would need to visit my parents' house the following day to check on everyone after the chaos of the weekend. Just the idea of being able to spend more time with my family after all the months on the road was a relief.

That night, extra guards from On Your Six were at the house double-checking some of the additional cameras and alarms that had been installed. While Derek drove to his place to gather some of his belongings, I checked the largest guest room to make sure everything was clean and ready for his stuff.

Ollie was still at her parents' house, but I felt sure she would return soon when she discovered live-in security would be on the premises.

For the next several days Derek and I lived in a sort of make-believe world where the two of us were like real lovers, spending every night exploring each other's bodies. With no plans during the first full week after the tour, I took advantage of my empty calendar by staying up late fooling around with Derek and sleeping in the following morning. There was no one around except the two of us.

During the day, I wrote new music while Derek ran down intruder leads based on information found in my fan mail files, but at night we would set work aside and just revel in each other's nakedness. It had been a long time since I'd enjoyed physical pleasure like that, and it didn't take me long to get used to having mind-blowing orgasms on a regular basis.

The following Monday, Derek had to go in to the office for several hours, so the security company sent a different bodyguard to stay at the house. It was strange. The man was nice enough, but not having Derek around gave me an unexpected feeling of wrongness. I tried to mentally laugh it off, but deep down I felt unsettled.

When he returned after eight o'clock that night, I tried my best to look unaffected, but inside my chest I felt a noticeable pressure ease. There was concern in Derek's eyes that hadn't been there before, and I resented the other guard's polite small talk before leaving.

Finally alone again, we sat down on the couch off the end of my kitchen.

"What is it, Wolfe?" I asked.

"Two things actually. First, the company is making me take the weekends off. Legally I can't work this much, so they need to make sure I'm off the job for a minimum period of time. They tried to get me to take a couple of days off immediately, but I talked them into waiting until the weekend."

My heart sank. It went without saying he couldn't be around me for nonprofessional reasons when another bodyguard was watching over me. That sucked. I tried to remind myself if we were only together for the sex, that just meant a two-day break. Easy peasy. Except I knew it was more than that for me. I'd grown to crave his body, sure, but I'd also grown to crave his companionship, his soft voice in my ear at night, his teasing when I played Taylor Swift songs but his singing along if it was Madonna.

"Well, that makes sense. No problem," I lied. "What else?"

Derek raised an eyebrow at my feigned nonchalance.

"Ari has been trying to reach you through Clint's office."

I nodded. "I know that. Clint told me after the LA show. But how did you know?

"Clint's office has to report to us all names of people trying to contact you so we can keep a database. The database then recognizes trends and anomalies. For instance, if someone named Karen Smith wrote you a letter, then six months later wrote another one, the system would alert that she's had repeat contact. We've been trying to use this system to figure out if there are any other threatening fans before focusing in on just Ari. But when I did search for Ari Crowe, his name was in there for multiple attempts," Derek said.

"Just since our trip to Los Angeles?" I asked.

"No. Jude, he's been trying to get a hold of you periodically for six months."

The news hit me like a ball to the gut. I didn't know what to say. Should I be angry or just plain frustrated? I made a decision and held out my hand.

"Give me his number," I demanded.

Derek's eyebrows went up. "Why?"

"You know why. Just give it to me."

"No," he said. "You already told him to get lost."

"He-Man, give me the goddamned number."

"*No*," Derek repeated, this time sounding quieter.

"Never mind," I said, pulling out my phone and dialing. When Clint picked up I spoke. "Hey, Clint, it's Jude. Listen, there's an old friend of mine from Nashville who's tried to contact me through your office recently. Can you please give me his call back number? His name is Ari Crowe."

Derek and I locked eyes while I waited for the number. He seemed a little too calm, and I narrowed my eyes at him.

"Sorry, man, I don't have it. I think I gave it to Wolfe. Ask him," Clint said.

I felt my nostrils flare. Jackass bodyguard. "Will do, talk to you later."

"You're an ass," I told Derek. "Don't treat me like a child. If I want to call Ari, that's my business."

"Keeping you out of trouble is my business. I'm sorry it's pissing you off, but no good is going to come from engaging this guy, Jude."

Suddenly I remembered the business card in my wallet. I left the room and closed myself in my bedroom. My hands shook as I dialed Ari's number, making sure it would show up on his end as an unknown number.

"Ari Crowe," came a voice so familiar that tendrils of memory snaked around my gut.

"It's Jude," I said.

"Jude, it's good to hear your voice. I've been trying to reach you."

"No shit. What do you want, Ari?" I asked.

"You," he said with a laugh. "Preferably naked and horny."

"Not going to happen. Is that the only reason you've been calling me?" I asked.

"The truth is, I just want to get this investment meeting on the books."

"Again, no. If that's all you wanted to talk to me about, I've got to go."

"Wait. How about this, the next time you come to Nashville, you give me thirty minutes. You don't even have to give us the business, just let me prove to my partners that I can get you in a room to listen to their pitch. Think of it as a favor for an old friend who helped drop kick you in the direction of your success," he said with a laugh.

"No thanks."

"Just think about it, Jude," he said. "The way I see it, you kind of owe me one, Bubba."

I hung up and stared at my phone.

Holy hell.

In the end, I knew I couldn't keep the call a secret from Derek. No, that wasn't quite right. I didn't *want* to keep it a secret from Derek.

When I joined him again on the little couch in the kitchen, I told him everything.

19

DEREK

I wanted to pound that cocky fucker into the ground. How dare Ari Crowe think Jude owed him anything after the things he said all those years ago?

Jude sat in the corner of the couch, arms wrapped around his knees.

"Damn it!" He flung a fat sofa pillow across the room. It hit a windowsill and fell to the ground.

I stayed where I was, letting him vent his frustrations however he needed to. His hands raked over his face and into his hair.

"Goddamned selfish son of a bitch," Jude ground out. "He's trying to play me. Just another fucking person from my past who wants a piece of me now that I'm rich and famous. Typical. How could I have been so stupid all those years ago? What did I see in that arrogant asshole? Was I so desperate that I thought I could trust him? Is there no one beside my family who doesn't want me for my money or fame? *Really?*"

I could tell he wanted to throw something else or punch a wall. I leaned forward, weight on my feet in case I needed to hop up and intercept him before he did something stupid.

His head whipped around, long hair trailing in an arc around his shoulder. "Say something, Wolfe. Tell me there's a way to make him stop this bullshit." The look on his face was chilling. Before I saw it, I had assumed he was pissed. But now that I was looking into those Jude eyes, I saw absolute, raw loneliness. As if he'd been reminded he couldn't even trust the people he'd been closest to.

I was on him before I could think, pulling him against me and wrapping my arms around him the way I'd wanted to all along. He fought me like a cat, and I let go in surprise, lifting my arms up and stepping back.

"Get off me," he cried. It was almost a sob and it broke my heart. "I can't do this. I just can't. I want... I... this is why I don't fucking do this."

Jude turned his back on me and started toward his room. "I'm sorry, Wolfe," he said over his shoulder before disappearing down the hall.

I stood there, staring after him, wishing he knew without a shadow of a doubt that he could trust me. He was gone before I could say anything, but all I could think was, *It's okay, I understand*. I just didn't want him to hurt anymore. Or feel alone anymore.

I didn't want to be one of the people in his life he had to second-guess. How could I possibly show him I understood when I'd never been in his shoes? Jude's words left me feeling helpless and a little stung.

I blew out a shaky breath and turned to make my way to the guest room. If he needed to be alone, I had to respect that.

After checking the doors and double-checking the alarm, I got into the shower. Alone. It had been a long day, one that started with teasing, playful sex and ended with the opposite. I couldn't push him to deal with this until he was ready. I slid between the cool sheets of the guest bed and tried to get comfortable. No dice.

My restlessness stirred the bedding up into an annoying froth of tangles and lumps. As I tried to straighten everything out with a grumble, I heard footsteps outside my open door. Before I had a chance to call out, I heard Jude's voice.

"Can I come in?" he asked.

"Of course," I said, sitting up.

The lights were still out so I couldn't see his face, just a vague silhouette of his body as he moved toward me in the room. Jude sat on the bed next to me and sighed before speaking. "I'm sorry, Derek. You didn't deserve that."

"It's okay Jude, I understand why you said it. In your position, I'd probably feel the same way. I can't imagine how hard it is for you to trust anyone. For what it's worth though, I hope you know you can trust me."

"That's just it, though. I do trust you. When I got into bed, all I could think about was the fact that I trusted you, yet I'd let that asshole scare me into pushing you away. That's not what I want. I want to touch you. I want to crawl in your arms and stay there. I'm sorry."

I pulled open the bedcovers in invitation and he slid in beside me and into my arms. We both let out a sigh of relief at the same time.

"I take it you don't want to talk about it right now?" I asked.

"Hell no. I want to have my wicked way with you," Jude said. I could hear the grin in his voice, and I laughed.

Before I could ask him if he was waiting for an engraved invitation, he climbed down my body. When he got past my waist, I heard him suck in a breath.

"Hmm?" I asked, knowing full well what had caused his breath to hitch.

"You dirty boy," he said from under the sheet. "I just assumed you only slept nude when you were with me. Were you that sure I'd come to my senses or you do sleep nude on your own too?"

I let out a laugh. "Always sleep nude, but I forget that I'm naked sometimes and wander out to get a drink of water. You caught me in a hotel suite one time, actually."

He bolted upright, removing his mouth from the skin of my abdomen and pulling the sheet off his head. "Did not. I would have remembered that, believe me."

"You were sleepwalking. We had an entire conversation with me holding a decorative basket in front of my junk. I think we were in

Portland. It wasn't until you asked me to remember to check on the birds before I got back in the pool that I realized something was off."

Jude was laughing too hard to stay focused on what he was supposed to be doing to my body. But a giggling Jude was the best kind of Jude, and I loved hearing him lose it. "No way. I don't sleepwalk."

"You definitely do. Another time you came into my room and yelled at me for getting the colors all wrong," I told him, chuckling as I remembered how pissed he was.

"The colors for what?" he asked.

"Beats me. I begged you to explain yourself, but you'd had just about enough of me at that point and threw up your hands in disgust before returning to your own room."

"You're making all this up." Jude laughed, straddling my hips and resting his hands on my chest.

"Nope. Ask your family if you sleepwalk. They'll tell you. Simone once told me that you used to get completely dressed for school in your sleep and would wake up surprised at how diligent you'd been in prepping the night before."

"Oh shit," he said, losing it again. "I do remember that now. Oh my god."

"I think it's cute. The best part is getting to see what crazy PJ pants you're wearing," I said. "Which ones do you have on right now?"

"They have sandwiches on them," Jude said. "Pete and Ginger's girls sent them to me for my birthday, remember?"

"Yeah. Yesterday you had the ones with party chickens on them," I remembered. "Those are my favorite."

"Right, the chickens celebrating their day off on Thanksgiving. Mom gave them to me last year. She thought it was funny since I'm a vegetarian. I don't think she put two and two together about how the day off for chickens isn't so great for the turkeys. But at least they're cute."

"What started you on the crazy pajama thing?"

"It's so embarrassing. When I was a teenager, my parents kept buying my clothes in the kids' section because I was so small for my age. As the youngest of five boys, you can imagine how much shit I took about my superhero pajamas from my fucking brothers. So even when I moved up to the adult sizes, they'd pick out cartoon ones or humorous ones to make it look like I was still shopping in the kids' section. It just became a thing."

"You know they adore you, right?" I asked.

"Yes, I do. They're amazing. What about you? You never talk about your brothers, so I assume you aren't close."

"No, but not for the reason you think. They're twins. So they've always been closer to each other, which sort of leaves me as the third wheel. I followed my father's footsteps and became a Marine, but my brothers chose the Army. Then they took the whole 'competition between branches' thing a little too seriously. I think the final nail in the coffin was me moving to the West Coast." I shrugged. "I envy what you have with your family. They're ridiculously wonderful."

"My mom would probably be willing to adopt you if she knew you were gay," he teased. Three of Jude's brothers were adopted through a gay youth program.

"It's worth considering," I mused. "I do love her cooking."

"Of course, then I'd be sitting on my naked brother right now," Jude said with a shudder.

"Gross. Maybe we should stop talking about your family."

"I think that's a great idea," he agreed, renewing his slither down my body.

I stopped him and pulled him up until we were lying face-to-face.

"Jude?" I asked.

"Hmm?"

"Are you okay? I mean, are *we* okay?"

He smiled the kind of smile that went all the way to his eyes again. "Yes, Derek. We're very okay."

"Good. I just want you to know you can trust me. I would never do anything to betray you or deliberately hurt you. Do you believe me?"

"I do," he said, kissing me sweetly on the lips before moving to spread wet kisses all over my body.

20

———

JUDE

"Jude, baby, *please,*" Derek begged, as I drove him crazy with my tongue.

After he came, I felt ridiculously proud of myself for bringing my gorgeous Marine to his release with my mouth. As silly as that sounded, it made me feel powerful. Derek had spent months standing quietly and calmly in the background of my life. Nothing fazed him, and nothing ruffled his feathers.

This big tough guy had been reduced to a begging, shaking, whimpering ball of need. And he'd called me *baby*. Fuck if that didn't push all my goddamned buttons almost as much as it did when he called me Bluebell. There was a part of me that wanted to be Derek Wolfe's baby more than I wanted my next hit song. But I couldn't go there.

Derek was a quiet, private man. If the media thought I was in a relationship with him, his life would no longer be his. That wasn't something I could do to him, and I knew he would never voluntarily put himself in that kind of position.

As he came back down from his climax, I climbed up to settle in beside him. His arm curled around me and I rested my head on his shoulder.

"Thank you," he whispered. "Your turn." I could hear the smile in his voice, but I could also feel his utter relaxation against my body.

"No, Derek. Sleep. I just want to lie here with you while you drift off."

"Mmm, you sure? I don't have the energy to argue." He turned his head and kissed the top of mine. "Night, Bluebell."

Shit. All the feels. If only he knew what that word really meant to me.

"Night, Wolfe."

As he fell asleep, I lay there enjoying the feel of him against me. The warm solid shoulder under my cheek, the coarse hair of his belly under my hand, his curvy calf muscles against my toes. After several minutes, he shifted us both in one smooth motion so he ended up spooning me. His large body surrounded mine in a protective curl and I snuggled back into him, pulling his arms farther around my chest and threading my fingers with his. I brought the back of one of his hands up against my lips and kept it there.

Derek's lips brushed the skin on my neck and I shivered. His hand came up to smooth my hair back from both of our faces. "'S like sleeping with a girl," he mumbled.

"You complaining about my hair?" I joked.

"Hell no. Love your hair. Sexy as fuck."

I smiled into the darkness, not wanting to fall asleep and miss the joy of lying in bed within the protective circle of this man's arms.

"Go to sleep, Jude Marian," he whispered into my ear. His voice was like aged bourbon going down, making everything inside me warm. And when he used my last name, it made me feel real. Like he saw the skinny awkward kid I'd been in the high school band and liked me anyway.

I CAME AWAKE to the feel of someone's morning wood nudging my ass. My mouth stretched into a grin as I remembered I was in bed with the sexiest man I knew. My ass pushed back into that glorious cock, and I heard a groan.

I did it again, but this time I wiggled too.

"Mmffhh," he said as he reached around to palm my cock. "Pants off," he said as he tried tugging them down.

After stripping them off, I climbed on top of his sleepy form. "Sleeping with you is like sleeping next to a fireplace," I said. "So hot, so good."

His sleepy face split into a grin. "Until summer returns, then you'll ride the side rail and growl at me if I even think about touching you."

Summer. Would we still be sleeping together that many months from now?

"I'm cold year round. Especially at home here in the Bay Area. But you already knew that." I leaned down to press my lips against a nipple and heard him hiss.

"Ah yes, the ever-present Jude hoodie for our little delicate flower. Maybe that's why you always fall asleep against me. You're a heat-seeking human."

"Either that or it's because you're sexy as hell. One of the two," I said, continuing to search his chest with my lips.

His hand pulled my face up to his and he began kissing me, reminding me he was in charge of this round. Derek's hand circled my throat, his thumb pressing lightly into it, and my cock stood straight up in response. God, what was it about his hand on my neck that made me so turned on? It was like striking a match.

"Mmm, someone likes that," he teased as he felt my erection throbbing against him. I whimpered in response. His lips moved over to my ear where his words lit the fuse. "Do you want me to manhandle you, Jude? Hold you down and fuck you like I own you? Your dick is hard enough to pound nails right now, so I think you do. And that's hot as hell. Stop me anytime, Bluebell."

My eyes might have rolled back in my head as I nodded my consent and awaited the explosion.

21

———

DEREK

As if I didn't think Jude could get any hotter. When he responded to my own desire to dominate him, it was like flipping a switch inside me. My cock went rock hard and my heart began to thunder in my chest. I gripped the back of Jude's head and pulled him in for a blazing hot kiss, all lips and tongues and nipping teeth.

Every move my hands made was strong and decisive. I flipped him onto his back and pushed his knees over his shoulders, lowering my mouth onto his gorgeous tight hole. My mouth rimmed him while my hands caressed the backs of his thighs.

I flipped him onto his stomach and pulled his ass back toward me hard, gripping his hips and rubbing my hands over his tight ass before swatting it.

"God, you're so fucking sweet," I said before leaning down to bite one of his cheeks. My mouth moved back to his hole and I dove in again. By the time I was ready to don the condom, Jude was practically vibrating with need. As I slid it on, I leaned back up to Jude's ear to ask, "Are you ready for this, Jude?"

"Oh my god Wolfe, please, *please* fuck me," he whimpered, pushing his ass up in invitation.

I took him in one swift thrust. The channel gripping me was tight, hot and one hundred percent Jude. My hips pounded into him, spurred on by his cries for more. Harder, faster, deeper.

Leaning over his back I whispered into his ear, telling him how good it felt to fuck him, how tight his ass was, how much I wanted to own his pleasure and make him scream. With each word, his cries became whimpers and his breath hitched faster. My hand reached around to grasp his cock finding it hard as a rock. Precum bloomed from the tip and I used it to stroke him.

Just as swiftly as I'd entered him, I pulled out, lifting him up and rolling onto my back before lowering Jude's ass on top of me in a straddle.

He looked dazed, but his body knew what it wanted. He moved to ride me, reaching back to guide me into his body. I gritted my teeth in an effort to keep from shoving up in one big stroke. Finally, he was seated on me fully, and it felt amazing.

He began to move, sliding up and down on my shaft, seeking his own pleasure. I grabbed both of his wrists and held them together behind his back forcing his chest to arch and his hips to buck even faster.

As his body moved in a frenzied haze of pleasure, I told him how wanton he looked, how sexy he was, how I was going to lose my shit when I came deep inside of him. I released his wrists and moved to stroke his cock with one hand while the other returned to his neck in a light hold, reminding him once more who was in charge.

It didn't take long before his eyes rolled back in his head and a full-body shudder wracked his small frame, white ropes of come shot across my chest, and I grabbed him by the back of the neck to pull his mouth to mine in a crush.

As his orgasm continued to spill into my hand, his cries vibrated against my lips, making my insides pulse with white-hot pleasure. My own grunts of release went into Jude's mouth as I felt the pulse of my orgasm rocket up from my groin to my chest. Eyes slammed closed, muscles contracted, and full-body shudders racked through me.

We lay together in stunned silence while the sounds of our rapid breathing seemed to bounce around the room. It was a while before either one of us could catch our breath and form a coherent thought.

I could get used to starting off my days like that.

WE SPENT the rest of the week in our normal routine of work during the day, followed by cooking dinner together and then pretending to watch TV but really humping all night instead. When Saturday morning rolled around, so did my mandatory time off. By the time we'd taken showers and gotten dressed for the day, it was time to face the music. "I have to go back to my place."

He looked over the kitchen island to catch my eyes. "I know. Stay for some breakfast first?"

"Okay. Mike should be here in about twenty minutes. I think Ollie's back too." After leaving her parents', she'd decided to visit her sister in New York before Jude's schedule picked up again.

"She is," Jude said as he gathered items from the fridge. I told him I would meet him at the recording studio on Monday morning and take over from Mike then. He went over what he thought the rest of the week's schedule was going to look like while he cooked a simple breakfast of eggs and fruit.

After we finished eating, I moved to the small couch to finish my coffee, and Jude came over to sit next to me. Not polite, *daytime* next to me, but naked, *nighttime* next to me. Practically in my lap. His head leaned against my shoulder and I felt my body relax against his touch.

He smelled like soap.

Damn it.

"Okay, can I admit that I'm going to miss your presence here when you're gone this weekend?" Jude blurted.

I couldn't help but laugh. "Only if I can admit that I'm going to miss seeing your gorgeous face while I'm away. I'm probably going to sleep like shit too, if last night's initial attempt was any indication."

"Same here. I sleep way better with you next to me. Maybe it's all that heat," Jude said with a smirk.

"Mm, maybe. Or maybe it's because you're getting a regular orgasm each night that's helping you sleep better," I suggested, running my hand through his long hair.

"Either way, I'm pretty happy with you being around. I hope you know that."

"Me too, Bluebell," I said.

We sat together in comfortable quiet for a few minutes, putting off the inevitable.

"Derek?" he asked, pulling his head back from my shoulder to look at me.

"Hm?" I answered, caught in his warm brown gaze.

Jude put his hands on my cheeks. "Thanks," he said before leaning in to kiss me softly. His lips were his voice and the tender touches of his tongue were his words. I heard how grateful he was with every move of his mouth, and I responded in kind.

Before we were ready to pull away and be professional for the day, there was a knock on the door. We jumped apart but made eye contact before I got up to answer the door.

It was Ollie, and she hit the ground running, going over the day's social media plans and demanding to hear all the juicy gossip from Simone's crazy wedding weekend.

I stood to leave when Mike arrived, catching Jude's eye over Ollie's pink hair. When I shot him a wink, he blushed deep pink, and I knew Ollie would notice and give him hell about it after I left.

All I could tell myself to stop the nerves beginning to swirl in my stomach was that I was only going to be gone for the obligatory two days off.

If only I'd known that a family emergency would turn those two days into two weeks.

22

———

JUDE

Even though we weren't physically together, we continued flirting casually during the weekend break. We'd been texting almost constantly throughout the couple of days apart, but Derek went quiet for several hours on Monday morning when he was supposed to be meeting me at the studio. Finally, just before lunch, he texted me.

Derek: *My brother Aaron was in a bad accident. He's in a hospital in Germany and I have to take my mom over there. Dad can't go and my brother Kyle is in Japan. At airport now. Going thru security.*

Jude: *Oh shit, Derek. I'm so sorry. Is he going to be okay? What can I do to help?*

Derek: *I don't know. Just forgive me for leaving on such short notice.*

Jude: *Don't be ridiculous. Safe flight. Text when you land?*

Derek: *Will do. Go easy on Mike and stay safe.*

Jude: *Nah, we're skydiving today and learning how to swallow swords after that.*

Derek: *Be sure to tell your mom ahead of time it was not my idea. I can't imagine my life without her cooking.*

Jude: *I see where your priorities are.*

Derek: *If you're not around, I'll have to put the moves on Aunt Tilly in order to stay near your family. She's my favorite Marian besides you.*

I laughed at that. My aunt Tilly was crazy. A foul-mouthed sailor disguised as an eighty-something little old lady, and she thought Derek was a tasty treat.

Jude: *Don't make me laugh. You know she'd sex you up in a skinny minute.*

Derek: *After that many years on earth, she's gotta have some killer moves.*

Jude: *Pls change subject. If you die in fiery crash, I can't have our last conversation include dirty grannies.*

A minute later my phone rang. I was by myself in my home gym trying to distract myself with some exercise.

"Hey, Bluebell," he drawled in his smooth, calm voice. My heart started hammering in my chest like a traitor.

"Hey. I'm sorry about your brother. Do you have any details?"

"His unit was attacked and the truck he was in flipped over, trapping him. Has some bad burns on his body, but we won't know more until we get there. I couldn't let my mom go alone."

I tried to think of how I wanted to word my next thought. "Wolfe, do you want me to come with you? It sounds like you could use a friend."

There was silence for a moment, and I felt my face heat up at the thought that I might have just crossed that relationship line we were trying so hard to avoid.

I began to backpedal. "I mean, I—"

"No, Jude. But thank you for offering. Really. That means a lot. I really would like your company, but I'm afraid you being there would make things too weird."

"Right, of course. I completely understand," I said. And technically, it was true, even if my heart had a hard time accepting it.

"I have to go. They announced my flight."

"Be safe, Wolfe," I told him.

"Now who's trying to protect whom?" He laughed.

"If you don't come back in one piece, I'll blame the Air Force for not training you properly," I teased, knowing full well what his response would be.

"Marines, asshole." His laugh rumbled over the line before the call disconnected.

During the next few weeks, new music began pouring out of me, and I scrambled to keep up with it. I convinced myself that finally recovering my sleep and spending some much-needed time in my own home had made all the difference.

The day after Derek arrived at the Army hospital where Aaron was, he was told the biggest risk was infection. Aaron was expected to recover from the burns with some scarring on his back and one leg. He was in a lot of pain, and their mom was having a hard time handling it.

After the first week of Derek's absence, I had the band over to share some of my ideas. They loved what I was creating and helped me tweak it so we could get ready to record. I stopped stressing about having enough material for our new album. We were already more than halfway there, and I felt like I still had more to write. Ollie arranged a practice schedule for us to begin working on the new songs. I had a sound studio at my house that we would use until it was time to record the final versions.

I took advantage of my time alone to keep the media happy and take Jae out a couple times. We met for a very public lunch down-town and then again for dinner and dancing at a club with her friends. She was just as vapid as I recalled, and I was thankful I wasn't giving up something more fun on those occasions in order to be with her.

In the evenings Ollie and I would cook dinner together and binge-watch Netflix. I caught her looking at me strangely a few times but ignored it. It was one night, late into the second week of Derek's absence that things with Ollie finally came to a head. We had ordered pizza, and Ollie met the delivery person at the front door. While I was pulling out plates and napkins, my phone buzzed with a text from Derek.

Derek: *Finally on my way home. Should be at your place by dinnertime tomorrow.*

Jude: *Thank god. How's everyone holding up?*

Derek: *Fine. Mom's still upset, but better. She's staying until he's ready to come home.*

Jude: *Good.*

Derek: *What about you? How'd it go today with the band?*

Jude: *Productive. They had some great ideas for tweaking two of the new songs. We're ahead of schedule for once.*

Derek: *Whoa, look at you. And I haven't even been there rushing you.*

Jude: *No shit. Or distracting me. Maybe that explains my productivity.*

Derek: *Ouch. Should I stay away?*

Jude: *No way, He-Man. Get your smoking hot ass back here and distract me. Distract me please.*

Derek: *That's the plan. Rest up, Bluebell. See you tomorrow.*

"Oh. My. God." Ollie stood in front of me looking at me like I'd suddenly shaved my head. "I finally figured it out. You're getting laid."

I looked up from my phone, pressing the button to darken the screen.

"What?" I asked, feeling a traitorous flush heat my cheeks.

"You have a lovesick grin on your face, and you didn't hear me calling your name," she accused.

"Bullshit, fuck you." I laughed.

If it was possible, her eyes got wider. "Spill the beans, baby cakes."

"What beans? There're no beans to spill," I said, reaching for the pizza box.

"You're such a liar. You will tell me, and you will do it right now."

"There's nothing to tell," I tried, grabbing a slice and slipping it onto my plate.

"Who were you texting?" she asked while getting her own slice. We sat down at my kitchen table, Ollie with a beer and me with a glass of ice water.

"Oh that? Derek texted me to say he'll be back tomorrow," I said in my best nonchalant voice.

The screech took me by surprise, and I jumped, the pizza slice sailing through the air to land on the other side of the table.

"Oh my god, you're in love with Derek Wolfe," Ollie cried.

My stomach dropped as I stared at her, desperately trying to concoct a mature response to her accusation. I could do this. I'd just deny it. After all, it wasn't as though I was actually in love with Derek. Maybe just with his penis.

Be cool, Marian.

"Am not." It came out sounding like a whine. *Well done, idiot.*

"Are too," she sing-songed.

"Dude, what?" I said, continuing my display of maturity. I always thought Ollie suspected I was gay, but we'd never talked about it.

"Tell me everything. Have you slept with him? Wait, should I pop some popcorn? Is the story going to be that good? What am I saying? Of course it is." She got up and pretended to look in the pantry for popcorn.

"Sit your ass down and eat your pizza, drama queen."

"Start talking, Jude," she said after taking her first bite of the veggie-laden pizza.

I stalled, taking a bite of my own slice while I made a decision. There was nothing I wanted more than someone to confide in and ask advice. I'd known Ollie for almost twenty years. We'd been friends in school and grew even closer when she started working for me years before. The only reason she didn't know about my hookups and relationship with Ari was because we didn't live near each other during those years and I hadn't wanted to tell her over the phone.

"Fine. I'm not in love with him. But I might be in lust," I admitted.

"And?" she encouraged.

I took a minute to think about what I could tell her. Derek wasn't out of the closet. It wasn't my place to out him to anyone, but did that include Ollie? I had to assume it did until and unless I heard otherwise.

"And what?" I stalled again.

She gave me that look; the one that says, *Cut the bullshit.*

"Hypothetically speaking, if I was hooking up with someone who wasn't out of the closet, it wouldn't be my place to tell anyone, right?" Now it was my turn to give her a look; one that said, *We all know what I'm saying.*

"I completely understand," she said with an innocent smile. After a few more bites, she started again. "I have a friend named Jack. He's been in the closet forever, and he's hooking up with this new guy he works with. The guy's name is Darryl. I'm so curious about what Jack is thinking. Not only do I want to know how my friend is feeling, but I also want to be able to help him navigate what must be a challenging situation. You see, Jack is a famous… politician. And it can't be easy for him to pursue a relationship while he's in the public eye."

I rolled my eyes at her but decided to play along.

"I'm sure it's not. It must be excruciating. Probably actually easier to just be celibate for the entire time he's been in the public eye."

"Shit. Why would he do that?" she asked.

"Dunno. Maybe because he dated an asshole who told him he was worthless and would never amount to anything," I mused.

Before I knew what was happening, I was engulfed in a tight hug. Ollie was like an Amazon with great boobs, and she gave the best hugs ever.

"But he isn't worthless. And look what he amounted to. He's the most amazing politician ever," she whispered into my ear.

"I'm sure he knows that, but it's still hard to hear otherwise."

"Do you think Darryl is any better for him than the ex-asshole?" she asked, pulling back to return to her dinner.

"Yes, but they're probably just friends with benefits," I said, eating my own food.

"Why?"

"Maybe it's easier that way. No expectations, no hurt feelings. You know, no worrying about the messy stuff that comes with relationships," I explained.

"Shit, Jude. But what about all the good stuff that comes with relationships? Joy, comfort, and companionship?"

I shrugged. "Is it really worth the risk?"

She stopped eating and stared at me with something like pity in her eyes. I couldn't look at her.

"Hell yes it is. And my friend Jack deserves to be loved. Not just fucked. The fact that you don't believe that seriously breaks my heart. Do you think Darryl doesn't deserve that either? What if he wanted a relationship instead of just a booty call?"

"He doesn't."

"Maybe that's just what he says. Maybe he really cares about Jack. Maybe I can tell by the way he looks at my friend. As if my friend Jack is the most beautiful, amazing human being in the world. Because he is, Jude. And if not, maybe he should ditch Darryl and look for someone he could really build a life with."

My eyes stung. "I'm pretty sure if he wanted someone to build a life with, it would be Darryl. But I'm equally sure Darryl is better off without the hassle. Being with a politician isn't worth it."

"Oh shit, baby," she said before hugging me again.

23

———

DEREK

I was restless on the drive from the airport to Jude's house. It didn't even occur to me to swing by my place. There was nothing in that bland apartment I wanted or needed more than Jude Marian's naked body against mine. I hoped to god he didn't have any plans for the rest of the day other than lying in bed receiving pleasure from me.

By the time I pulled into his driveway, my nerves vibrated almost to the point of snapping. I kept chanting to myself, *Keep it together, Wolfe.* It was imperative I hide my desperation until we were alone, however long that took.

When I walked in the door, I saw Mike sitting at the kitchen table.

"Hey, Mike," I said, reaching out to shake his hand. "Thanks so much for taking over for me."

"No problem," he smiled. "How's your brother?"

"Getting better, thanks. Where's Jude?"

"He just went back into his bedroom. I should probably wait around to say goodbye."

"Nah, I'll tell him for you. You deserve to get out of here and have some fun. Tell Kathy and the girls I said hello," I said, remembering his wife and kids.

His face broke into a grin. "I will. It's Annie's birthday tomorrow so I have to pick up the cake on the way home."

"Go on then. Enjoy. I'll hold down the fort."

"Thanks, Wolfe. See you next weekend."

When he was gone, I locked the doors before going to find Jude.

I came around the corner to the hallway with the bedrooms when Jude came flying at me, jumping up and landing with arms and legs wrapped around me. If he'd been any bigger, I might have stumbled and lost my footing, but he was just the right size. I held him tighter than I should have and let out a deep sigh of relief.

"Thank god." I said into his hair.

"Mm-*hm*." He exhaled into my ear.

I stood there for a minute, just holding him. Breathing in his scent and letting the familiarity of his body relax me. I knew I'd missed him, but this? This was different. The feeling of relief and happiness at having him in my arms wasn't sexual at all. Sure, I wanted him. My throbbing erection was proof of that, but it was more than that. I forced those thoughts away and turned my head to take his earlobe into my mouth.

"You, me, naked, bed," I murmured into his ear.

"Yes, please," he rasped.

We didn't even make it into the bedroom. Within seconds we were ripping each other's clothes off and shoving tongues into each other's mouths. Both of us dropped to our knees at the same time, making us laugh before he tackled me on the thick carpet of the hallway.

Our bodies naturally flipped until we were sucking each other off frantically at the same time, curled around each other like a dirty yin and yang symbol. There was no such thing as enough. I couldn't touch enough of his skin, lick enough of his hard shaft, smell enough of his familiar musk, hear enough of his mewling sounds as his pleasure built to its climax. My senses were overloaded.

It was quick and frenzied and determined. Loud sucking sounds mixed with moans and grunts until finally I couldn't take any more. My brain stuttered and stars began flickering along the edges of my vision.

"Jude," I gasped. "Baby, I'm gonna come."

The hot rush of Jude's own release hit the back of my throat just as mine began shooting. I almost choked at the combination of convulsing through my own release and trying to keep up with Jude's as well. My arms clutched around his lower back tightly, one hand grasping an ass cheek. I felt my muscles quivering.

"Fuck," Jude said between puffs of air. "Fuck."

"You okay?" I asked.

His laugh came out stuttered. "Uhh, *yeah*. That was... God, Wolfe. That was overwhelming. In a good way."

I sat up, pulling him with me and scooting back so I was leaning against the wall. His body was pliant and relaxed, moving easily wherever I pulled him. When I settled against the wall with my legs stretched out in front of me, Jude ended up resting his head in my lap.

My fingers ran lazily up and down the smooth skin of his back. Jude's hair covered his face like a curtain, and I took a moment to push it back behind his ear. His dark eyelashes rested against his cheek and the familiar planes of his face were flush with color.

"You're so beautiful," I whispered before I had a chance to think about it. He leaned back to look up at me.

After a brief hesitation, the smile he gave me was the full-Jude version and it nearly took my breath away. "Thank you."

I gently pulled him up to straddle my lap, leaning forward to touch his lips with mine, drawing a light swipe across his bottom lip with the tip of my tongue before pulling it away. Our foreheads touched, then our cheeks, then an almost kiss. Our eyes met and I gently brushed his nose with mine. Two mouths danced close to each other without actually touching. My heart was thundering in my chest, and I could feel Jude's breath hitching through the hand I held on his back.

His tongue grazed my lip, and mine chased it lazily. Jude's fingers came up to trace my eyebrows and cheeks, jawline, and lips. Time stopped for us, and my heart felt like it might explode. I could feel it clogging my throat, and that scared me.

Something must have shown in my eyes because Jude's own warm brown ones shuttered, his body language changing. He began standing up as his gaze shifted away. I wondered if I'd somehow screwed things up between us.

"You hungry?" he asked.

"Uh, yeah. Sure," I replied. Jude reached back for my hand and gave me a smile. When I stood, I realized I felt sticky and sweaty.

"Let me take a quick shower first," I told him, unsure if he'd want to join me.

"Want some company?" He smirked up at me. I let out a breath, sensing we would be okay after all.

"Abso-fucking-lutely." I grinned.

We showered and changed into comfortable clothes before heading into the kitchen to fix something for dinner. Jude turned on some music and I noticed it was a regular rock selection instead of country.

"Did Mike tell you about the two other houses in the neighborhood that had break-ins similar to yours?" I asked Jude while he chopped some vegetables on a large cutting board.

His hands stilled and his head came up. "What? No. Tell me."

"I just heard about it on the way here. Forgot to ask Mike for more details since I was in such a hurry to get him to leave." I laughed. "The guys at the office said one of the houses broken into was a state representative. They got surveillance video, but it's not very clear. The cops are busy trying to run it down since you and the politician are high profile."

"Was anyone home during the other break-ins?" Jude asked.

"No, and they couldn't determine that anything was taken. Makes it tough to link them together. For all we know, they aren't connected. Or they are, and there are others that the police haven't come across yet," I said.

"Shit, Wolfe. Maybe it's not the crazy fan after all."

"Maybe. Maybe not."

I grabbed two beers from the fridge and gestured to ask if Jude wanted one. He nodded. I placed his beer on the kitchen island, purposefully leaning my chest against his back as I reached past him to set it down. He hummed his approval of my move, and I took a minute to enjoy the feel of him.

"Want me to make the chicken since I'm the only one eating it?" I asked.

"Nah, just relax. If you make it, it'll end up fried in lard," he teased, stretching his head to one side to offer up his neck. My nose found the thin skin behind his ear and my tongue soon followed. I felt Jude shiver under my touch.

"Up yours," I said before pinching his ass and stepping away for the sake of my empty stomach. "Just because I'm from the south doesn't mean I fry everything I eat. You're probably going to steam the chicken and make me eat the vegetables raw."

"I was thinking I'd steam everything until it's good and bland before chucking everything in the Vitamix for a chicken-and-veggie smoothie," Jude said with a straight face. "Maybe add some kale too. Don't worry. You can't—"

"Taste the kale," I finished with him while rolling my eyes.

We both laughed until there was a knock at the door.

24

JUDE

When we heard the knock at the door, Derek looked to me with a raised eyebrow as he made his way to the kitchen door.

"I'm sure it's Ollie," I reminded him. "We've been having dinner together most nights."

Sure enough, it was Ollie. She was dressed in our nightly uniform of comfy pajamas and she was carrying a couple pints of ice cream.

When she saw Derek's large form in the doorway, she stepped back to take him all in. He was drool-worthy, dressed in low-hanging track pants and an old black T-shirt with faded gray writing. I knew from memory it said, *What doesn't kill you makes you stronger. Except a Marine. A Marine will kill you.*

"Well, hello, handsome. Look who the cat dragged in." She smirked.

"Ollie, good to see you," he said, pulling the door open wider in invitation. After she moved past him to put the ice cream in the freezer she turned and hugged him. An "oof" sound punched out of him, and his eyes snapped up to meet mine. I shrugged.

"I'm so sorry about your brother," she said against his shirt.

"Thanks, but he's okay. It didn't take him long to recover his snarky personality. Actually, the pain made him mean as a snake there for a while," Derek said with a chuckle, pulling back from the embrace. "And how are you?"

"Good. I've been looking after your boy here in your absence." She smirked again. I rolled my eyes and got a nervous feeling in the pit of my stomach. If Ollie dared let on what she knew about the way things were between Wolfe and me, I'd have to murder her right there in my kitchen.

"Thanks, Ollie. I appreciate it. And here I thought Mike was doing that." Derek laughed. "Should have known better."

"What's for dinner, baby cakes?" Ollie asked me. Before I could worry what Derek would think about having her join us, he spoke up.

"Jude here is making chicken-kale smoothies, and I've decided ladies first on tasting it." Derek grinned.

Ollie laughed. "You joke now, buddy, but you know he'd do it. One time he made me drink a smoothie he'd hidden edamame and bok choy in. I didn't speak to him for days."

"I'm on a strictly no-kale diet, so you can have my portion. What flavor ice cream did you bring? Maybe I'll just have an ice cream smoothie while you two get your health food on," Derek teased.

"I'm making a stir-fry, jackass. You're going to love it. Teriyaki sauce with plenty of processed sugars in it just the way you like. I'll even make white rice since I know serving brown rice will make you fake being hungry again in thirty minutes," I told him.

"I wasn't faking it. I never fake it," Derek began. Ollie laughed again, causing Derek to blush. "I mean, I never fake being *hungry*. Jesus, you two."

Ollie looked at me and we laughed even harder. "Derek Wolfe blushing? Now this I'm not sure I've ever seen. Call the press, it's a banner day," Ollie teased.

"You've seen him blush before," I reminded her. "Remember when that waitress said she wanted to have his babies? We were in Kansas City, I think. Somewhere in the Midwest anyway."

Ollie squealed. "Oh my god, yes! She just blurted it out the minute she saw him like she couldn't help it. And his face turned lobster red."

Derek put his hands over his face but we could still see his crimson ears. "Don't remind me," he mumbled through his hands.

"And the time at a mall when that little boy asked him to open his shirt and show him his superhero costume?" My laugh almost turned to a giggle at the memory.

Ollie's eyes began tearing up through her laughter. "And Wolfe just looked at him like the kid had requested a lap dance."

"Shut up," Derek begged. "He asked me to take off my clothes. I didn't know he thought there was a superhero costume under my shirt. What was I supposed to think?"

I giggled again. "Olls, I forgot to tell you, but after the rehearsal dinner in Napa, Aunt Tilly kept begging Wolfe to dance even though it was a hotel bar with no dance music or dance floor. He was trying so hard to be polite, but the rest of us were dying laughing. Finally, she began spouting off wolf jokes. 'Hey Wolfe, I bet I can make you howl all night long,' 'He's so fine, I could just Wolfe him right down,' and something about wanting to be a sheep inside Wolfe's clothing. Then Granny yelled across the bar, 'Tilly, stop crying Wolfe. That hunk can huff and puff and blow me any time he wants!' Oh my god, I thought Derek was going to have a seizure right there."

Derek finally succumbed to laughter. "That woman, I swear. But I thought you were too drunk to remember all that."

"No way," I laughed, catching my breath. I looked over at him. "She asked about you at Sunday dinner last week."

"Did she?" he said, meeting my eyes across the kitchen.

"Yes. Said it was strange to see me there without my shadow," I admitted.

"I thought about that when I had to take that weekend off before Aaron's accident. That I'd miss Sunday dinner at your parents' house. If I take weekends off now, how the hell am I ever going to taste your mom's cooking again?"

No one said anything for a few minutes while I finished preparing the ingredients for the stir-fry. The rice was already cooking and I'd pulled out extra chicken when Ollie came in.

I thought about the times during the tour we were able to come to town just long enough to join my family for our usual Sunday dinner before flying out again to the next city. Derek had gotten to see how my family worked and learn who everyone was. I was one of nine children, and when we got together every weekend, it was always eventful. Even though he usually stayed in the background, Derek was able to see the dynamics among the siblings.

When I'd been there the Sunday before, I kept looking over to see his reaction when someone said something interesting or funny, but my eyes landed on Mike instead of Derek. Every time that happened it was like taking too many steps off a staircase, foot landing awkwardly and stomach lurching a bit.

Derek began to tell Ollie about the new break-in information, and I got the feeling he was trying to fill the silence. Ollie sat across the kitchen island on a stool with a glass of wine while Derek and I cooked and gathered plates and silverware. He and I had cooked together several times in the weeks before his brother's accident, and we moved in sync through the kitchen. At one point, I caught Ollie watching the two of us, and I wondered what she was thinking.

Once the food was ready and we were sitting at the kitchen table, Ollie began her interrogation.

"So, Wolfe. Tell me more about your family. All I know is that you have brothers and are from the south."

"North Carolina, yes. My twin brothers, Aaron and Kyle, are a few years younger than I am, and they're both in the Army. Aaron is the one who was in the accident. My dad is high up in the Marines, so my parents live near Quantico now in Virginia."

"Why did you leave the military?" she asked.

"Olls," I interrupted, not wanting Derek to feel on the spot.

"It's okay, Jude. I left because I was injured in Afghanistan. It was a roadside bomb and some shrapnel was left over in my leg and hip. They considered it too risky for me to stay on."

"I'm sorry. Do you miss it?" she asked.

"I did for a while, but not anymore," he said before glancing over at me. My stomach flip-flopped and I looked down at my plate.

"Mm," Ollie said knowingly. "That's good. I'm sure it's much more fulfilling to keep adoring fans from loving Jude to death."

Derek laughed. "Maybe not as fulfilling but just as adventurous, I assure you. I'm not the only one women blurt stupid shit to, remember?"

Ollie broke into laughter. "The funniest one happened before you were with us, actually. The band was playing a concert in Florida a couple of years ago and between songs, a woman in the second row screamed out, 'You're my baby daddy!' I thought Jude's jaw was going to hit the ground, and I could just envision the media headlines the following day. Immediately, the woman's girlfriends chimed in with, 'But you ain't got no baby.' The woman looked pissed when she answered, 'Not yet bitches. Not *yet*.' Then she gave Jude a sultry look and put a finger telephone up to her ear mouthing, *Call me*."

Derek snorted. "What about that time Jude was signing autographs and that forty-year-old weirdo asked him to make it out to the best piece of ass he'd ever tasted?"

We all gagged at the memory. "Ugh, that guy wasn't even cute," Ollie complained. "Gross."

I shuddered at the memory. "I ended up signing it to the biggest ass I'd ever met, but I don't think he noticed."

Derek looked over at me. "How many times would you say someone has slipped you their phone number?"

I felt my face heat up again. "Dunno."

"Liar." He grinned. "Guess."

"A few," I admitted.

"Hundreds," Derek said. It was not a question.

"Maybe." I chuckled.

"Have you ever been tempted to call one?" he asked.

"Never." And it was the truth.

"Why not?" He looked surprised.

"Fans are crazy. And I always assume they'd turn around in a skinny minute and sell the story of their Jude encounter."

"Sad," Ollie said. "But true."

I decided to lighten the mood again. "If I was ever tempted, it would have been that middle-aged woman with the tattoo of me on her boob. Now that shit was hot."

Both of them laughed again. "That was heinous," Ollie corrected. "First of all, she practically had to untuck the boob from her waistband to show it to you, and secondly, it was an image of you making out with Walker, Texas Ranger."

Beer dribbled down Derek's chin as he struggled to swallow through his laughter. Without thinking, I reached out and swiped it off with a finger. He kept laughing, hardly noticing the gesture, but I saw the minute Ollie noticed. Her eyes widened and her hand froze halfway to her wineglass.

"Well, kids. Sorry to eat and run, but I have a date with a good sci-fi novel. My grandma is having her hip replaced tomorrow, and I'm the one taking her at the crack of dawn," she said, standing up and taking her plate to the sink. "And I'll be honest, I'm not even going to feel guilty about leaving the dirty dishes for you to clean up."

"What about the ice cream?" Derek asked.

"No, thanks. Consider it payment for dinner and the dishwashing," she said with a wink. "Welcome home, Wolfie. I'm really glad you're back."

25

———

DEREK

After she left I asked Jude to dance with me.

"What?"

"Dance, Bluebell. That thing you do on stage when you shake that gorgeous ass of yours."

"But right now? Here, in the kitchen? Why?" he asked.

"That conversation about Tilly reminded me that I've been itching to dance with you. I love to dance, and I love watching you dance. Since I can't very well take you out to a club, dance with me. Please." I found some music on my phone and pressed play.

We danced for at least an hour. Fast silly dances, slow romantic dances, and finally hot-as-hell grinding, taking turns pressing cock against ass. The alternating dry humping quickly morphed into alternating blow jobs that left us half-dressed and sprawled on top of each other on the couch. Jude looked at me with stars in his eyes, and I thought he'd never looked more alive and beautiful. The feelings I had for him scared the shit out of me.

"We need to shower before we ruin your furniture," I suggested.

Jude laughed and got up, pulling me up and then cleaning some remaining items around the kitchen. I watched him move in his graceful way as I made my way to check the door lock.

"Thanks for asking me to dance, Wolfe. I can't remember the last time I danced with someone I liked besides Ollie."

After I set the alarm, I turned to Jude with a smile. "She's the best. Why doesn't she have a boyfriend?"

"Did you know she's divorced?" Jude asked.

"What? No. Jesus, I thought she was your age. How did she have time to get married and divorced?"

"She was different when we were in high school. She succumbed to peer pressure and turned into a clone. The Ollie I'd known in grade school and middle school became Olivia, wannabe cheerleader and girlfriend to the star basketball player."

"No shit? I can't even picture that," I said.

"It was pretty bad. We grew apart as a result, and she ended up following the guy to UCLA. Only, she spent more time helping him with his classes than working on her own. He popped the question and they were married before he graduated. As soon as she was engaged, he officially moved her into his apartment and encouraged her to give up her classes. Said she wouldn't need her degree since he had money from his family."

"What a jackass. Then what happened?"

"She quit school, they got married, and ten months later, he beat the shit out of her."

My heart stuttered, and I looked over at Jude, who was standing nearby while I loaded the dishwasher.

"Who is he, Jude? Where does he live?"

"Easy, killer. Let me finish," he said with a smile. "She immediately called 911 and told the ER staff what happened. They involved the police and arrested him. Did you know that Ollie's father and two of her three brothers are SFPD?"

"Oh my god." I couldn't help but bark out a laugh. "Did they murder the guy?"

"Close, they stayed on the case and made sure he got jail time. He did two years in county jail," Jude said.

"God, Jude. How did I not know about this? I've spent hours and hours with Ollie over the last six months."

"She doesn't talk about it. Says it happened in another lifetime when she was in her stupid phase. I can't disagree. She really wasn't herself. Once Scott was in jail, she seemed to find herself again. Mom gave her a job at the veterinary clinic and she moved back in with her parents for a while. As soon as I was able to, I hired her."

I started the dishwasher and walked over to him, putting my hands on the counter on either side of his hips, caging him in.

"You're a good man, Bluebell. I didn't realize how good at first."

His hands came up to land on my chest. "What do you mean? You thought I was an asshole?"

"No. I just thought you were all about your public image," I confessed. "A showboat. But I wasn't able to see what you were like in private. Selfless, generous."

He seemed uncomfortable under my compliments so I tried to temper it with humor. "Really good at sucking—"

He smacked me on the chest. "Shut the hell up, Hulk." He laughed. "If you think I'm good at that, you must be desperate. I'm six years out of practice."

"Not anymore," I teased. "But if you think so, I'm willing to go back to your room and let you practice some more."

Before Jude had a chance to answer, I scooped him up in a fireman's carry and walked toward his bedroom, fondling his ass with my free hand as I went.

When we were finally naked on the big bed, Jude took over. He pushed me onto my back and climbed my body like a field of boulders, teasing every inch of my skin with fingers and tongue. By the time I convinced him to put me out of my misery, my cock was so hard it was painful and dripping. He seemed smug when he noticed my desperate state. I didn't care.

"Please," I begged. "*Please.*"

He put the condom on me and lubed himself in front of me. I squeezed my eyes closed and concentrated on breathing. Finally, I felt the sweet familiar heat and squeeze of his channel enveloping me, and I groaned out his name. Now it was his turn for eyes squeezed shut as his sounds became choked.

The sight of Jude Marian riding my body for his pleasure was overwhelming. His abdominal muscles splayed out under my appreciative fingers, his hair long and messy, and his head tilted back to expose the long, sensuous expanse of his throat. The man was stunning.

His eyes opened and caught me staring. "Derek," he breathed.

Yes, I wanted to say. *Yes, baby. Anything.*

Instead, I reached my hand up to pull his face down to me for a kiss. I tried to show him with my mouth what I could never say. *More. I want more. All of you.*

I felt the same words come back to me through his touch and his taste, and for a brief moment, it felt like maybe this was it. Maybe we'd cut through our bullshit excuses and found each other for real. I watched a bead of sweat slide down Jude's chest and land in the nest of curls at the base of his cock. I trailed my finger after it.

And just like that, the moment passed.

Our eyes skittered away from each other and he came off me, surprising me when he climbed off my body and got on the bed beside me on his hands and knees. I got the message and knelt up behind him, sensing face to face was suddenly too much. Instead of feeling stung, I felt relieved. It wasn't something either of us wanted. In the light of day and with rational heads, the reality of a relationship between us was a nightmare.

But here? In bed, when our bodies were joined? It was a dream.

I entered him with a groan of relief and began to thrust. My arm came around his front and I laid my front over his back, dropping kisses onto his shoulders and running my tongue along the salty surface of his skin.

His arms bent and his face landed on the sheet, ass still propped up against my hips. My hands moved to his round ass cheeks as I leaned back up on my knees and searched for the angle that would wreck him.

When he cried out, I knew I'd found it. I continued to pound the right spot until he came in a rush, screaming curses and gasping.

His body's tight clasp around mine pushed me over the edge as usual. I stroked as deeply as I could one more time, and felt the tingle in my balls burst into electric shocks moving outward to the tips of my fingers and toes.

The buzzing in my ears dampened my own cries and I collapsed against Jude's side in a satisfied heap.

"Fuck, Wolfe," Jude said through gasping breaths. "Don't ever leave again."

"No shit."

26

JUDE

Almost two weeks after Derek's return from his brother's accident, we found out two people were arrested for the break-ins in the area. The surveillance footage had finally turned into a useful lead. When they found the thieves, one of them was wearing one of Jude's concert tees and another was wearing a pair of shoes stolen from the politician's house.

It turned out to be a pair of homeless teenagers and that fact bothered me tremendously.

It was October and we were on our way to my parents' place in Hillsborough for family dinner when Derek gave me the update about the judge giving the teens community service instead of formal charges.

"Oh thank god," I said.

My stomach turned at the thought of two homeless kids going to jail for stealing food. I had three brothers who'd been homeless as teens, and I'd heard what it was like to be young and desperate. People pushed to the edge had to make awful decisions in order to survive.

I couldn't help thinking of my brother Griffin.

"Did you know that Griff was homeless for a long time before he found the shelter?" I asked. "He had to do some horrible shit to survive, Wolfe. I can't stand the thought of those kids in jail for trying to find food and clothing. They could have stolen my Grammys or my computer. Hell, they could have stolen any number of expensive items I have just lying around the house. But they didn't."

"I know, Jude. It's okay though. They'll get some help and a fresh start."

"Do you think Ollie can keep track of them so I can help them get on their feet?" I asked.

"I'm sure she can. That woman is a computer wiz."

I bit my lower lip and looked out the window as we passed through downtown San Francisco. "It shouldn't have happened, Derek."

He looked at me with furrowed eyebrows. "You're taking this really personally, Jude. Are you going to be okay?"

"Yeah. It just reminds me how lucky I was to grow up in the family I did. Why me? Why can't all kids be safe, fed, and sheltered?" I put my hand over on Derek's leg in the driver's seat. "I'm just a little thrown by this, you know?"

His hand came down on mine and squeezed. "Yeah, I know."

When we got to my parents' house, almost all my siblings were there with the exception of Jamie and Blue.

My mom came around the corner from the kitchen to greet us.

"There they are. Derek, come give me a hug, sweetie," she said before wrapping her arms around him.

"Rebecca, it's nice to see you again," he said.

"I'm so sorry about your brother, honey. How're he and your mom?" she asked.

"Both doing better. I talked to her yesterday. It sounds like her friends at church are keeping her company with emails to her iPad."

"Good, good. I'm glad you could rearrange your work schedule to join us. You boys come through to the kitchen. We're going to eat inside since it's so windy today," she said, leading us into the kitchen.

I greeted everyone with a wave and gave a tight hug to my sister,

Simone. She was still smarting from her breakup, and I could see rings around her eyes.

"How are you holding up, baby girl?" I asked.

"Like shit, if you really want to know," she confessed. "I was thinking about going to see Jamie in Denali just to get away for a little bit."

Pete overheard and chimed in. "And freeze your ass off? No. I have a better idea. I've been trying to get Ginger to get away for some relaxation in the sun now that her big fundraising gala is over. Why don't I send you two to Cabo or something for a little while? That way you can get away and it'll force her to finally take some time off."

"Shit, Pete. Do you really mean it? I would love that. What do you say, Ginge?" she asked our sister-in-law.

"I'm in. I just didn't want to go alone, and none of my girlfriends are Cabo-worthy. You are though. That would be perfect. Let's do it."

Aunt Tilly appeared from somewhere deep in the house and gave Derek a hug that lasted an inappropriately long time. He politely extracted himself from her embrace, locking eyes with me over her silver head of hair.

"My, my, Derek Wolfe. We haven't seen you around since Simone's *Scandal*," she said.

Simone groaned. "I told you that's not a thing, Aunt Tilly. Stop trying to name it."

Tilly waved her hand dismissively at my sister and kept her attention on my bodyguard. "Sorry about your brother, big guy. But rest assured I'm happy to provide a nice, comfortable bosom to rest your weary head on."

"Uh, thanks, Tilly. I'll keep that in mind," he replied. As he turned away to offer my mom some help in the kitchen, Tilly snaked her hand out to smack him on the ass. Derek jumped and sucked in a breath. I laughed.

"Aunt Tilly, Jesus. Give the guy a break. That's sexual harassment. He's on the clock, for crying out loud," I warned.

Derek quirked a brow at me, and I felt my face flush.

Tilly snickered. "Jude, honey, don't tell me you haven't noticed what a nice ass he has. I mean, mmm-hmm."

My father sighed and my brother Pete barked out a laugh.

"I'm not going to deny the man is in good shape," I admitted. "But that doesn't mean people can just grab his ass any old time they want to."

Derek twisted his tongue between his teeth to keep from calling me on my bullshit. I happened to be a person who took great pleasure in grabbing his ass any old time I wanted to, assuming we weren't in public.

My brother Maverick came to Derek's rescue. "Leave poor Derek alone. He's used to staying quiet in the background and now you guys have him pinned in the spotlight and are discussing his glutes like he's a prize bull at an auction."

"Speaking of auctions," Dad said, "I heard your guitar lesson brought in over thirty thousand dollars for the children's cancer group. That's fantastic, Jude."

My stomach dropped at the reminder of the Ari encounter. I mumbled a thanks and busied myself making a pitcher of ice water to take out to the dining table.

I heard Wolfe chime in. "It was really something, actually. Lawrence Hammond matched the donations, so another thirty-two thousand went to Wounded Warriors in Jude's name."

"Actually," Simone said, "it went to Wounded Warriors in your name, Wolfe."

I heard a lull in conversation and chose not to turn around.

"What?" Derek asked in his usual calm voice. I was starting to learn the nuances of that voice, however, and that calmness belied a promise that this subject would be covered whether it was now or later.

"I only know that because I helped him organize the donation distribution from the auction. The woman who normally does it was on maternity leave. I do all of that work for the animal shelter so he knew I could stand in for Brenda."

"Speaking of Brenda," I chimed in, "has she had her baby yet?"

Leave it to news of a new baby to get the conversation rolling in a new direction.

Late that night after we'd returned to my place and vigorously wiped the two days of celibacy out of our memories, he brought it up again.

I lay on my back with my head leaning against Derek's calf and my feet up by his shoulders. His hand ran a delicious trail up and down my bent leg as we enjoyed our post-orgasmic stupor.

"You didn't tell me you sent that donation in my name," Derek said. "Thank you."

I opened my mouth to make a joke but forced myself to give him the respect he deserved. "You're welcome. Thank you for your service."

Derek leaned up on an elbow to look at me. His eyes were searching mine and I reached out to smooth the line between them.

"You're welcome, Bluebell. I would say it was my pleasure, but it definitely wasn't." A shadow darkened his face. It was one I'd seen before and had been too scared to ask him about. That conversation was for lovers, partners. It wasn't for fuck buddies.

"No, I guess not."

"You ready to take a shower and go to sleep?" Derek asked. "It's late."

"Hm? Oh, sure," I said, following him into my bathroom, still envisioning what he could have gone through to bring those shadowed memories to his face.

I took my time sliding soapy hands along the expanse of his muscled back and torso, giving special attention to the broad, rounded shoulders and biceps I liked to clutch when Derek was on top of me. Just as his mouth began to turn up in a smile that could only mean good things for me, the perimeter alarm blared angrily.

27

DEREK

I scrambled into my clothes while still dripping wet and barked at Jude to stay where he was. Racing out of the bedroom, I heard phones start ringing and knew it would be the alarm company calling Jude and On Your Six calling me.

We discovered a crashed drone in the driveway with a transmitting video camera on board. The SFPD officers suspected it was most likely some sort of media attempt to get private photographs of Jude in his home. They had learned from LAPD that drones were being used more and more to spy on celebrities.

The situation brought into focus that even being together behind the closed doors of Jude's home could be dangerous. I couldn't imagine someone from the media getting a shot of Jude in a compromising situation with me or otherwise. Even a photo of him making breakfast fully clothed would be a massive invasion of his privacy. A photo of the two of us having sex was unthinkable. It would be worth an obscene amount of money.

After the police and security company responders left that night, it was obvious Jude was still shaken. His eyes were wide and he was pale. I had already closed all the blinds and curtains in the house and made note of the few windows that didn't have any type of covering.

He could get Ollie to look into fixing that the following day while I researched any possible way of disabling drones around the house.

I couldn't help but triple-check the window and door locks before resetting the alarm. Jude was in the kitchen making a cup of hot tea and asked if I wanted any.

"You know I hate tea, especially that stuff you drink," I said, filling a glass of ice water instead.

"It's good for the voice," he explained.

"I know. Maybe that's why it tastes like shit."

"Maybe." He smiled.

"You okay?" I asked him.

Jude shrugged. "Not really. I'm pissed off. Times like these make me wonder if it's worth it."

"You've given up a lot for your career. But you have food in your kitchen, a roof over your head, good health, and a loving family. Lots of people would sacrifice plenty for any one of those things. Remember that."

He rubbed his hands over his face. "You're right. Thanks, Wolfe. I needed to hear that tonight."

"Let's go to sleep." I pulled him up from his stool and led him by the hand toward his bedroom. "It's beyond late. Things will look better in the morning."

Once we were in bed, Jude fell asleep pretty quickly. His warm body was attached to my side, and my fingers ran through his hair as I thought about what he'd said about success being worth the sacrifices of fame.

The concept of something good being worth a certain amount of sacrifice was something that I'd been confronted with my whole life. Growing up in the military taught kids that national security was worth missing their parents for months on end, that promotions and adventure were worth the heartache of saying goodbye to friends. That sometimes saving someone's life was worth sacrificing your own.

Worth it.

That keeping my family blissfully ignorant of my sexuality was worth hiding my true self. I wondered what Jude thought about it. Was his success and fame worth being celibate for six goddamned years of his life? Was protecting his heart from another betrayal like Ari's worth not letting anyone get close?

For that matter, were we really succeeding at keeping our emotional distance from each other? It didn't feel like it. It felt suspiciously like a relationship. One in which we cared about each other, missed each other when we were apart, and took comfort in climbing into bed together after a long night, even with no plans to have sex. Just what kind of sex-only relationship was that? We were kidding ourselves.

What Jude and I were falling into was a relationship.

I tried to decide how I felt about that realization. My two biggest reasons for avoiding emotional entanglements were the risk of being outed to my family and my inability to commit to someone when I was hardly ever home.

Both of those excuses were moot with Jude. He didn't want to be outed either, and when I wasn't home, it was because I was with him. I lived with him, for god's sake. I slept in his bed five nights out of seven.

Would it really be so bad if I opened myself up to a relationship with Jude Marian? Maybe. But it didn't have to be all or nothing. I could let go of some of my hesitation. Be open to him and open to finding out what would come next if we allowed our... whatever it was, to go where it naturally wanted to go.

I shifted us both until I spooned against his back. My lips pressed a kiss on his bare shoulder, and I was tempted to kiss him awake and then pleasure him back into oblivion. I resisted the urge in favor of letting him sleep and forced myself to sleep as well.

WHILE JUDE PRACTICED with the band the next morning in his home studio, Ollie and I worked side by side at the kitchen table on our laptops.

We had ended up together like that several times over the weeks and enjoyed each other's company. I had started to get the feeling she suspected something was going on between Jude and me, and I was surprised to realize I didn't mind her knowing. If Jude could trust her, then I could too.

That morning Clint dropped by with some huge news. Ollie and I were arguing about whether or not she should change her hair color to orange for Halloween when the doorbell rang.

I escorted Clint down to the studio with Ollie hot on my heels. She must have known he wouldn't drop by unless he had something interesting to share.

Jude saw me through the window of the studio and his whole face lit up. God, he was fucking adorable when he smiled. He was beautiful all the time, but there was something magical about being on the receiving end of that incredible grin.

The music stopped and Jude pushed the door open.

"Hey, guys, what's going on?" he asked.

The band trickled out and made their way to a cluster of large couches arranged in front of a bank of television screens hanging on the wall of the basement TV room. It was the kind of space most men would use to invite their friends over to watch a big football game, but it was more likely to be used for movie marathons or video games in Jude's house.

While my body wanted to follow Jude to a spot on the sofa, my brain remembered I was on duty as a bodyguard. A bodyguard stayed in the background against a wall and remained invisible. I quietly wandered away a professional distance.

The look on Jude's face confirmed I wasn't the only one who felt a new strangeness at this dichotomy between our personal time and professional time. It had been a while since I'd been in bodyguard mode around Clint and the band.

Jude's eyebrows furrowed and I could see his eyes flick toward me every few minutes. I did my best to retain the stoic neutral face I had perfected in the military.

Clint greeted everyone and announced he had some very exciting news.

"I got a gig for you in early February in Nashville," Clint began with a big grin on his face. My stomach knotted at the word "Nashville," and I tried to contain my outward expression of annoyance to a clenching of my jaw.

I looked over to Jude, whose eyes were already on mine and full of worry.

"At the Ryman?" Fiona asked with raised brows. "Please say it's the Ryman. I love playing there."

"No, I'm afraid it's at the stadium," he said. There was a smattering of disappointed sighs. Surely he hadn't come to Jude's house just to tell them about a regular old concert.

"They want you to sing the halftime show at the Super Bowl."

Silence for a beat. Jude seemed as though he was getting ready to stand up, but quickly settled back down.

Beck, the drummer, jumped up and shouted. "Woo-hoo!"

Fiona looked shell-shocked. "Are you for real? Oh my god. Are you serious right now, Clint?" she asked in a hushed whisper.

Sutter and Joey high-fived and whooped their excitement before Sutter told everyone it was a dream come true. Even Jude couldn't help but smile in response to the news. It didn't matter where the game was, being asked to play in front of 100 million viewers worldwide was like reaching the pinnacle of an artist's career.

As the excitement bubbled through the room, Clint made sure to remind everyone they had to keep the news confidential until they signed all the paperwork and the NFL made the official announcement. No one could even tell their families.

After realizing they wouldn't get any more productive practice in for the day, everyone moved up to the kitchen to celebrate with a drink. Clint told everyone that after he called to accept the offer, they could expect paperwork by the end of the day.

Again, I stayed in the background while everyone celebrated. I gave Jude a smile of congratulations, and he thanked me with a grin. Ollie made a point to stand near me and engage me in bits of conversation. She'd always treated me as a coworker or friend more than a bodyguard and even on tour, she was uncomfortable with my invisibility routine.

It seemed she was even more uncomfortable now, which led me to believe she really did know things were more than bodyguard and client between Jude and me. I'd have to ask him about it.

I'd also have to think about how to plan Jude's security while we were in Ari's hometown.

Before Clint and the band left for the day, he made one last announcement. The band would travel to Nashville a few weeks later to hammer out production plans for the show with the event committee. Hundreds of people would be hired to help facilitate the halftime show, and it was a massive undertaking that required coordination and practice.

I wondered if it would be possible for Jude to travel to Nashville for the planning meeting without Ari finding out.

28

JUDE

Hearing about the Super Bowl gig was unbelievable. No one could deny a band's success once it played that halftime show. It truly was a dream come true for all of us.

I couldn't wait to tell my family, but more than that, I couldn't wait to talk to Derek about it. When Clint had announced the news, I almost jumped up and ran over to Derek. Was that crazy? That the first person I wanted to share the excitement with was my bodyguard?

Whatever was happening between the two of us was getting complicated. I was feeling less in control of my ability to hide my feelings for Derek from anyone, including myself. He was quickly becoming the person I told everything to. But more than that, he was becoming the person I *wanted* to tell everything to. And I wasn't sure how he would feel about that.

Once everyone had left, Ollie gave me a quick hug and disappeared too. I finished locking the door behind her and turned to Derek. He stood leaning back against the kitchen counter with his hands resting on the edge by his hips. His face sported a killer smile and my heart did a little jig.

"So," I said with a grin.

"So," he replied with a smirk.

"Guess what happened at work today?" I teased.

"C'mere, Bluebell." He held out his arms and I jumped him, landing with my arms around his neck. I felt the vibration of his laugh against my chest and the tight clasp of his arms around my back.

"Congratulations, Jude. That's really something," he said into my ear.

"Thanks, Wolfe. I can't wait to tell my dad. He and Pete will flip out."

Derek laughed again. "They sure will. Ginger too."

I pulled my face back to look into his green eyes. "How should we celebrate?"

The green intensified. "Naked."

"Hot damn," I agreed with a grin. "Lead the way, Marine."

Derek led the way to the bedroom, removing an article of clothing every few steps. Following that trail of discarded clothes through the house was like following a treasure map where X marks the spot of my next orgasm. Each piece felt warm under my bare feet, and I thought about the heat from his body in his clothing all day.

Damned lucky pants.

As I walked, I did the same stripping routine except mine was done in secret. He never looked back, so when I tackled him buck naked onto my bed, he gasped before laughing.

Our bodies rolled together as our hands memorized skin and our lips found each other. Derek's fingers accidentally brushed against a particularly ticklish spot, and I forgot to hide my reaction. Once he knew my weakness, he exploited it mercilessly.

"Uncle, *uncle*," I gasped through laughter, unable to catch my breath as his fingers assaulted that spot. "Baby, stop."

He stopped and locked eyes with me. I replayed the endearment in my mind and felt my face flush. My teeth gripped my lip to keep from apologizing for being too familiar. What was I sorry for? He'd called *me* baby before, and I loved it. Why was it weird for me to do the same?

Derek's mouth stretched slowly into a wide grin before it lowered itself onto mine in a slow, sensual kiss. The kiss told me all was well. More than that, all was magnificent.

Our lips slow danced before my fingers turned grabby. I ran my hands up into his hair and pulled his head back, exposing his throat. My mouth moved in wet kisses down to his Adam's apple, where it sucked and teased until I dipped my tongue into the cleft at the base of his throat.

He tasted like Derek. My Derek. For a moment, I was overwhelmed by the familiarity of his taste, his smell, the feel of his skin against mine. I felt a burn behind my eyes and squeezed them closed to block it out as my mouth continued moving along the top of his shoulders, my nose desperately wanting to bury itself in his neck to suck in his scent and lose myself. I resisted, afraid the move would push my already strangled emotions over the edge.

"Jude?" he whispered.

"Mmm?"

"I love the way you make me feel," he said in that sexy voice of his.

My chest swelled with relief and something more. I raised my head to meet his gaze straight on.

"What do you want, Wolfe? I'll do anything you want to make you feel even better."

I felt his heart speed up under the hand I had resting on his bare chest.

"I want you on your back the entire time. I want to be able to see you when you come," Derek said.

I swallowed. The few times we'd started off in missionary position, it had been too intense. We inevitably ended up back to front in some way before our orgasms hit. What he was asking for wasn't about a sex position. It was about making a connection.

I nodded. "Okay."

His face relaxed into a smile of gratitude, and, in a heartbeat, he was plucking all of the right chords on my body. I felt whatever control I had slip away as my whimpers turned into slutty sounds of begging and pleading.

Derek looked into my eyes and slowed for a brief moment while he reached to brush long strands of hair off my face. That tender gesture in the midst of hot, sweaty lust took my breath away.

"*Derek*," I whispered.

"Yes, baby," he responded in a soft voice.

I couldn't grasp the words to say what I was feeling. They were blocked by fear and nerves, feelings that were becoming all too familiar. So I didn't say anything. Everything I wanted to tell him came out through my touch.

As he entered me, I cradled his jaw and stroked my thumbs over his cheeks. With each slow stroke he made into my body, I traced a part of his face with my fingers— his lips, his nose, his eyebrows. He lowered his mouth onto mine and kissed me with the softness of dandelion fluff, and I had to reach behind his neck to pull him in harder. Tenderness morphed to frenzy as our pace quickened.

We kissed deeply and feverishly, our bodies thrusting together and our breathing beginning to trip.

Derek's body was slick with sweat, and I raked my fingers through his short hair, leaving it sticking up in damp spikes. His curses were muffled where his lips pressed into my shoulder and his hands came up to cup the back of my head. My skin tightened and my nerves tingled.

"*Jude*," he breathed before biting down hard on the skin of my shoulder.

Oh my god.

Suddenly, without warning, energy pulses shot through my body as my climax rolled through in wave after wave of gratification. My head fell back in surprise and my body arched up as I cried out my release. Warm shots landed on my chest and abdomen, even catching Derek under the chin. My hands were still firmly attached to his shoulders and I had a dim realization that I'd come without either of us touching me. I squeezed my eyes closed in disbelief.

His orgasm hit shortly after mine. I opened my eyes again just in time to see his flushed face tighten and eyes lock onto mine as he pounded into me one last time. His large hands wrapped around the back of my head were the only thing keeping me from being shoved up into the headboard. I felt his growl as much as heard it, and it was unlike any noise he'd ever made in bed with me. It was primal in a way that both excited and unnerved me.

I brought my legs down to land my feet flat on the bed next to Derek's legs. His heaving chest was pressed against mine, propped up only by his elbows. I kissed his face, tasting the salt of his skin and relishing in the knowledge he'd earned that sweat in the pursuit of my pleasure.

My thighs squeezed against his sides even though they trembled. I wanted to embrace him with my whole body. Hang on to him and not ever let him leave my bed.

Derek's forehead laid against my shoulder, his face turned in toward the side of my head. I felt soft lips graze my ear, and I breathed out a sigh.

I loved him.

We stayed together like that for a few moments in silence, the only sounds our ragged breaths and the whisper of lips on skin. I turned my head to look at him and saw him watching me.

"I'm so sorry," I whispered.

His eyebrows raised in confusion.

"For what?" Derek asked.

I felt my heart begin to peel apart and wanted to stop the words before they came out.

"I can't do this anymore."

29

DEREK

I tilted my head, assuming I had misunderstood Jude. My heart felt like it was being shoved up into my throat.

"What do you mean?" I asked.

"This, us. Friends with benefits or whatever," he blurted.

"Okay..." I said, wondering what he was trying to say.

"It's not working, Derek... I just... I... ugh!" he said in frustration, pushing me off of him. He got up and strode to the bathroom, closing the door behind him.

What the hell had just happened? Was he telling me he didn't want to sleep with me anymore? Pain snuck in and settled sharp knives in my gut. I didn't know whether to be hurt or angry.

We had originally agreed on sex only. No relationship, no feelings. It was better for both of us. So what if I'd developed feelings for Jude? He didn't want that. Maybe this was his way of informing me he knew things had changed for me, and he wasn't interested in someone with feelings.

When he didn't come back out immediately, I realized he was probably waiting for me to get the message. What was I waiting for? He'd said he couldn't do it anymore, didn't he? What more was there to say?

I stood up slowly and forced myself to walk out of his bedroom. Each step I took was like a hammer hitting the ends of the knives in my stomach, and I clenched my teeth to keep from cursing.

It took all my concentration to gather my discarded clothes from the hallway and make it to the sanctuary of the guest room. The hot shower was a balm to my shaky body and over sensitized skin. I felt raw and used, flayed open and then spit on.

The whole thing was my fault. I knew going into it I wouldn't be able to stay just friends with Jude after sleeping with him. And I knew better than to risk my employment stability by screwing around with a client. Would I really be able to stay on Jude's security detail after this? It would certainly be a true test of my maturity.

I was still standing under the water with my eyes closed when I heard the bathroom door slam open.

"Are you fucking kidding me right now?" Jude shouted.

I jumped and bumped my elbow against the hard tile wall.

"What?" I asked.

"That's it? After what just happened, the connection we made and then me trying to talk to you about it, you just walk out?" He was naked and angry as a hornet. God, even when he was stark raving mad, he was stunning.

"You said you didn't want to do the friends-with-benefits thing anymore and I said okay. Why are you mad at me, Jude? I'm trying to respect your wishes," I said.

He opened the shower door and stepped in behind me.

"Right. Except I can't be your fuck buddy because *I have feelings for you*, asshole. I just couldn't figure out how to put the words together to tell you. I was scared of saying the wrong thing."

My heart rate hitched up as I tried to figure out what he meant by that.

"So... are you saying we're not done, we're just done pretending it's casual?" I asked, afraid of making assumptions.

His brown eyes shot angry darts at me and I would have given anything to be able to read his mind.

"Just tell me what you want, Bluebell. I'm obviously clueless here," I added.

"I care about you, damn it. I thought maybe you felt the same way. Was I wrong?"

"No. Jesus, no, which is why I don't want to hurt you. No matter what happens, I can't handle hurting you," I told him, reaching out to grab his elbows. "You said you didn't want a relationship, so I've been trying to keep my feelings to myself. I didn't want to put any pressure on you."

Jude let out a big breath. "I know that's what I said, Derek. But sometimes you can't help it when you start falling for someone. I was an idiot to ever think otherwise."

The sound of my first name spoken by Jude's beautiful voice never failed to stop me in my tracks. I felt my mouth widen in a shit-eating grin as I pulled him closer. "Get back to the part where you said you're falling for me."

"Fuck you," he muttered as he came willingly into my embrace, wrapping his own arms around my waist. I stepped us back until the warm spray ran over both of us.

My heart was hammering with relief. Jude hadn't given up on us. He was here, and he wanted to be with me.

"You're not the only one who's falling, Jude. But what are we going to do about it? I'm not ready to come out yet, and I don't think you are either," I said.

He shrugged. "I'd come out if you wanted me to, but I'd be terrified of the media invasion on your life."

I shuddered in revulsion at the thought of what that exposure would be like. "No, thanks. I can't even imagine the scrutiny. I've never understood how you do it."

"Right. So why don't we just acknowledge that we've moved past the sex only stage into an actual relationship? Oh, and you promise not to sleep with anyone else while we're together," he added with his own grin.

"I'm not sleeping with anyone else, and I sure as hell expect the same from you, superstar."

That earned me a laugh.

"Right, He-Man. Because I'm the one out there clubbing for dicks on my days off."

I smiled at his rare display of jealousy. So fucking cute. "I'll have you know I haven't touched another person in months. Since before you and I got together. I've hardly had the time, not to mention I sure as hell haven't had the inclination." I began lathering his skin with a bar of soap. "If we're going to be exclusive, maybe we could talk about getting rid of the condoms. I've been tested recently, and I'm sure you have too."

He smiled. "Yes, I have. And this conversation has officially done a one-eighty. Kind of makes me want to drag you out of the shower and lube you up again."

"I'm not opposed to that, but isn't Ollie going to turn up for dinner sometime tonight?" I asked, leaning down to drop light kisses on the bruise forming where I'd bitten his shoulder.

Jude pouted. "I guess you're right. We should finish and get dressed."

We spent a few more minutes fondling each other with the soap before I thought of something.

"Do you want to tell Ollie about us?"

Jude stopped and stared at me. "Would that be okay with you?"

"If you trust her, then I do too. Plus, I think she already knows. It'd be a lot more comfortable when we hang out together if we didn't have to worry so much about it. Sometimes I catch myself right before touching you and it puts me on edge. And I'd especially like to be able to sit next to you when we watch movies together. As things are now, I end up sitting in a chair while you two cuddle. It sucks."

Jude's face lit up. "That would be great. I'd love to tell her. She adores you, you know. Of course, she won't for much longer if you steal her cuddle partner."

"Maybe we'll have to work on finding her a boyfriend. What about your brother Thad?"

"Nah, I think he's been talking to Tristan's cousin Sarah over Skype since they met in Napa."

"Hm. Well, we'll need to think of someone else."

"Speaking of Tristan, I was hoping to go up to the vineyard to see Blue next weekend now that he's back from London. Can you change your schedule and come with me?" Jude asked.

"Probably. I'll send Mike a text after we get dressed."

We finished up and were settled on the couch off the end of the kitchen when Ollie arrived for dinner. Jude plucked out a new tune on his guitar while I watched the kickoff of a Monday Night Football game on mute.

Ollie knocked before letting herself in. It was her turn to cook, and I was looking forward to something a little more exciting than Jude's healthy crap.

"Whatchu got for us tonight, darlin'?" I asked. "Please say it isn't green."

Jude reached out his foot to shove my leg. "You'll thank me one day when you're not dead from cardiac arrest."

"I am making an awesome spicy poblano corn chowder since it's finally gotten chilly this week, and then we'll have leftovers to eat on Halloween when I make you two watch all my favorite scary movies," Ollie informed us.

"Shit, Olls. You know I don't like scary movies," Jude said.

"That's okay, Bluebell, I'll protect you from the scary monsters," I reminded him with a laugh.

"You might have to protect him through the night, Wolfe. You know, like in his bed. Naked," she teased.

"I already do, sweetheart," I said, leaning over and kissing Jude right on the mouth, sliding my tongue through his lips and devouring him until his fingers accidentally plucked the guitar strings they gripped.

"Fuck, Wolfe," Jude gasped, tearing his mouth away from mine with a deep blush.

"Not right now, babe. Later though," I said with a wink and went back to watching the game.

Ollie laughed until she snorted. "You could have just said you were together, you know. No need to put on a display to make me both jealous *and* horny."

"Where's the fun in that?" I asked with a grin.

"Guess you're right. Thank god. It's about damned time," she said before turning and pointing her finger at me. "But don't think this means you can cuddle with him during the movie. I've had dibs on that for decades."

Damn it.

30

JUDE

As the time approached to travel to Nashville, I sensed Derek getting squirrelly. He requested additional security to travel with us and told Ollie to book us into a private condo rental downtown so there wouldn't be a hotel with our room information listed.

We'd had a great time at the vineyard, and I was even able to convince Derek to relax and play poker with us. We drank and played cards late into the night in Tristan and Blue's cabin, and I enjoyed seeing Blue's utter and complete happiness in Tristan's company.

The two of them were so open and easy with each other, which reminded me for the millionth time that Derek's and my relationship had an unfair handicap. I wanted so badly to be able to flirt openly with him, grab his hand when I wanted to, and lean on him without worrying who would see.

Never in a million years would I have expected to live my life in the closet. I grew up in San Francisco to liberal parents who volunteered with gay youth. *Five* of my brothers were gay, for god's sake. Of all people to be in the closet, I was the most ridiculous. It was frustrating. I wondered what it would take before I decided to come out.

The following week was Halloween. Ollie ended up going to visit her parents to help hand out candy, and I decided to pay a surprise visit to my nieces at Pete and Ginger's house. Derek was taking his days off, so Mike drove me over to Pete's in the afternoon to drop off some candy and Halloween books I'd picked up for the girls.

I'd had an ulterior motive in going out, and I asked Mike to drive us past his house before heading back to my place. He had kids who were trick-or-treating age, and I'd be damned if I was going to let him miss it.

I'd brought along candy and books for Mike's kids too, and the look on his face when I produced them was priceless.

"Jude. Shit, you didn't need to do this," he said.

"I know that. But if my dad had to work on Halloween, it would have sucked. I'm doing this for your kids, not you," I joked.

Mike and I walked his kids around the neighborhood and for once in more than five years, I was actually essentially ignored. Anytime someone's eyes roamed over me, they must have assumed I was dressed as Jude for the holiday. It was strangely liberating.

The following day I met Derek at the airport for our flight to Nashville. Since the whole band plus various people from Clint's office and Ollie were traveling with us, we chartered a plane.

Once we were on board, I smelled Derek's aftershave and felt myself getting hard. Luckily I had an oversized hoodie to hide the growing bulge, but it was still embarrassing to know how quickly I was affected in his company. I shifted in my seat. He must have known what was going on because he raised his eyebrow and smirked at me.

"Bastard," I muttered under my breath.

"I believe you meant 'sexy bastard,'" he muttered back. I narrowed my eyes at him.

"Shut up."

He barked out a laugh that got Ollie's attention.

"Why are you blushing, baby cakes?" she asked me.

"I'm not blushing. I'm just hot," I corrected.

"Yeah, you are," Derek mumbled through a fake cough.

I smacked his chest. "Dude, seriously. Stop it," I demanded. But I couldn't hold back my own laugh.

While we prepared to take off, Derek did his usual routine of trying to distract me with stupid stories. By the time I stopped laughing, we were at cruising altitude, and Clint asked to switch seats with Derek so he could talk to me about some details of the new album contract.

After our conversation, Clint stayed in the seat next to mine. I couldn't figure out how to tell him to switch back without sounding like a brat. Remembering it was a charter flight without the no-cell-phone rule, I pulled out my phone to text Derek.

Jude: *He's not budging.*

Derek: *I figured.*

Jude: *He doesn't smell as good as you do.*

Derek: *Why are you sniffing him?*

Jude: *I'm not. But I wouldn't mind sniffing you some more.*

Derek: *I'm sitting next to Sutter and he smells like ass.*

Jude: *Now who's inappropriately sniffing people?*

Derek: *Think he'd be up for the Mile High Club?*

Jude: *Don't make me come up there.*

Derek: *Is that a threat or a promise?*

Jude: *I really feel like whining. Can't you come put a sleeper hold or something on Clint? We can move him without him ever finding out.*

Derek: *A sleeper hold doesn't cause amnesia. Plus, there would be witnesses.*

Jude: *But could you do it?*

Derek: *I'd tell you but then I'd have to...*

Jude: *Liar.*

Derek: *Okay, fine. I do know how to do a sleeper hold but I'm not doing it on Clint. I also know how to parachute, but we're not doing that either.*

Jude: *Do it to me later?*

Derek: *So many ways I could respond to that question, Bluebell...*

Jude: *Are we going to be able to sleep in the same room tonight?*

Derek: *Hope so. Ollie gave me some kind of strange wink when she told me she hooked us up with the condo. Either she worked some slutty magic for us, or she's coming down with pinkeye.*

Jude: *How am I supposed to snooze if I can't lean on your shoulder?*

Derek: *You need to figure it out and get some rest. If you sleep now, we can stay up late tonight.*

Jude: *Ooo! Can we watch infomercials?*

Derek: *Sure. Except instead of watching we'll be sucking. And instead of infomercials it will be cock. Other than that, exact same thing.*

Jude: *I like your version better. As long as when we get to the end you say, "But wait! There's more..."*

Derek: *If I recall proper infomercial nomenclature, there's always a special two-for-one offer. That sounds like an interesting challenge.*

Jude: *Yes, please.*

Derek: *Rest up, Bluebell.*

I slipped on my big headphones and fell asleep listening to some old Nanci Griffith music I loved. The song was "Outbound Plane" and certain lines stood out, "You may walk away from love but / You'll fall head and heels again."

Leave it to a country song to hit the nail on the head when it came to love.

THE TRIP to Nashville started off on the right foot. We had a friendly introduction dinner with the committee, which was thrilled to have us accept the invitation to perform. All the people seemed genuinely excited to put together a great show, and I was energized by the band's willingness to brainstorm fresh ideas.

Even better than the successful dinner was the private wing of the condo Ollie had rented. The master suite had a bedroom next to it down one hallway while the other two bedrooms were on the opposite end of the condo. Obviously Derek made a show of setting up in the room next to mine while Ollie and the other bodyguard settled into the other two.

As soon as we went to bed, Derek snuck into my room and fulfilled his promises of mutually beneficial sucking and multiple orgasms. After we showered, my gorgeous bodyguard spent the night with a country music singer clinging to his large, warm back like a turtle shell.

The next day started off with a planning meeting led by the event managers, and we settled on the performance details. The public relations teams hammered out the press release language and the team separated to spend the evening doing whatever they wanted before the next day's press conference. With one exception.

Clint had roped me into a charity dinner with one of the

members of the Super Bowl committee who had been instrumental in bringing the event to Nashville. Dominick Floros was the CEO of one of the banks headquartered in Nashville and wanted to request my participation in some kind of veteran fundraising event his bank was spearheading.

As usual Ollie begged off, so it was just Clint, Derek, and me in the limo. The other security guard, Diego, had been with me in the afternoon while Derek met with the security team managing the stadium during the Super Bowl, but Derek had asked him to accompany Ollie that evening in case she wanted to go out. Derek didn't want to risk her being out on her own in Nashville just in case Ari knew about her.

When we got to the restaurant, Mr. Floros met us at the entrance.

"Good evening, Jude, Clint. So nice of you to come. We are just through here in the private dining room."

We shook hands with the tall man and I thanked him for inviting us.

"It's nice to meet you Dominick," I said.

"Dom, please. I've invited a few others involved in planning the fundraiser, and I can't wait to introduce you. Please follow me," he said before leading us to a private dining room.

It shouldn't have surprised me to see Ari in that dining room, but it did.

31

DEREK

I couldn't decide who I wanted to kill more. Ari for being there, or my boss, Joel, for not finding out where Ari was going to be every minute we were in Nashville.

My hand came to rest on Jude's lower back instinctively when I saw Ari standing in the room. I quickly removed it to place my hands behind my back as I remained standing behind him.

Sure enough, when Dom tried to introduce Ari to Jude, Ari tried coming in for a big hug. I wasn't about to let that happen no matter how rude it would make me look. I deliberately dropped my phone and then bumped against Jude while I leaned down to grab it. When I stood back up with the phone, I was magically in between Ari and Jude. Imagine that.

Hug denied.

While I stammered out a fake apology, I heard Jude cough-laugh. Slipping my phone back into my pocket, I turned around to wink at him before taking my spot against the wall by the door.

The dinner was the typical bullshit small talk that had originally given me the false impression Jude was shallow. He said all the right things and played the game to perfection. Knowing him the way I did now, though, I could see through it like glass. It was a complete front. His fingers lightly tapped out the rhythm of one of his new songs against his thigh under the table. When the food came, he carefully selected each bite to make sure it was the same size and then chewed it twice as long as usual. He was bored out of his goddamned mind.

He wasn't the only one. My mind wandered in a million different directions in an attempt to stay alert. At one point, I realized I was basically paid to stare at my hot boyfriend all day. The thought almost caused a bark of laughter to bubble up, so I bit my tongue to keep it from escaping. He was seriously beautiful though. Even before we were together I had moments of feeling insanely lucky to be paid to watch him. Sure, there were long hours, loads of travel, and so much time on my feet that it hurt, but Jude Marian was a joy to watch.

He carried himself with a casual grace and was always attentive to the people around him. His voice was hypnotic and his smile was—

I sighed. God, I was pathetic. There was no denying how hard I was falling for the man.

After dinner Jude excused himself to the men's room and I followed. When we were out of earshot of the others, he turned to look at me.

"I want you to order something for dinner to take back with us. Don't argue with me. I'll pay for it, okay?"

I could tell he was going to fight for this one, so I shrugged. "Okay."

His eyebrows went up. "That's it? You're not going to argue with me?"

"Do you want me to?" I asked with a smile.

"No." He laughed. "But you're usually pigheaded. You must be feeling sorry for me tonight."

"Well, I am. But I'm also hungry, and one of those steaks looked amazing. You're not going to make me order something vegetarian, are you?" I already knew he didn't mind me eating meat, but I liked teasing him about it.

"You can order the steak. I'll just have to donate the equivalent price to the ASPCA in your name. It's no big deal," he said with a straight face.

I barked out a laugh. "Have at it, Bluebell. Totally worth it. Be sure to mention the pig whose life was sacrificed for the bacon bits on the loaded potato I'm getting too."

"You'll have to write a sympathy card to the potato's mother. Are you sure it's worth it just for one meal?"

"Throw in a slice of cheesecake and I'll get my boyfriend to double his donation. He's rich. He can afford it. Plus, he's a total pushover for a good cause. Why, just tonight he agreed to donate a certain amount of money to a charity event, but I know he'll secretly write the check for twice as much."

Jude blushed and looked away. "Shut up," he muttered. "Except the boyfriend part. That part you can say as much as you want."

When we returned to the dining room, there was a new face in the room. The older gentleman was about Dom's age and looked similarly wealthy and distinguished.

Ari was the one to make the introductions.

"Jude, I'd like to introduce you to my father-in-law, Joseph Crawford. Joe, this is Jude."

"Nice to meet you, Joe," Jude said with a polite smile. "I met your daughter a few months ago. She's a lovely woman."

"Thank you. You're very kind to say so. Listen, Jude, Ari and I were hoping to keep you after dinner for a few minutes to talk to you about something. Could you spare time for a drink with us after dessert?"

What was he supposed to say when put on the spot in front of everyone? I almost leaned forward to remind Jude of an important function he needed to get to, but I knew I wouldn't be able to sell it. Plus, I had to trust him to manage his own shit the way he saw fit.

"I can only stay for one more drink," Jude said. "I'm afraid we have an early press conference in the morning that I still need to prepare for."

After dessert, everyone left except Jude, Ari, and his father-in-law.

And me. I continued to stand by the door with my hands clasped and my neutral face glued in place.

Mr. Crawford began the conversation. "Jude, Ari here tells me that he has introduced the idea to you of letting our company handle your investments."

I almost barked out a laugh. Assuming that's what this was about and hearing it spoken aloud were two different things. Pathetic.

Jude nodded.

"Right, well, I'd like to personally explain what makes our firm different from the others and give you the opportunity to—"

"Joe, I'm going to stop you right there," Jude broke in. "While I appreciate your coming out tonight to meet with me, I make it a policy never to mix business with pleasure. Regardless of how successful your company is, I do not hire financial advisers based on personal relationships or past friendships. While that may seem counterintuitive to you, it's what I've found works best for me. Now, if you'll excuse me, I'm going to get back to my bandmates for a late meeting."

I was stunned and impressed. This wasn't the sweet Jude I knew. This was someone who had enough and wasn't going to listen to a minute more. Finally.

I fucking loved that man.

Oh, shit.

I really did.

Jude stood up and gave a winning smile to Joe Crawford while reaching out to shake his hand. *No hard feelings*, his smile said. *Just business.*

When Jude turned to Ari, Ari shocked the hell out of both of us. He winked at Jude and mouthed, *Thank you.*

Jude turned on his heel and walked out of the private dining room. I followed him until he made it out to the town car waiting in the parking lot. When we got into the car, he finally took a breath and looked at me.

"Did you order the steak?"

I blinked at him, trying to hear what he was asking. In my head, all I could hear was the repetitive pounding of a phrase I'd never uttered to a single person outside of my family.

I love you.

I wasn't sure I'd ever be ready to say it out loud, but I knew in my heart it was the complete truth.

32

JUDE

November and December went by in a flash. The days were spent recording our new album and the nights, as usual, were spent worshipping Derek Wolfe's body.

The two of us fell into a happy routine that actually kind of resembled dating, like normal people. We even went out to dinner and to the movies a few times together, even though we avoided any kind of PDA like the plague.

Many nights we stayed in and cooked. Either just the two of us or with Ollie. I even thought about telling my family about Derek but had to keep reminding myself that once the circle of trust grew larger, at some point it would break.

We were happy together. One night he surprised me with a visit to a rock climbing gym. Ollie had helped him arrange the gym to stay open after hours just for the two of us, and I repaid the treat the following week by taking him camping at Big Basin. I thought it was cold as shit, but he loved it. Since sleeping with Derek was like sleeping near a roaring fire, I survived.

Camping was most definitely not my thing, but I remembered stories he told about how much he'd loved going with his brothers when he was growing up. Once we arrived at our campsite, he took over building the fire and cooking the food. I had deliberately chosen weeknights so the campground was virtually empty and we could enjoy some privacy.

During the day we hiked on trails among the redwoods, and at night we danced with each other by the campfire and then feasted on each other in the tent until we were too spent to stay awake any longer. Derek made s'mores by the fire, and I pulled out my guitar to play for him. I ended up admitting one of the songs on the new album was written about him.

We were sitting by the fire late one night, and I'd just finished playing James Taylor's "Something in the Way She Moves." Derek asked me to play one of the new songs, so I took a breath and let out a laugh.

"Are you ready for me to get a little corny?" I asked.

"Cornier than playing guitar around a campfire?" he said with a wink.

I felt my face heat up. "Never mind. It's too much. I can't do this without embarrassing myself."

Derek shifted over until his arm was around my waist. "I'm sorry. I didn't mean to make you feel self-conscious. I was just teasing you. I'd love to hear any song you'd like to play for me."

He pushed the hair back from my face and kissed my temple. His lips were soft and warm on my skin. I turned my face to his and kissed him on the mouth, tasting the graham cracker and chocolate on his tongue and setting my guitar aside so I could hold his face while we kissed.

Derek deepened the kiss and put his hands on my waist until I ended up straddling him on the wooden picnic table bench.

"I've had a great time with you here, Jude. Thank you for bringing me," Derek said.

"Mm-hmm," I agreed happily into his mouth.

"Babe?" he mumbled against my lips.

"Mmm?"

"I know you're trying to distract me from your corny song, but it's not going to work."

"Wanna bet?" I asked, lifting up the hem of his fleece pullover to reach his fly.

His hands came down on mine with a laugh. "First the song, then the nookie. If I like the song, I'll even make you the sole focus of the nookie."

My face was surely beet red, but I gathered up my courage and slid back to my own spot on the bench. Grabbing my guitar, I began to strum the intro to the song.

"This is called 'Invisible,'" I said. "It's, ah, kind of about you."

My fingers played the strings while my voice sang the mellow tune.

> You stand behind me — Invisible
> But I see your shadow.
>
> You run beside me — Invisible
> But I hear your footsteps.
>
> You watch me, all-seeing — Invisible
> But I see all of you.
>
> Always watch over me like you do,
> But who watches over you?
>
> Protection Perfection — I need you.
> You stand tall and walk proud — I walk with you.
> Your green eyes are sparkling — I laugh with you.
> Our words have a rhythm — Please share with me.
>
> Always watch over me like you do,
> And I'll watch over you.

I couldn't look at Derek while I sang it, so I sang it to the campfire instead. When I was finished, I put the guitar down and stood up nervously to hold my chilled hands out to the warmth coming from the flames.

A giant embrace engulfed me. Derek's strong arms wrapped around my front and he pulled my body so tight to his chest that my feet barely touched the ground. His stubbled cheek scraped against my own as his face slid next to mine.

His voice was low and gravelly, almost hoarse. "That was amazing. I don't know what to say. No one has ever done something so sweet for me in my life, Jude."

I shrugged. "Yeah, well, I think you're pretty incredible, Derek Wolfe."

He turned me around and pierced me with his emerald stare.

"I love you, Jude."

My heart hammered at the words while my brain replayed them, looking for a mistake or misunderstanding.

"Thank god," I blurted, hopping up into his arms and wrapping my legs around his waist.

He laughed and grabbed me under the ass.

"That wasn't exactly the response I was expecting."

I kissed him and then pulled back to peer at him with a smile.

"I love you too, Derek, so much."

We kissed with stupidly smiling lips. I kept my arms and legs wrapped around him and he held me easily. I basked in the joy of the moment, knowing I'd found a kind of happiness I'd never known before. Things would be okay. We would figure it out. As long as we had each other, it was going to be fine.

We kissed and laughed our way into the tent where we did very naughty naked things to each other. The day we'd arrived at the campground we'd agreed to keep our sex noises as silent as possible on the off chance anyone could hear us. It had actually turned into a fun game of pressing firm hands over mouths to muffle moans and screams.

That night, Derek stuffed his T-shirt in my mouth when I wouldn't stop whimpering.

"The ranger is going to think I'm murdering you in your sleeping bag if you don't quiet down." He laughed in between vigorous sucks on my shaft.

"Feh uhh guhh," I whimpered through the shirt. *Feels so good.*

He laughed and went back to work, stroking and sucking until I felt like I was going to turn inside out.

I yanked the shirt out of my mouth and gasped, "Fuck me, goddammit. Want you."

He was already hard as a rock from stroking himself. I had tried to go down on him, but he'd reminded me I'd earned all the attention that night. Who was I to complain?

When he pushed into me, I couldn't help but let out a moan of satisfaction, which earned me the gag again. His green eyes twinkled as he thrust into me lazily. Too lazily.

Asshole.

I scrambled to grab at the backs of his thighs to pull him in tighter and faster, but he just smirked at me some more. My breathing was stuttering, and I began to feel desperation clawing at me. Wanted, needed him faster, harder.

God I wanted him *so* badly.

The shirt came out again, and my begging became real.

"Baby, please," I whispered frantically. "*Please.*"

"Love you," he said.

Sweet man, stop distracting me from my lust-filled desperation.

I felt like I was going to break apart. My eyes smarted, and my heart thundered.

"*Derek,*" I whispered in a broken voice.

His mouth landed on me with gentle kisses. I lost track of everything when his mouth began caressing mine. My twitchy muscles settled, my frantic need simmered, and the buzz in my ears quieted. Christ, how that man had me under his spell.

Suddenly he pulled out and was sucking my cock again. I threw my head back and almost swallowed my tongue as I felt two fingers enter me in search of my prostate.

Found it.

After the next suck, he flipped me over onto my stomach and

grabbed my hips, pulling my ass back toward him swiftly in a move that never failed to roust my inner slut.

"Oh god, *yes*," I cried.

He slammed into me, putting one hand on my lower back and the other between my shoulder blades to push my chest and face down hard into the cool slick surface of our sleeping bags. Derek Wolfe knew exactly how to make me crazy.

As he thrust into me, one large hand reached around to stroke my throbbing hard-on, and I blurted a noise of approval. He leaned his warm body against my entire back and rubbed his stubbled chin against my shoulder to grumble words into my ear.

"Jesus, fuck, you're so sexy. Your ass in the air, your hair wild. God, Jude."

I was past the point of being able to speak. My climax hit like a thunderbolt and white jags shot through my vision, blotting out everything except the rolls of delicious pleasure wringing me out.

I felt Derek pull out and heard him growl behind me before I felt his warm, wet release land on the cool exposed skin of my back.

Holy shit, that was hot.

My body collapsed in a heap like a spent dishrag, his heavy warm body landing partly on my back and partly beside me. Heavy breathing sounds filled the tent, and Derek's hand moved to push the damp hair off my face. I turned to look at him and he laughed.

"What?" I asked.

"That was insane."

"Pfft," I replied.

He laughed harder and rolled off me onto his back, pulling me over to snuggle against his side with my head on his chest.

Sometime later I awoke to the feeling of Derek maneuvering us into the joined sleeping bags. He slid in beside me and pulled me against him again.

"I really do love you, Derek. I'm so lucky you came into my life," I murmured into the darkness before feeling soft lips against mine.

33

DEREK

When Christmas came Jude and I headed to the vineyard where Blue and Tristan were hosting the family for the holiday. It was a nice, relaxing few days, but I sensed Jude's frustration when I continued to behave as his bodyguard around the family.

The situation was starting to wear on both of us, and I was unsure how we were going to be able to go on tour together without outing ourselves by accident. When we were at home in the city, it was easier to be together. We had time and privacy in Jude's house, and we didn't spend very much time in the public roles of celebrity and bodyguard.

When we did have to slip back into those roles, they didn't fit anymore. It was awkward and strange. There were so many small moments that bothered both of us, and I wasn't sure how long Jude was going to think I was worth the trouble.

I tried to push off worrying about it until after the Super Bowl. The tour wouldn't begin until mid-February so I needed to remember not to put the cart before the horse.

This time when we were at the vineyard we took the risk of sneaking me in and out of his room. There was no way we were going to sleep apart during Christmas.

On Christmas morning we awoke to the sound of Jude's alarm.

Pete had warned him the night before that Santa presents were opened earlier than humans normally awoke. If Jude wanted to see his nieces go nuts over their haul, he needed to be tree-side by seven sharp.

I reached for his phone and hit the snooze button before rolling over to kiss the back of his shoulder.

"Merry Christmas, sleepyhead," I mumbled into his warm skin.

"Mphf," he grumbled into the pillow.

I ran my hand down his bare back onto his perfectly rounded ass and squeezed. My cock was already awake and the feel of Jude's tight ass made it even harder.

Grabbing the bottle of lube that was still on the bedside table, I quickly climbed on top of his sleepy form.

"Mmm," he hummed in agreement.

I pressed into him and hooked my arms under his shoulders to hold on to him. He smelled like sleepy Jude, which was one of my favorite smells. I buried my nose in the back of his neck after pushing his hair out of the way.

I reached around to grasp his own morning wood. Whispering dirty shit into his ear, I managed to speed up the thrusts and strokes to make us both hot enough to come together in a shuddering rush.

After I caught my breath I jumped up and smacked him on that gorgeous ass.

"Chop-chop, we have kids waiting on Uncle Jude out there. Make it snappy, Bluebell."

"Ugh, you're such a goddamned morning person. And I hate it when you rush me."

"You love it. Now get your ass in the shower. I need someone to soap up all my hard-to-reach places."

Jude reluctantly got up to follow me into the bathroom. "The last time I got in the shower with you before we were supposed to be somewhere, we were half an hour late," he reminded me.

"This is a platonic shower. Just two dudes washing each other's naked bodies by hand. Nothing gay about it," I said with a straight face.

He laughed and grabbed my ass cheeks with a squeeze.

"Mmm, this ass. I just want to fondle it all the time. Would you ever let me top you?" Jude asked.

I turned on the faucet before turning around to look at him. "Is that something you've been thinking about?"

"Yes. You have a gorgeous ass, and it's been tempting me more than usual lately. But if you don't want to, that's okay too."

My heart sped up and I felt blood rushing south again. I reached down to tell my dick to shut it.

"I've never bottomed before, but I'm willing to try. Can we wait until we get home though? I'm not sure I can relax enough when I know your family could be in the next room. Can you imagine me yelling, 'Harder, Jude, pound that ass,' while your mom or, god forbid, Aunt Tilly listens through the door?" I asked, my words causing Jude to shudder in disgust.

"Christ, that's disturbing," Jude said. "Be careful or I won't let you come anywhere near me again until we get home."

"Liar," I accused.

"Fine," he said. "I admit to being a predictable wanton harlot. Now fucking wash my dick like you mean it so we can go act like strangers in front of my family."

Christmas Day with Jude's family brought several surprises, including a spontaneous decision for the Marians to go to Maui the following week to see Blue and Tristan tie the knot. Jude's friend Wayne Travis offered to loan the family the use of his Maui estate for the trip, which made planning exponentially easier.

Jude called Ollie to ask if she could arrange a charter jet, before also asking if she wanted to join us there. She said her father's retirement ceremony from the SFPD was too important to miss and she spent the rest of the evening sending Jude pitiful texts about how she always missed out on Marian weddings.

He promised her she would not miss out on his own. Just the idea of Jude marrying someone made my stomach twist. I couldn't decide if it was twisting with nerves that the someone would be me or nerves that it wouldn't.

All of this wedding talk just brought home the fact that there would come a time when we had to decide what the future of our relationship looked like. And that thought terrified me.

WHEN WE GOT BACK to his house the following day, Jude and I exchanged our own Christmas gifts before Mike was scheduled to arrive to take my place for two days. Leaving Jude was getting harder and now it was beginning to really piss me off. The whole situation was unfair.

I was nervous about exchanging gifts with Jude because he was a multimillionaire, and I was barely a multi-thousandaire. He was usually sensitive to the difference between our financial situations because he knew it messed with my pride.

I handed him a wrapped package and sat next to him on the couch in the kitchen. He turned to face me with his back against the arm of the couch and his socked feet on my thighs. My hands instinctively rubbed his legs under the cuffs of his jeans, and I relished the feel of his shapely runner's calves.

"Hmm," he mused, shaking the box next to his ear. "Breakable?"

"That poor kitten is probably concussed now, Jude. You're just plain cruel."

He gave me a big beautiful grin and began to open the package. Once he got the box open, he pulled out the first item and looked up at me in confusion.

"It's a guitar pick punch. Kind of silly but you can use it to punch out a guitar pick from things like old credit cards or gift cards." I shrugged. "I just saw it and thought it might be fun to play around with."

"That's cool. We'll have to look around for something to try it on. I'll bet a postcard would work too, at least until the pick got soft. Thanks, babe," he said with a smile, leaning up to kiss me.

I pulled back from the kiss and pointed at the gift box. "But wait, there's more," I said in my infomercial voice.

Jude grinned and pulled out the next item. I had separated the three items with a set of dishtowels. Each one had a different humorous saying on them. The first had a simple drawing of a few brussels sprouts with the phrase *Every Day I'm Brusselin'* written on it.

The second had a similar drawing of two kale leaves with the phrase *Kale Yeah!* on it, and the last was my favorite. It had a drawing of a beet and said, *Let the Beet Drop*.

His face lit up when he saw what was next.

"Seriously? My very own As-Seen-on-TV Veggetti?" he exclaimed dramatically. "Do you have any idea what this baby can do?"

I laughed. "No, why don't you tell me about it?"

"Did you know you can make noodles out of many different vegetables?" he said, continuing in his melodramatic announcer voice. "But when you make noodles out of veggies, you don't call them noodles. Do you know what you call them, Derek?"

"Uh..." I pretended not to know. "Vegoodles?"

"Why, zoodles, of course!" He laughed and climbed onto my lap.

"Thank you, Wolfe," Jude said with the sweetest smile over his soft brown eyes. "You and I both know I really wanted this but was too embarrassed to admit it." His lips came down on mine in an appreciative kiss. "You know what this means, though, right?"

"That I'm having spiralized vegetables every night for the foreseeable future?" I asked.

"Yup. You lucky dog. All veggies, all the time. They'll probably taste just like pasta once they're shaped like it. Don't you worry."

I rolled my eyes at the blatant lie, and he laughed.

"Why do you think I waited to give it to you until I was getting ready to leave for two days? You can serve Mike all the zoodles you want."

"What's the last thing? I love these towels, by the way."

He pulled out the last towel and found the small box underneath.

"Now it's my turn to get a little corny. I felt like I owed it to you," I said while trying to hide my nerves.

Inside was a slim leather bracelet like the kind he sometimes wore. Stamped into the surface was the refrain from the song he wrote for me.

> Always watch over me like you do,
> and I'll watch over you.

"Derek, oh my god, I love it," he said, shining brown eyes meeting mine. "It's perfect."

He was in my arms again, and I buried my face in his neck.

"I'm glad you like it. That song means so much to me and I wanted you to know I felt the same way."

We kissed for a long moment until Jude sniffed and pulled back, wiping his eyes and laughing at himself.

"Shut up. I know I'm a sentimental sap." He handed the bracelet to me to put it on him.

"I love that you're sentimental. Well, maybe not when you're watching commercials during football games," I teased.

"That was one time, Wolfe, and those puppies were orphans, for god's sake," he said.

"Okay, my turn," I said. "Gimme. I'm hoping you saw the Maserati catalog I left in your bathroom a few weeks ago."

He leaned over to grab a gift off the coffee table.

"As a matter of fact, I did see it. I ordered one for Aunt Tilly," he said. "She returned it because she said the backseat wasn't big enough for making out at the drive-in movies."

"I believe it." I chuckled. "Can you even imagine that woman behind the wheel of a sports car?"

"Yes, and it terrifies me. Open your present."

I opened the small box and saw a bundled up T-shirt. It was an exact replica of my favorite Guns N' Roses T-shirt. I had gotten it at the last concert I went to before my deployment to Afghanistan, and it had practically disintegrated months before. When I unfurled it, something fell onto my lap. A key on a keychain. It wasn't a Maserati key; it looked like a house key.

"Jude, I already have a key to your house. What's this for?"

34

JUDE

Why was I so damned nervous about this?

"It's not a key to the house. It's a key to the apartment over the garage. Ollie is moving out, and I was hoping you might want to move in and get rid of your apartment."

Derek stared at me for a minute, and my stomach really began to lurch.

"If not, I mean, if that's not something you want to do, I completely understand," I stammered in my usual stupid, nervous way. "Don't feel pressure or obligation or anything."

I forced myself to stop stammering and take a breath. Somehow I'd ended up with my back pressed as far into the opposite side of the couch as I could get from Derek. My nerves were taut, and I was afraid they were going to snap with disappointment when he opened his mouth.

"Shit," I muttered.

Derek crawled over to where I sat huddled in a ball with my arms wrapped around my knees.

"Jude Marian, I would love to move into the apartment over your garage," he said, intense green eyes penetrating my defensive shell.

"Really?" I squeaked like an idiot.

"Yes, really," he said, straddling me in a comical reversal of our usual positions on the couch. His large hands cupped my face, and he continued locking eyes with me.

"Leaving you each week to go back to my lonely apartment is killing me. Being here where I know you're under the same roof will make a big difference to my peace of mind. But please know you can change your mind at any time, okay? If you decide it's too much or it's not working for you, be honest. I don't ever want to make you feel uncomfortable."

I broke out in a jagged laugh. "You're crazy if you think I'd ever want you to leave. What I really want is for you to move in with me, but we both know we can't do that right now. At least with the apartment, it will pass as a mere convenience factor. And we've been together long enough that everyone knows we're friends now."

"How much is the rent?" he asked with a twinkle in his eye.

"Fuck you. I'm not even going to dignify that with a response, asshole."

"What if I insisted?" he teased.

"Then I'd demand payment in sexual services rendered. You can work it off with your mouth," I replied.

"Can I start right now?"

"Hell yes," I said, pushing him off me and racing for my bedroom. Heavy footsteps ran closely behind.

Before he had a chance to take charge I spun and tackled him onto my bed, and he let me. My hands shucked off his shirt and began working on his belt buckle.

"Oh, I almost forgot about the second part of your present," I said.

"You're going to suck me off too?" he teased. "Why, thank you. I accept."

"Okay, I meant, I almost forgot about the third part of your present." I smiled up at him while my fingers continued to remove his pants. "I want to bring your family to the Super Bowl."

Derek propped himself up on his elbows. "Really? God, Jude. My dad and brothers will flip. Are you sure?"

"Yes, I'm sure. Ollie said she can book their flights with my frequent flier miles so they don't think it's a big expense. They'll be in the box seats that were given to the band, so you can just tell them it was an easy way for me to give you an end-of-the-year gift. My dad is coming too, with Pete and Ginger. None of the rest of my family really cares that much about football."

My hands had already started their appreciative fondling of my favorite Derek parts and I could see the conversation portion of our exchange coming to a swift end.

"Thanks, Jude," he hissed, and it was somewhat unclear whether he was referring to the Super Bowl or the fondling. I didn't give a shit.

"Mm-hmm," I murmured as I licked and teased him with my tongue.

Derek's stomach muscles contracted and I ran my hand over them in appreciation of their bumpy definition. I set a mental note to never rush his nightly routine of crunches and pushups.

"Why are you still dressed, goddammit?" he growled, grabbing for my shirt.

He helped me strip down and then grabbed my hips and lifted me up onto his face. A hot, wet tongue found my ass, and I gasped, "Fuck *yes*."

Derek's mouth assaulted me while I scrambled to hold on to the headboard.

He brought me back down until I was lying on top of him kissing his mouth and running my hands through his short hair. His face was dark and his eyes were blazing green with desire.

I leaned over to the nightstand and grabbed the lube, squeezing some out and slicking his shaft before my own.

Derek's hips kept arching up into me and I positioned myself to let him in. Once he was fully seated inside me, I let out a breath and laid my forehead on his chest.

"God, you feel so good," I murmured.

Large hands came up to brush my hair behind my ears. I tilted my head to look up at him and smile before I began moving. He threw his head back and moaned, pushing his thick shaft up into me as I came down onto him.

My own cock stood stiffly off my body, throbbing with want and need for Derek's touch. He must have read my mind because his eyes took on a smug glint and his hand wrapped around it.

"Fucking finally," I grumbled under my breath. His eyebrows shot up and his mouth turned up in a devious grin. Oh *shit*.

Before I knew it, I was flipped over onto my front and fucked to within an inch of my life. My body was half numb with pleasure, and my breathing was in serious danger of shorting out. The noises coming out of my mouth were nonsense carried on a bit of drool. I wanted to cry from the sheer overload of emotions I felt when Derek owned me like that.

His mouth came down by my ear and a husky growl caused my balls to tighten even further.

"Love holding you down and taking you like this. Hearing those sexy-as-hell noises that come out of you. You are *mine*, Jude Marian. And don't you ever forget it."

I wanted to cry with relief. I wanted to scream that I couldn't possibly forget it. Not only was I his, but I wanted to be only his for the rest of my life.

Derek's arms wrapped around me and pulled me upright onto my knees in front of him. His body pressed against my back and one hand wrapped around my throat, the other around my rib cage. Hot words continued to blow into my ear, and I felt my eyes prickle as my hands grabbed a hold of his and held on for dear life.

When it was over, I swiveled around and launched myself onto his front in a tight hug. My face was turned into his neck, and I felt his arms tighten around me as much as mine did around him.

We knelt there holding each other as tightly as we could for a few minutes. Both of us knew that when we got dressed it would almost be time for him to leave.

The only consolation was knowing that pretty soon, his leaving wouldn't take him so far away from me.

35

DEREK

During my two days away from Jude, I spent plenty of time at the gym and caught up with my family on the phone. My dad and brothers lost their collective shit when I told them about Jude's offer to bring them to the Super Bowl with us.

"Holy cow, Derek! Is he for real? Is this a joke?" Kyle asked.

"Not a joke. The guy has seven brothers but only one of them is interested in coming. That leaves more than enough room in the box for you guys," I told him with a smile.

"Shit, man. It's no wonder they don't give a crap about football. Half his brothers are fags. They're probably more interested in going to a beauty pageant than a sporting event."

My breath caught in my throat as the slur hit me out of the blue.

"What the hell, Kyle?" I snapped. "You're seriously going to insult the guy who's giving you a gift worth thousands of dollars?"

"I didn't say *he* was a fag. I was talking about his brothers."

"You're a fucking idiot. Let me talk to dad again before I change my mind about letting you come to the game," I said.

"Jesus, sorry, Derek. What's got you so sensitive today? Spending all that time with the Marians over Christmas made you all emotional?"

I hung up on him. There was no point in staying on the phone with any of them when I was this pissed off. The conversation with Kyle reminded me of why I was in the closet, and the reminder was like a bucket of ice water to the groin.

After lacing up my running shoes, I drove to a storage place to buy some boxes. I had been on a month-to-month lease for the last six months in my apartment, so I didn't have to wait to move out. I'd texted Ollie to ask why she was moving, and she told me her grandmother couldn't live alone anymore since her hip replacement hadn't been a complete success. Instead of her grandmother having to sell her home, Ollie elected to move in with her to help her out.

I asked if she was sure about the move, and she assured me she was. Finally I had to leave the subject alone after reminding her more than once that if she ever changed her mind, all she had to do was let me know.

While I was out running errands, I got a coffee and stopped at the bookstore to pick up a couple of books to read during the Maui trip. I loved flying. It was one of the times in public when I didn't have to be on the lookout for Jude's safety and could just sit next to him and relax. I chose an interesting memoir and a new spy thriller along with a couple of newsmagazines.

While I was standing in a long line to check out, my phone buzzed with a text from Jude.

Jude: *I made a salad for lunch and spiralized every single vegetable except the lettuce. Jealous?*

Derek: *You read my mind. I was just sitting here eating a Snickers bar wishing it was a spiral of zucchini.*

Jude: *Don't worry. I'll make you one when you come home.*

My chest tightened at his use of the word "home," and I thought of how much I wanted to share a home with Jude.

Derek: *Oh goodie. Speaking of home, I picked up some boxes to start packing. Wishing I had time to make the move before we go to Hawaii.*

Jude: *Maybe if we do it together. I'll come over and help.*

Derek: *No thanks. I'm afraid you'd be more of a distraction than help.*

Jude: *What if I put my hair in a man bun and wore flannel? Then you wouldn't be tempted.*

Derek: *Believe it or not, I'd still be tempted, Bluebell. I don't have that much stuff to pack actually. I'm going to get rid of some of my things and buy a bigger bed and new couch.*

Jude: *You had me at bed.*

Derek: *Thought so. It'll be kind of fun to invite you to my place from time to time.*

Jude: *I've been to your place before. Remember when I made fun of your old tube tv and we had sex on the kitchen table?*

Derek: *Yes. I remember that every time I eat breakfast and get a boner. I'm getting rid of the tv too. Going to go full He-Man and get a big flat screen.*

Jude: *I'm on board with that. I might have to get you the kind of coffee maker I like though.*

Derek: *I already bought the same one before we went to Napa for Christmas. Didn't want to tell you for fear your beautiful head would get too big.*

Jude: *Aww, someone gave up his instant coffee and joined the new millennium. Good for you, babe.*

Derek: *Jackass. I'm headed to the mall to get a bathing suit for Hawaii. You need anything while I'm there?*

Jude: *I'm sorry, what? I was busy imagining you in a speedo.*

Derek: *Funny. I'll take that as a no. And get your hand out of your pants.*

Jude: *My hand isn't in my pants, smart ass. ... I'm naked.*

Derek: *Jesus, you're cruel.*

Jude: *Text me pics from the dressing room, Wolfe. Promise me.*

Derek: *No way. You'll sell them to the highest bidder. I know deep down you're a money-grubbing whore.*

Jude: *Ah, he finally learns the real source of my wealth. Hot spank bank pics. Lucrative business. Yours would go for a pretty penny, especially if I added in the naked ones I take of you at night while you sleep.*

Derek: *Nice try. You sleep nestled so tightly against me that I notice every time you get up. Btw, you haven't been sleepwalking since we've been together. Actually, I take that back. You did once, but it was quick.*

Jude: *What? When?*

Derek: *That night at my place. I thought you were getting up to pee but you went to the kitchen and came back with a measuring cup. Got right back into bed and held the measuring cup against your chest until I took it away from you.*

Jude: *You're a terrible liar, but I love you anyway.*

Derek: *You only wish I was lying. Deep down you know it's true because I saw you notice the measuring cup on the nightstand.*

Jude: *I thought you were into some kind of measuring kink. Didn't want to ask you about it for fear you'd tell me.*

Derek: *I love you too, Bluebell. Call me tonight.*

I went by the mall and found some swim trunks that didn't look as ratty as my old ones. After stashing my clothing purchases in the car, I returned inside to shop at one of the furniture stores, selecting a nice leather couch and two overstuffed chairs to go with it. I could picture Jude curled up in one of the chairs and realized I'd rather wait on the purchases until I got his opinion.

Finally I made my way home and began to pack. It wasn't until almost midnight that I got the call from Mike telling me that someone was at Jude's gate.

36

JUDE

I was sitting at the kitchen table working on some song lyrics I was toying with for Blue's wedding surprise when the driveway gate buzzed. The sound startled me, coming as it did in the silence of the late night.

Mike had gone to bed in the guest room about an hour before. I hated to bother him, but I knew better than to deal with a visitor on my own, especially at midnight.

As I rounded the corner to his room, I saw the door open and Mike step out. I forgot his phone would have sounded an alert.

I could tell he'd been sleeping, but he had pulled on some clothes and shoes before following me back to the kitchen to answer the intercom.

"May I help you?" he asked.

"I'm here to see Jude. Tell him it's his biggest fan," the slurring voice responded through the speaker.

"Name please?" Mike asked.

"He'll know. We met after the Hollywood Bowl concert."

My stomach dropped and I felt my heart speed up. Mike immediately pulled out his phone without even looking at me.

"Derek, it's Mike. I think that guy from the LA hotel room is here at the gate." He listened for a moment before agreeing to whatever Derek said and hanging up.

"What did he say?" I asked.

"He said to stall until he gets here. Is that okay with you? If not, I'm happy to deal with him myself."

"Uh..." I began.

"If it makes any difference to you, Jude, I'd like to wait," he told me. "Derek has more experience in reading people's body language, and he knows way more about this guy than I do. I only know that he's some fan who showed up at the suite in LA. If we can stall, Derek can get some more information out of him since the LAPD wouldn't give us anything."

"Okay, yeah. Let's wait," I agreed.

Sour vapors steamed in my gut while we waited. After a couple of minutes the gate intercom buzzed again.

"Hello?" the guy said. "I'm still out here waiting."

Mike tapped the button to respond. "Sorry, I've tried to get Jude, but he's locked in his music studio. It'll just be a couple of minutes longer."

The drive from Derek's apartment usually took twenty minutes, but with no traffic, he made it there in about fifteen.

The man had buzzed again in the meantime, and I came on to tell him to hold his horses. I realized I was in my pajamas, so I raced back to my room to change into jeans. Before I finished getting dressed, Derek walked into my room.

I looked up and met his eyes.

"Hi," I said.

"Hey," he said as he stepped forward to hug me. His hand came up to brush hair back from my face and plant a kiss on my forehead. "I missed you. You okay?"

I nodded before leaning in to kiss him, lips soft and sweet like he'd eaten pineapple for a midnight snack. God, I loved kissing Derek. His mouth was delicious and his responsiveness made me stupidly happy.

My hands came up to cup his rough cheeks as my mouth moved over the rest of his face.

"So glad you're here," I breathed against his ear.

Derek pulled back. "Mike's out front with the guy. He refuses to talk to anyone but you. It's definitely the guy from the hotel incident. We're waiting for the cops."

"Should I go out there and talk to him?" I asked.

"Hell no. That's not a good idea. Plus, he's really drunk. I don't want to leave Mike much longer, but I wanted to check on you."

"I'm fine. Go ahead. I'll just wait in the kitchen."

A little while later Derek and Mike surprised me by telling me that we weren't pressing charges. I could tell by the look on Derek's face that I could ask questions later when we were in private but it would be best to keep them to myself around others. When everyone had finally left, including Mike, Derek turned to me and pulled an envelope out of his pocket.

"What's that?" I asked.

"Photos," his eyebrows were furrowed with worry. "The man was threatening to give them to the media if you wouldn't come out of the house. I convinced him to keep his mouth shut for a few days until I contacted him." Derek handed me the envelope. "I didn't look at them, Jude."

I looked down at the small envelope in my hand like it was a grenade. I wracked my brain to try and remember any time I'd let anyone take any photos of me that would be inappropriate in the media.

I remembered the media drone in my yard as my vision blackened around the edges, and the highlight reel of every interaction I ever had with Derek spun through my mind. My adrenaline spiked, leaving me feeling faint and breathless.

After Derek walked over to the sofa at the end of the kitchen, I threw the envelope across the room with a strangled curse. Regardless of what was inside, I knew I wasn't ready to look at it.

37

DEREK

It was time to face the music. The envelope was on the floor where Jude had thrown it, but I wasn't about to be the one to pick it up. I wouldn't go near it until and unless he wanted me to. I had told the police that it was a misunderstanding and to let the man go. After what he'd said, I didn't want to take the chance of him saying something revealing to the cops.

While Jude quietly freaked the fuck out, I sat calmly on the couch, pretending to check email on my phone as Jude paced around the envelope trying to ignore the damned thing. Finally, I lost my patience. Our reputations were in that envelope.

"Want me to flush it down the toilet?" I asked calmly.

His head whipped around. "What? No, are you crazy? We need to know what's in there," he said.

I gave him a look.

"Mpfh," he grumbled, realizing who exactly was acting crazy. He snatched it up from its spot on the floor and came and sat down next to me on the couch.

He smelled like soap. *Dammit what that does to me.*

As he ripped open the envelope, I tried to keep my eyes on my phone screen to give him a measure of privacy. But I was desperate to know how bad the damage was.

He sighed and tossed the envelope in my lap, turning his head into my body and burying his face in my side. "It's not as bad as I could be. But still. Goddamned asshole," he rumbled into my shirt.

I put an arm around him and picked up the envelope. The photos weren't at all what I had expected. They were of Jude and *Ari*, standing on what looked like a balcony in New Orleans. They had towels wrapped around their waists and it looked like they'd just gotten out of a shower. The photographs captured them kissing, Jude's hand cupping Ari's ass over the towel. Clearly it was taken several years ago, but my stomach still knotted painfully at the images as the unfamiliar swell of jealousy tightened my gut.

Only one of the five shots had a crystal-clear view of Jude's face, but it was unmistakable.

"Who took these?" I asked. "How did this random guy get them?"

"I have no idea. Does it matter?" Jude said.

"Well, yes. Do you think this guy, Martin, is the one who took the photos? That maybe he's been stalking you for that long? Is that even possible?"

"Who knows? Looking back, I remember seeing someone on a balcony nearby taking photos of us, but I thought it was just a pervert or a tourist. There's no way I'd remember what he looked like. I wasn't famous and we weren't naked, so I didn't really think much about it. It's not like we could try to track down the guy in another building and tell him to give us the images. They were legal since we were in public." He let out a breath and looked at me. "I'm just glad they're not of you too."

"C'mere," I said, pulling him onto my lap and wrapping him in my arms. I felt his body sag against me as he let out a breath. "Let's sleep on this and figure it out in the morning, okay? I think we'll have to call Joel and ask for his help."

After a few minutes of letting me hold him, Jude pulled back and met my eyes.

"I love you," he said. "Thank you for putting up with all of this shit."

His words went straight to my heart, and I kissed him. "You're worth it."

When we were undressed and curled around each other in bed, I tried desperately to think of a solution to the photo problem.

Jude's head was against my chest and my fingers played with strands of his hair.

"Derek, I think I should come out. Take away his hold over me and just be done with this stress once and for all," Jude said.

I didn't say anything at first. Couldn't. Part of me wanted to answer him based on what *I* wanted, not what was best for him.

He lifted his head to stare at me. "Babe, your heart is hammering. What are you thinking?"

"I'm thinking I want to kill that psycho and bury him in the desert," I admitted, remembering every word he said and threat he made to the man I loved. The man I was supposed to protect from harm.

"Oookayy, let's make that plan B, shall we?" He sat up next to me and leaned back against the headboard, running fingers through his hair before smoothing a hand down his chest. My eyes couldn't help but follow its progress, my body wanting to slither all over Jude's, but my mind kept tripping over the other situation. I blinked.

"And plan A is you coming out because some obsessive freak decides he wants to have you all to himself?" I said. "God damn it, Jude."

Jude swiveled around to straddle my abdomen. His hard-on was right there in front of me. Surely he was asking for it. I couldn't think straight. The feel of him, the smell of him.

"Wolfe, do I need to fuck this pissy attitude out of you before we can have a productive conversation about this?"

At the word "fuck" spoken in that sultry voice of his, my cock stood up and I shuddered. I tried assessing his question. On the one hand I didn't want to ignore the giant stalker-shaped elephant in the room, but on the other, dear god did I want that man's mouth on me.

"Yes, please," I answered with a sigh.

Jude laughed and kissed me hard, his tongue finding mine in a passionate rush. While our breathing sped up, his hands were everywhere. Part of me was even grateful to the stalker for giving me the excuse I needed to be naked in Jude's bed that night.

Jude began making his way down my chest. His warm tongue danced down along my happy trail as he looked up at me. I was struck by those warm brown eyes, no longer filled with the weight of the world. They shimmered with mischief. Happy.

That was just how he was. The man could be threatened by an obsessive, manipulative bastard one minute and look at me with loving kindness the next. I don't know how he did it.

Before long, I was losing myself to the pull of Jude's greedy mouth. I balled my hands into fists to keep from grabbing his hair and pulling his head toward me harder and faster. My hips pushed up in search of more. Jude pulled off and sucked his finger with a wet smacking sound.

Oh shit.

At the realization of what was coming next, I tensed before taking a breath and remembering how much I trusted Jude. And maybe he needed this tonight. To control someone else for a change. As if he didn't control me every moment of every day just by being himself.

His mouth landed back on my cock and I sucked in another breath, this time forgetting all about that wet finger until it entered me a minute later and sent bolts of excitement through me.

Jude's pace was too slow and I realized he was trying to be delicate with me. Well, fuck that.

"More," I demanded through closed teeth.

Jude's eyebrows shot up and his grin widened. "Yes, sir, drill instructor, sir," he teased.

He fumbled the cap open on the lube while I stroked my cock. I felt the cool drizzle land on my overheated skin and sucked in a breath.

Jude's lip was caught between his teeth in concentration, and I couldn't look away.

Two fingers entered me this time and I felt more discomfort. Was I really going to bottom for this guy who was so much smaller than me? Even though Jude was little, his cock most definitely was not. The whole thing would be laughable if I wasn't so damned turned on by the thought. I loved topping Jude, so a part of me wanted him to have that experience, to feel as good as I felt when I was inside him. Wanted him to press into me and feel the tight squeeze of a lover's body pulling him toward a climax.

Jude's eyebrows were drawn together in concentration as he began to push himself into me. I focused on relaxing and stroked myself for distraction. Jude probably would have been more helpful if he hadn't suddenly fallen into some kind of trancelike state.

"Holy fuck," he breathed with eyes squeezed closed. "Ho-ly *fuck*."

I held my legs back and watched as my body accepted him. His eyes opened and stared glassily at me.

He leaned in to kiss me and I had to lean forward to reach him because of our height difference. We kissed for a minute while he gently rocked his way farther into me.

As he began to pull out, his cock brushed against my prostate and I grabbed his ass cheeks to hold him right there.

I managed to stutter, "S-stop, wait. Do that again."

Again with the mischievous eyes on mine. "Mm-hm, thought so."

Smug bastard.

He stroked my prostate with that magic dick again, and I nearly lost my shit. He grabbed for my cock, stroking me with his hand while he thrust in and out of my ass.

It felt so damned good. His hair fell in curtains on either side of his flushed face. His shoulder muscles worked and rippled as he stroked me with one hand and held his weight with the other. His dark eyelashes fluttered up and down as his own climax began to test his rhythm, but Jude never faltered. Rhythm ran in his blood.

Our orgasms came only a moment apart, my cock shooting so violently I was pretty sure a porn studio would have paid big money for a video clip. I roared Jude's name as he screamed out a curse. He lay sprawled across my body like a glorious Jude-skin blanket, but I no longer had enough energy left in my arms to appreciate that skin with my hands the way I normally did.

"Well?" he asked after a little while.

I shrugged.

38

JUDE

Whoa.

Topping Derek was pretty amazing. I was busy basking in the afterglow when he responded to my question.

Hold up.

I lifted my head to stare daggers at him. "A shrug? That's what you have to say about it? *A shrug?*" I asked, sitting up. I noticed the shit-eating grin on Derek's face and snorted. "You really are an ass sometimes."

"Did you see me come? I've got some on my ear and I'm pretty sure there's some on your neighbor's house too."

I crawled farther up his body and kissed him.

"Yes, G.I. Joe, we're all very impressed with your virility. Would you like to stand up and take a bow? Maybe flex your muscles a bit for the ladies?"

My body felt his vibrating laugh before it came out of his mouth. "Nah, the only lady I care about has already seen my muscles." He winked.

"You're calling me a lady right after I just nailed you in the keister. That's pretty funny, Wolfe."

We stood up to head to the bathroom, and Derek seemed to be

feeling the result of his devirgination. He winced while I started howling with laughter.

"You totally deserve that for trying to rain on my alpha male parade," I accused.

"Damn, does it hurt like this every time?"

"No, only after you get hammered by someone extra-large such as myself. I've never been sore after you fuck me, for instance," I said with a straight face.

I felt the sting of a pinch on my ass and found myself flipped over Derek's meaty shoulder. God, I loved being thrown around by those muscles.

He smacked my ass until I admitted he had a big, beautiful slab of man meat, and I spent our entire shower nicknaming it ridiculous terms of masculine endearment and even sang an ode to it until he was red in the face.

We fell asleep laughing, which is the best way to fall asleep with the person you adore most in the world.

It wasn't until the following day that the stalker's threats came rushing back to my mind and began to drive a vicious wedge between us.

We spent hours discussing what to do. He even brought up the idea of contacting the FBI to report the threat. I was fairly sure I didn't want to go that far and kept reminding him it was probably time for me to claim my sexuality and move forward with my life anyway.

The problem was Derek. Whenever I mentioned coming out, the subject inevitably changed to the issue of *his* coming out. And he refused. He made the point that me going public would put extreme speculation on who I was dating and there would be no way to keep it a secret. He also claimed he'd be damned if some psycho asshole would be the reason he did any of this.

Derek's staunch refusal to consider changing his mind began to break me down bit by bit. I didn't even realize how much until we were in Hawaii with my family. It was New Year's Eve and we sat at a patio table by the pool with my brothers Maverick and Griff. Mav asked Griff about the guy he'd been seeing and Griff scoffed.

"It was a nonstarter. I realized after the third date Mark was still in the closet at work and with his family. Fuck that. I'm not interested in being with a guy who doesn't have the balls to live his life honestly. Too much drama for me," Griff said. I felt my shoulders tense and assumed Derek was experiencing the same.

Maverick pursed his lips. "Shit, Griff. I'm sorry. If it's any consolation, I agree with you. Remember when I went out with Jordan in college? Every time we visited his parents he made a big deal about us being buddies and described all these fake dates with women just to set his parents' minds at ease that he was 'normal.' It took me awhile, but I finally realized he was never going to have the guts to be honest. It made me feel worthless. I ended up so depressed that Mom showed up at the dorm to sit me down."

I remembered it clearly. Mom had told me that she was worried Mav was depressed and considering dropping out of school. I was in Europe somewhere on tour and felt disconnected from the family, but I remember thinking Maverick deserved better. He deserved to be loved by someone who was proud of him. My heart was heavy with the memories.

"She said that when the time was right, I would find someone who couldn't wait to shout it from the rooftops." Mav smiled. "I'm still holding out hope."

"That makes two of us." Griff laughed. "I went clubbing last week with some friends and got hit on by the weirdest people. One guy kept calling me pet names, and I couldn't help but laugh. Every time he spoke to me, he included an endearment."

Mav smiled. "Like what? Tell us."

"Like 'Hey, sweet cheeks, you wanna drink? Why don't we dance, kitty cat? Oooh, tiger, let's go out back for a quickie.' Finally, I just started doing the same to him and spent the rest of the night giggling. 'Sugar bear, why don't you get us some more drinks? You know what would feel good right now, punkin? Your lips on my dick.' Gotta say, the guy gave massive head with that sassy mouth."

We were all groaning and laughing by the time he finished describing it.

"I mentioned it to a friend of mine who works for a magazine and he suggested I write a humor piece about it," Griff said.

"You totally should," I said. "That would be a great article. It reminds me of that one you wrote for Huffington Post about tough businessmen who still get yelled at by their grannies. Hilarious." I couldn't help but laugh remembering the way he'd written it. The article had gone viral and been adopted by feminists as an example of misogynist hypocrisy in the workplace. Griff was good at using humor to make a point about societal idiosyncrasies.

"Thanks, Jude. You know that was Aunt Tilly's idea. Don't you dare tell her how successful it was or I'll have to front her poker buy-in later."

"I heard that," Tilly said from the lounger we'd all assumed she was sleeping on. "Go back to the part about that guy giving you a blow job at the club."

"Jesus Christ, Aunt Tilly," Maverick said before burying his face in his hands and blushing beet red. "She's going to kill me one of these days."

That set Derek off laughing, and I was struck for the millionth time by how much I loved him. He was striking. The body of a Marine with the sweetness of a kitten. I wanted him to stay with me so much it took my breath away, but I couldn't keep living in fear and in the dark.

A little while later we sat together on the far side of the pool with our feet dangling in the water. The sun felt warm on my skin and the clear blue sky was a nice break from the San Francisco winter.

I kept my voice low so my family couldn't hear us.

"Derek, I can't hide who I am anymore. I know you're not ready, and I get that. I'm trying to respect it. But this situation with the photos is bringing it to a head. You and I both know I'm not going to give in to the threat. That means he's going to out me anyway. It would be way better for my career if I'm the one controlling the announcement."

"I can't do it, Jude. I'm sorry." Derek didn't look at me while he spoke, and I wanted to grab his chin and turn it toward me to force his eyes on me. I put my hands under my legs instead.

"What are you more afraid of, Derek? People finding out that you're gay or the media scrutiny because you're with me?"

He finally looked at me. "I don't know, and I'm not sure it really matters."

"It matters to me. I love you. I don't want to do something to upset you or hurt you. Please tell me how I can fix this," I begged him.

He sighed and looked out over the sparkling water of the pool. "I don't have any answers."

I began to feel the first sting of resentment slither through me. "Well, I have to do something, Wolfe. I can't simply let this threat sit out there until he finally decides to follow up on it. I don't have the luxury of saying I don't have any answers."

His jaw tightened and his lips drew together. "I'm aware of that."

"And?" I asked.

"And I don't have any answers," he repeated through his teeth.

I felt my eyes begin to burn and I refused to cry out there where anyone could see me. God forbid my gigantic fucking family catch wind of my heart breaking. Standing up, I grabbed my towel and strode into the house, bypassing someone's questions about what I was going to wear for the wedding ceremony.

When I got to my room, I stepped into the shower and let go. Tears of frustration mixed with the hot water, and I felt familiar emotion bubble up from its recent hibernation.

Loneliness.

39

DEREK

Attending a wedding was either a blessing or a curse depending on the state of your own relationship at the time. That night's wedding was a goddamned curse.

Not only were Jude and I unable to hold hands or share intimate looks during the celebration, but we were also barely speaking to each other after the discussion by the pool.

Jude did a fairly decent job of pretending to be happy and excited for his brother, but I saw the return of his lonely gaze and it shattered me. I couldn't stand being responsible for his unhappiness.

Throughout the night I watched him interact with his family. He danced with his mom, his sister, and Aunt Tilly. His hips swayed with the grace and natural rhythm that had always mesmerized me. His hair was pulled back, and the tiny lights strung around the patio accented the lovely angles of his face.

At midnight there were fireworks. The family and guests were spread out around the patio, pool deck, and backyard. Couples shared kisses while they gazed upward at the colored light bursts. I was hit by the unfairness of not being able to kiss the man I loved in front of everyone ringing in the new year. I looked over at Jude just as one of the bursts of light landed on his face, reflecting off tears.

Fuck.

I took several long strides to get to him and grabbed him by the elbow. He jumped at my touch and turned to look at me.

"Inside, please. I need to talk to you," I said in a low voice.

He followed me inside the house to my bedroom and stood in the semi dark while I closed and locked the door behind me.

Despite quick swipes of his fingers, his cheeks were still wet. His eyes searched mine and I could see furrows of confusion on his forehead.

"Please don't leave me," I whispered. My voice sounded foreign to me as the unexpected words came out on their own.

His eyes grew wide and he came toward me, reaching his arms out tentatively until I met him halfway in an embrace so tight it lifted him off the ground. Jude's legs came up to wrap around my waist, and I turned to sit on the end of the bed, holding him.

We stayed like that for a while, faces buried in each other's necks and wet eyes leaking onto each other's skin. Our arms stayed tight around each other and I savored the familiar smell and feel of him.

Mine, I thought.

"I love you so much, Jude," I whispered. "I'm terrified of losing you now that I finally found you."

Jude leaned back and looked at me. "I'm not the one going anywhere. When and if this ends, it's going to be because you leave me, Derek."

His eyes. God, they were so desolate I could hardly stand it.

But he was right.

"I don't want to leave you. Ever." I tried to assure him, but I knew it sounded like the non-promise it was.

"I know you don't, baby. But you're not going to leave because you don't love me. You're going to leave because the media situation will wear you down until you just don't have the energy to fight for it any longer. I get it. It's why I was alone for so long before I met you. It's why I told you from the very beginning I wasn't sure if it was all worth it."

I leaned toward him, kissing his damp cheeks softly and running my hands up under his shirt to the skin of his back. He allowed me to replace the difficult conversation with lovemaking and we treated each other with exquisite tenderness.

When we came together a little while later, his fingers traced the lines of my face and his eyes fogged over with desire. We didn't speak with words. We used our hands, mouths and bodies to demonstrate just how much we loved and needed the other.

Even our climaxes were silent and we finished wrapped so tightly in each other's arms that I wasn't sure if he could still breathe.

Eventually, we took a quick shower and got back into bed, immediately wrapping our arms around each other again before falling asleep. I didn't realize until later we hadn't wished each other a happy new year.

It never occurred to either of us that Jude's own bedroom door stood open in the hallway for everyone to see that he hadn't slept in his own bed that night.

~

IF ANYONE NOTICED the open door, they never mentioned it. I left Hawaii in complete denial of how tenuous our relationship was. Once home, Jude sat me down and broke my fucking heart.

"I don't want to live like this anymore, Derek, I'm sorry.

We sat on the little couch in the kitchen with our jackets still on from the ride home. The flight back from Hawaii had been uneventful until someone recognized us in the charter terminal and people swarmed Jude. After wrangling him out to my car along with the right suitcases, I was looking forward to coming home and having stress-relieving sex with my boyfriend one more time before Mike showed up, and I finally began moving my stuff over from my old apartment.

Nope.

"Talk to me, Jude," I said.

"This whole thing is just too much. The pressure. The media. I chose this life, but you didn't. I think it would be better if we break it off now so we can move on and find other people."

My throat felt like it was filled with sand, and I had to struggle to breathe.

"I don't want to find other people," I whispered. "I already found you."

His eyes filled, and he looked away. "I know, Derek. But I want to be with someone who can be completely with me. I'm tired of hiding. Sitting there at my brother's wedding was fucking brutal. I couldn't touch you or kiss you or even look at you with the love I felt in that moment. It sucked. That's not how I want to live. I'm going to come out."

I felt my eyes sting and clenched my jaw tight to keep from yelling at him. It wasn't his fault. He wasn't asking for anything he didn't deserve.

Jude looked up at me, the motion of his head causing the tears to overflow. I wanted to reach out and smooth them away, but I kept my hands to myself. Had I touched him, I would have dragged him onto my lap and refused to let go.

"Are you going to say anything?" Jude asked me.

"I want to tell you it doesn't matter, but I'd be lying. I can't handle the scrutiny, Jude. Being laid bare by the press. That's the opposite of the kind of life I imagined. You know how private I am."

He gave me a watery smile. "I know, babe. And that's okay. I understand. And I would give it all up right this minute if I thought it would make a difference. But once you've reached a level of fame, you're always going to be in the spotlight. Even if I retired from music tomorrow, I don't think it would offer you any additional protection from gossip rags."

Jude paused and looked away before continuing. "I'm not asking you to stay, Wolfe. I'm telling you to go.

A loud knock sounded on the door, causing me to jump.

I wiped my eyes and noticed Jude quickly exit the kitchen as I went to open the door. "Wolfe, I've been knocking for five minutes," Mike said.

I cleared my throat. "Sorry about that. Hope you're well?"

"Yeah, doing great. Happy new year," he said with a big smile and a hug. I felt numb as he hugged me, and I wondered how it was possible he didn't realize I was falling apart right in front of his eyes.

"I'm, ah, just going to find Jude to tell him I'm leaving," I stammered.

"Yeah, no worries. I told my parents I'd give them a call, so tell Jude I'll just be a minute if he needs anything, okay?"

I nodded and walked back to find Jude in his room.

40

JUDE

I made it to my room and closed the door, crawling onto the bed and curling up in a ball. How the hell was I going to survive a life without Derek in it?

A few minutes later I heard the door open and didn't look up. The bed sagged as Derek crawled over and spooned around me.

"I'm so sorry," he whispered in my ear. "I love you."

I knew that to be true the way I knew that loving someone didn't always mean you could make a life with them.

"I know," I said. "I love you too."

His arms squeezed me tight and his lips pressed kisses onto my neck before he climbed off the bed and out of my life.

I spent the next two days under my duvet and would have stayed longer if Ollie hadn't intervened.

"What the hell, baby cakes?" she accused. "Did something happen with the Hulk? He called me and asked me to check on you."

That sweet fucking jackass.

I pulled a pillow over my head and turned away from her.

"Aw, shit," she muttered.

She sat down on the bed next to me, kicking off her shoes and rubbing my shoulder.

"What happened?" she asked.

"He's gone," I mumbled through the pillow. My voice cracked from disuse and I felt fresh tears immediately soaked up by my pillowcase.

"What?" she asked. "I'll kick his ass. Why the hell did he leave you?"

"I told him to," I admitted, pulling the pillow away and turning to press my forehead into the side of her leg.

"Aw, honey. Why? What happened?" she asked as she began to run her fingers through my hair. "Did you guys get into a fight or something?"

"No. I told him I was going to come out of the closet. He doesn't want to, and he sure as hell doesn't want the media scrutiny of being with me."

"Well," she said, thinking for a minute, "I guess you can't blame him for that. Are you sure you want to come out?"

"Yes, I am one hundred percent positive that it's the right thing to do. At first I was doing it under duress." I told her the truth about the stalker and the photos of me with Ari, and she listened carefully.

"But then I thought about the reasons I was hiding my sexuality to begin with, the idea that country music wasn't ready for a gay star. But that's bullshit. Nobody's ever ready. It takes someone coming out to help people change. What about all of the closeted youth out there who feel trapped because they don't have role models showing them how to stand up and be proud of themselves? It's the right thing to do, Olls. I just wish I could come out and still have Derek too. I shouldn't have to choose."

She stayed with me and eventually forced me out of bed and into the shower. I dressed and came out to the kitchen in time to see a strange man standing with Mike.

"There he is," Mike said. "Jude, this is Kevin. He's taking over for Derek as your primary bodyguard."

I had known it was coming. There was no way either Derek or I would be able to be near each other without being together, but meeting his replacement was like a kick in the teeth.

"Uh, hi, Kevin. Nice to meet you," I said, taking his offered hand for a shake. "This is my assistant, Ollie. She lives over the garage."

Kevin's face notably lit up at the sight of my beautiful best friend.

"Hi, Ollie," he said. If I wasn't mistaken, he blushed as he spoke to her.

"Hey there, cutie," she said with her usual flirty smile.

After Mike left, I excused myself from the room, telling Kevin and Ollie I was going to go into my sound room and work on some music until it was time to fix dinner. I knew Ollie would stay and appreciate the chance to flirt with her new(est) victim.

I hadn't picked up my guitar in days, and it felt strange in my hands at first. Within the first few chords, however, my hands settled back into their rhythm and the instrument became an extension of myself.

Music flowed from my fingers while my mind floated away.

At some point Ollie came to find me for dinner. We ate quietly, Ollie and Kevin carrying the conversation. Apparently Mike had told Kevin I was sick, which, let's face it, was the truth. I was heartsick.

The following day I called Clint and asked him to come to my house for a meeting. He was worried about me since I'd skipped work at the studio immediately after being gone for a week.

The meeting with Clint sucked. He seemed almost giddy with the news of my sexuality. Not surprised, just excited. I told him about the stalker and the threats, but I didn't tell him about Derek.

"Clint, you seem happy about this. Why?" I asked when he wouldn't stop bouncing his leg under the table.

"I know you've heard it before, but it's true. There's no such thing as bad publicity, Jude. Plus, I think the fact that you're playing the Super Bowl will bring you even more into the mainstream music scene than you already are. Once you're there, the critical mass will support your coming out. The good old boys will be in the minority. I think it'll be fine."

"Okay, how do we do this? I need to tell my family first, and I can't do that until Sunday."

"We schedule an intimate interview with one of the big names on a major network. I think it would actually work out well if you were seen out in public before then doing or wearing something that hints at your sexuality. The media speculation will begin and the news will hit softer."

"What about the timing with the Super Bowl?" I asked. "Do we do it before or after?"

"For sure before. If anyone's turned off by your news, they won't be able to help falling back in love with you on Super Bowl Sunday."

"Okay. Well, I'll let you set it up. I'll tell the band in the morning at the studio."

The next day the band took it in stride like I knew they would, and afterward, damned if Beck didn't pull me aside to tell me he was bisexual. *What the hell?*

"Why didn't you ever tell me?" I asked him incredulously. We'd grown up together and known each other for decades.

He shrugged and laughed. "I thought you might be bi or gay. I assumed if you were keeping it to yourself, you had a reason. That's when I decided just to stay low key about my own shit. It's not like I've ever been in a serious relationship."

"That's because you sleep with everything that moves," I said before thinking. "I mean, what I meant was—"

He laughed. "It's okay. It's true. Why be in a band if you can't sleep your way around the world when you're on tour? I fucking love my life, man. And it's all thanks to you. I just wanted you to know there are no hard feelings about any of it. In fact, let me know if you want to go try out a gay club, and we can bust that cherry together." He winked before walking off to take a phone call. What in the world had just happened?

When Sunday came, I arrived at my parents' house to find absolute chaos. Simone was screaming at Pete for setting her up on a blind date with a moron, Thad was teaching my two nieces how to make paper airplanes that currently littered the whole house, Blue and Tristan had brought their dog, Piper, who kept jumping up to try and catch the airplanes out of the air, and Aunt Tilly had brought her two raunchy best friends, Tristan's granny and her wife, Irene.

My brothers Griff, Maverick, and Dante sat at the kitchen island laughing with Pete's wife, Ginger. My parents were nowhere to be found.

Blue asked where Derek was and I explained he wasn't with me that day.

I sensed Kevin shifting on his feet behind me.

"Welcome to crazy town. This is the Marian family. I have eight siblings and they're all nuts. This isn't even all of them if you can believe it," I told him.

Aunt Tilly noticed fresh meat and came toward Kevin. "Hey, Jude, what happened to Hottie #1? And helloooo, Hottie #2." She held out her hand to the bodyguard so he could kiss it. As if she was royalty. Kevin looked at me for a hint about what to do and I shrugged.

"Derek changed security details and now Kevin is watching me," I told her.

Tilly's face lit up in a devilish grin. "Is this *the* Kevin? As in the imaginary Kevin who's been sleeping with your dad for years?"

I felt my face flush as Blue barked out a laugh and Kevin looked like he wanted to go crawl under a car somewhere.

"Ah, no," I stammered before turning and beginning a futile attempt to explain the family inside joke to my new bodyguard.

Before I could explain, Mom and Dad appeared from the direction of their bedroom looking recently, um, exercised. I sighed and looked away, trying to mentally bleach the thought of what they'd been doing from my abused brain.

"Hey, honey, where's Derek?" Mom asked.

Jesusfuckingchrist with the questions about Derek.

"He's not here. Kevin took over for him," I said again.

"Welcome, Kevin," Mom said sweetly. After exchanging pleasantries, she glanced worriedly over at me.

Griff stood up and raised his voice to be heard over everyone. "Well, now that Mom and Dad are finished banging, and we've all met Dad's long lost boyfriend, we can eat. Everyone grab your plates. Let's go."

Dad's face flushed the color of Christmas and Mom swatted at Griff's shoulder as she walked by him.

"Nothing wrong with a healthy sex life, Griffin Marian. From what I've heard, you've been getting lucky with some sweet-talker out at the clubs lately. I think you should tell us all about it at dinner."

Now it was Griff's turn to blush. "Never mind. Forget I said anything."

"Oh hell no," Dante piped up. "Ask him who the newest sweet-talker at the clubs is, Mom."

Mom's eyes twinkled. "Thank you, Dante. Griffin, care to explain?"

Griff kept trying to weasel his way out of telling the story as we took turns filling our plates. I used the distraction to pull Blue aside to ask for his help designing a new T-shirt.

By the time we all sat at the big dining room table, he was forced to begin.

"A magazine wants me to write the article about the sweet-talker, so I started a little experiment to get some funny stories," Griff began hesitantly.

"Tell us about it," Dad said with a smile.

"Basically, I take a seat at the bar and try to pick up whatever guy happens to sit on the stool next to mine. Obviously if he's there with someone or in a relationship, I leave him alone, otherwise he's fair game."

He took a sip of his beer and continued. "I start with, 'Hey, foxy, can I buy you a drink?' When the drinks come I just start flirting, but every sentence I say includes a term of endearment of some kind. I time how long it takes to get them to ask me, ah," at this point he looked at our young nieces, who seemed oblivious, "how long it takes them to ask me *over for dinner*," he finished.

Simone choked on her beer. "Dinner, right. And do you enjoy *several* dinners a night, baby brother?"

Griff glared at her. "No. No dinner with them. I eat alone when I get home. Depending on how *hungry* the experience made me, some-times I eat two or three times."

Now it was my father's turn to choke, and Aunt Tilly lost her shit. Tristan's granny's dentures came loose, and Granny's wife Irene flushed a pink deeper than Ollie's hair.

Tilly couldn't very well be left out of a conversation like that so she piped up. "Too bad you don't eat out. Granny and Irene have been begging me to try it with them. Speaking of eating out, Rebecca, your taco is delicious," she said as she bit into the crunchy shell, causing juice to drip onto her plate.

And that was when I gave up trying to eat my dinner.

41

DEREK

The weeks without Jude felt like they'd never end. Every day took forever and I did everything I could to stay busy. After work in the office, I went straight to the gym and worked myself to the point of exhaustion.

When night came, I begged for sleep to give me a break from thinking of Jude but it was no use. Jude was in my dreams too.

In the mornings, I would wake, and for a split second think I still had a boyfriend. Then I'd remember, and my stomach would fall.

I worked from early in the morning until late at night until Joel finally insisted I take some time off and visit my parents out east. He knew I'd spent Thanksgiving, Christmas, and New Year's "working" with Jude, so he convinced me I owed it to my family if nothing else.

When I got to my parents' house, exhaustion hit me, and I was thankful Joel had insisted I take time off. I was able to watch some football games with my dad and Aaron as well as keep my mom company in the kitchen while she cooked for us.

I had obviously thought about the possibility of coming out in order to get Jude back. During the first few days at home, I almost blurted it out several times. But I realized that wasn't really going to solve my dilemma. It was the media scrutiny I was more worried about.

My family was getting very excited about the Super Bowl trip. I wondered how they'd feel after they learned the truth about Jude.

Joel had told me I was still on Jude's detail for the trip since they needed several people. My plan was to work day shifts only so we would never be alone or together at night. I could also do some of the advance work and team coordination so I wasn't close to him even when I was on duty.

Ollie texted me one Wednesday to tell me Jude's interview was going to be aired that night on TV at 9. I felt my nerves kick up when I switched over to the appropriate channel for the interview.

When Jude's face came on the screen, he looked as gorgeous as he always did. Even my mom made a comment about "that good-looking man." My dad worked on his laptop at the kitchen table and my mom sat next to me on the sofa. Aaron lay back in the recliner, letting Mom baby him by bringing him a bowl of ice cream.

The interview started off with questions about what he'd been working on, the new album, and his upcoming tour. Then the interviewer asked questions about Jude's brothers getting married.

"So, Jude, rumor has it that two of your brothers were married recently. Is that correct?"

Jude laughed. "You make it sound like they married each other. My brother Blue married a man named Tristan Alexander of Alexander Vineyards, and my brother Jamie married Theodore Kodiak, last year's winner of the Gramling Prize for Wildlife Photography. They are both very nice men, and I'm proud to welcome them to the family. They are well aware of what a crazy crew they've joined, I assure you."

He was charming the pants off her.

The interviewer laughed. "What do you mean *crazy crew*?"

"I have one sister and seven brothers. I also have a wonderfully irreverent great-aunt who has adopted a couple of new friends who fit right in. We're a motley crew of strong personalities, but it works for us. I'm very lucky."

"An unusually high number of your brothers is gay, correct?" the interviewer asked.

Jude continued to smile. If you didn't know him well, you'd think it was genuine.

"I'm not sure, Anna. What's the *usual* number of gay brothers for someone to have?" he asked with a wink.

Score one for Bluebell.

"Oh, sorry, I guess what I meant to ask is how many of your seven brothers are gay?"

"I'm not going to discuss my brothers' sexuality. That's their private business. I'm sure if they wanted to talk about it, their manager would contact you about scheduling an interview," he said pointedly, still wearing the smile.

"Right. Let's move along then. Yesterday you were spotted at a restaurant here in Los Angeles wearing a T-shirt that said, and I quote, 'Spoiler alert: I'm totally gay.' Would you like to explain that to our audience?"

A photograph of Jude wearing the shirt popped up on the corner of the screen, and it seemed to have been taken by paparazzi while Jude and Ollie were having lunch outside at a café. I wasn't sure what everyone else thought, but I knew for a fact it had to have been a planned paparazzi stunt, probably meant to get the word out before the interview hit the airwaves.

"My brother made it for me. I'm not sure it needs additional explanation, honestly," he teased.

"Come on, Jude. Your fans want to know. Are you really gay?"

"Yes. I am really gay," he said. His tone had become more even, and the grin was replaced by a familiar look of brave determination. My heart thundered so loudly in my ears I almost didn't notice the reactions from my family members.

"Holy shit, Derek," Aaron blurted. My mom snapped her head around to hiss a warning about bad language. "Sorry, Mom. But seriously, dude. You had to have known. Did he make you sign some kind of agreement?"

"I can't discuss it," I said automatically.

My father grumbled in the background, but I tried to tune him out.

Next, the interviewer asked the question I was waiting for.

"Are you seeing anyone?"

Jude crossed his ankle over his opposite knee and cleared his throat. "Not right now, no."

Fuck. Even though I knew it, it hurt like a bitch to hear him say it.

The interviewer's eyes lit up. "Well, well," she said with a grin, "I'm sure there are plenty of men out there who find that news both surprising and exciting. What do you think, Jude?"

"If they do, they're probably just starstruck," he joked. "Dating someone whose life is under a media microscope is harder than you think. I spent several years avoiding dating anyone because I was afraid to put someone through that."

"And now?" she prompted. "Are you hoping to find that special someone?"

"Honestly, Anna, I've already found that someone special, but it didn't work out. So for the time being, I'm going to lick my wounds and concentrate on my music. I'm lucky enough to have a loving family, a fabulous best friend, and a highly talented and hardworking band behind me. Right now, I can't say I'm lonely."

Liar.

"You're set to play the big Super Bowl halftime show next weekend. Tell us how you think your news will affect that performance," the woman asked.

"There's probably some kind of no-sex rule at the Super Bowl stadium, so I thought I'd just sing instead," he said with a smile. "I don't expect my sexuality to ever have any effect on my music performance. If someone thinks this announcement has anything to do with my ability to do my job, I'd like to know how."

"What would you say to a parent out there who decides that your sexuality is a negative influence on their child?"

"I would like to say their negative judgement of others is a negative influence on their child. In reality, though, I would tell them that maybe, by watching this interview, and seeing me finally being true to who I am, their children won't feel so alone if they're feeling different than they're expected to be. I hope I can encourage others to be brave enough to fight for the love they deserve."

"Is there anything else you'd like to say about it before we wrap up our interview?"

Jude turned to the camera and leaned forward. "If any of you are scared and feeling lonely, whether about your sexuality or any other kind of struggle you may be having, please reach out for help. You can call the National Suicide Prevention Lifeline at 1-800-273-TALK (8255) for help. Whatever you do, don't do it alone. I know it's scary telling someone your struggles, but be brave— you can do it."

"Thank you. That lifeline number along with links to many helpful organizations will be available on our website after the show. Jude, why don't we end this chat on a fun note? While preparing for tonight's interview, several of my coworkers submitted questions for you. One of the men in our sales department wanted me to ask you for your number." She smiled.

Jude blushed and chuckled.

Goddamned sales guy. Asshole.

"Ah, no, thanks, but tell him I'm flattered. I guess," Jude managed to say.

"Another person wanted to ask what your type is. If a friend set you up on the ideal blind date, what would the guy be like?"

I thought I might throw up. Jude on a date? With someone besides me? Dear god, *no.*

Jude continued to blush as he looked up and thought about it. "First of all, he'd need to love being mobbed by throngs of excited fans," he joked. "He'd have to accept some of my quirks, like the fact that I love all dogs except pugs, I'm a nervous flyer, and I only like my vegetables shaped like spirals." He said the last part with a small smile.

"What about looks?" the woman asked, pushing for more.

"Well, I'm pretty flexible about looks. It takes way more than outward appearance to interest me, but I'll admit I'm a sucker for someone tall and well built. I am most attracted to people who are kind, attentive, a good listener as well as a good conversationalist, and physically affectionate. Don't stereotype me too much, but I'm a cuddler," he admitted, blushing even deeper.

Good god, America had to be eating this shit up. The man was adorable as fuck.

"Tell me about the last man you dated," she prompted.

Jude looked up in surprise and the blush reappeared, spreading over his face and neck. "The last man I dated... He's all of those things and more. Just a kind, beautiful man. I miss him very much."

He scraped his upper lip with his bottom teeth in an uncharacteristically nervous gesture.

I shifted on the sofa and wondered if I might actually be coming down with the flu.

"Can you tell us his name?" she asked.

"Not a chance." He blew out a nervous laugh. "Nice try though."

"Worth a shot," she admitted. "Thank you so much for joining us tonight, Jude, and good luck next week at the Super Bowl halftime show. Viewers, be sure to catch Super Bowl coverage here beginning—"

The broadcast cut off and I looked to see what happened. My father held the remote where he stood behind the sofa.

"Hell, son. Didn't you say you had to stay in his house overnight sometimes?" my dad asked. My stomach flipped over as I prepared myself for the horrible things that might come out of his mouth.

"I've spent lots of nights at Jude's house, Dad. I'm not sure what you're asking. But please, if it's something homophobic, I beg you to keep it to yourself."

He grunted and went back to his laptop, but not before muttering one more thing. "They're fucking everywhere."

A stupid, childish voice in my head retorted, *No, we mostly just fuck at home like everyone else.*

I chose that moment to go to bed in case my stupid, childish voice decided to lay some truth on my family.

My fingers twirled my phone around in circles until I couldn't help but text Jude.

Derek: *Just saw the interview. You did an amazing job. I'm so proud of you.*

Jude: *Thank you. We recorded it this morning, and I'm already back home, waiting for the world to end. Ollie says I should pop some popcorn and watch scary movies with her if I'm going to be freaked out anyway.*

Derek: *Tell her I said you deserve a back rub and some comedy. She has strong hands. Guilt her into it.*

Jude: *Good idea. Are you okay?*

Derek: *Not really, I'm at my parents'.*

Jude: *Ah. Sorry.*

Derek: *Are you still okay with my family coming to the game? It's not too late to cancel.*

Jude: *Shut up. Even if I wanted to renege, which I don't, I don't want a Marine general and his foot soldiers murdering me in a bloody revenge op thankyouverymuch.*

Derek: *Good point.*

I knew better than to continue the text conversation. My head pounded and all I could think to type was *I love you, I want you, I need you.* So I turned off my phone instead.

42

————

JUDE

I felt stung by his abrupt ending to our text conversation. Not that I didn't understand why he did it, but still. Obviously that night I was feeling extremely vulnerable. Ollie had offered to get me drunk, but I declined in favor of gorging myself on Swedish Fish.

The fallout from the interview wasn't as negative as I expected. People came out of the woodwork to thank me for being a good example, but I didn't feel like I was. I felt like someone who had spent my entire life up to that point trying to pretend to be someone other than myself. After the interview, I felt a kind of giant relief, but it was shaded by the knowledge that I still couldn't have it all. Coming out may have solved one of my problems, but it created another one that was ripping my heart out.

My family made a point of surrounding me as much as possible in the few days left before the Nashville trip, and their support kept me from losing it altogether.

Telling my family I was gay had been the exact combination of easy and emotionally explosive I'd anticipated. Of course it had been easy to tell them I was gay. More than half the freaking family was gay. It was the part where I hadn't told them about my sexuality for years and years and years that was the problem.

At Sunday dinner, after Griff told us about the article he was writing, I told everyone I had something to tell them.

"I decided to join the bandwagon and become gay," I said with a feeble smile.

"Irene owes me twenty bucks," Tristan's granny called out at the same time Ginger elbowed Pete.

"You owe me a blow job," Ginger said to her husband.

My mom burst into tears, Simone had started blaming people, and Blue had leaned his face into Tristan's neck as if he'd just gotten sad news. It had made me wish like hell Derek was there. Goddamned selfish asshole. I'd needed him and he'd bailed on me. On us.

My dad tried to remain calm, as usual. He placed his arm around my shoulder and kissed me on the cheek.

"You must have had a good reason to keep it to yourself all this time, Jude. Do you want to share that with us? If not, that's completely fine."

Being a Marian was like living inside group therapy sometimes.

"It was a combination of factors, but I don't want to talk about that part right now. Most recently it was because of my career."

I had asked Kevin to give my family some privacy before I began the conversation, so I was able to speak freely. I told them about Ari, and then I told them the truth about Derek.

"Oh, honey," Mom said. And wasn't that the most *mom* thing anyone ever said?

She came over and hugged me, holding me tight for a while.

"I knew there was something going on between you, but it seemed like the real thing," she said.

"That's just it. It was the real thing. We both love each other. We both respect each other and want to be together forever. But we can't. I can't live in the closet, and he can't live out of it."

Of all people, it was Aunt Tilly who got angry as a hornet. "Well, fuck that," she spat.

My mom's eyes bugged, and Tilly continued. "You tell that cocksucker to grow a pair. No one ever said life was going to be easy.

You don't get that many opportunities to find a good man and when you do, you hold on to him for dear life. God, what an ass. And I don't mean that as a compliment, even though that's also true. He does have a smoking hot posterior. Almost... biteable if you ask me. Are you saying he's single now? How attached is he to the D?"

Her rant kind of petered out at that point. She began to wax poetic about Derek's ass. Who could blame her, really?

There was a collective groan.

"No one asked you, old lady," Blue said to Tilly.

Tristan looked at Granny with narrowed eyes. "Not a word, Granny."

The tiny woman just shrugged and mimed zipping her lips, but I was pretty sure she mumbled something about a giant salami cock under her breath.

Thad reached across the dinner table to put his hand on mine. "Isn't he going to be at the game with his family?"

"I don't know," I said.

My family spent the rest of the evening rallying around poor me. Simone stopped blaming people when she ran out of names and began to coddle me instead. I overheard Tristan tell Blue he'd suspected this since Hawaii, and Blue replied he'd known about it since I was a teenager. Blue won that round.

Dante, who normally lurked around the edges in his quiet way, came up and hugged me. "I admire you, Jude. Thank you for telling us. I know it couldn't have been easy, even as cool as everyone is about it. Tonight was the easy part. When you do that interview, remember we have your back."

"Thanks, Dante. That means a lot."

Griff came over to hug me too and tell me he could come to Los Angeles with me for the interview if I wanted him to. I told him I would really like that. He was one of the most fun-loving laid-back guys I knew and would do a better job than most at distracting me without being silly.

I found Kevin waiting in the town car in front of the house. I apologized to him and told him about my upcoming announcement to the press.

"I just wanted to tell my family in private. Hope you don't mind."

Kevin turned to look at me with an understanding smile. "Of course not, Jude. That's fantastic news. I know how hard it is to stay in the closet as an adult. You'll feel better once it's all out."

"You're gay?" I blurted. The man looked like a bouncer at a club, and not the gay kind. More like the auto mechanic meathead kind. I found myself on a stereotyping roll.

He laughed. "No, but my uncle is. He finally came out after he and my aunt had been together for twenty years. Can you imagine? All that time living a lie. Makes me crazy to think about it. He said the minute he came out, it was like walking into a brand-new life."

"Wow. How's he doing now?" I asked, feeling happy for this stranger I'd never met before. He was finally getting to live his life without all the secrets and compartmentalizing.

"Great. Happily married to a nice guy named Phil who has two daughters about my age. I think the fact that Phil was also married to a woman before helped them understand each other better. They live downtown here in the city, so I see them often. My aunt is in Portland now. She hasn't remarried, but she has a great group of friends who travel together all over."

Kevin continued to tell me about his family while he drove us back to my house. At some point he turned on the radio and I dozed off listening to the familiar sounds of country music classics.

WHEN IT WAS time to fly to Nashville, I was as ready as I'd ever be. I boarded the chartered jet with Kevin in front of me when he turned back to tell me something.

"Oh, I forgot to tell you that Derek isn't coming. Joel has him working on something else, so he wanted me to tell you he was sorry to miss it. His dad and brothers will still be there, but Ollie will take care of them and make sure they have everything they need."

My heart dropped, and I was torn between feeling relieved and disappointed. So that was that, then. No more Derek.

Instead of singing in the Super Bowl show, I wanted to go back to my bed and hide under the duvet for the next several months. Or as long as it would take my shredded heart to find some way of patching itself back together again.

I found a seat and dropped into it. Ollie boarded a few minutes later and took the seat next to mine. For the first time in a year, it was Ollie's shoulder I slept on instead of Derek's.

THE FIRST FEW days of practice were grueling. The show producers had rented an enormous warehouse that gave us an area equivalent to the halftime stage we would use. The rehearsal space had already been used for the last few weeks by the hordes of accompanying dancers. Since our band would pretty much stay in one place on the stage to do our performance, we just needed to get some timing and movements right to make sure we were all in sync. Sounded easy, but it turned out to be anything but. It was Thursday before we finally moved everything to the stadium.

Entering Nissan Stadium wasn't as exciting for me as it would have been for other people. I wasn't a big football fan. Pete, Ginger and my dad, on the other hand, were over the moon. They'd flown out a few days early and Ollie helped them find places to sit and watch the rehearsals while keeping them company. Kevin spent the time meeting with stadium security confirming details that I was sure he had already double-checked over the previous days and weeks.

The song we were starting with was one of Beck's favorites because of the killer drum solo. It was called "Empty Bed," but the fans always referred to it as "Cold Sheets." It was a high-tempo, almost angry, revenge song about a breakup. It was our most popular karaoke song because people loved shouting out the line from the chorus, "I like the sheets cold anyway." One of the show producers had specifically requested the song because she thought the crowd would sing along and get ramped up by it. The dancing they'd chore-ographed was really funky and strong, almost like a country version of hip-hop.

Our second song would be "Mothering Hands," and it was slow and sweet. The dancers would weave around the stage and have flowing white silks billowing all around them. I couldn't wait to see the video of how it looked from above.

Next came the debut of a song off the new album called "Midnight Sparklers." The dancers, along with every single ticket holder, would have faux sparklers to wave around to the music. They were like skinny sticks with fiber optic twinkle lights on the ends. From a distance they looked incredibly real, but they were completely fire safe. It was going to be an energizing crowd-pleaser.

We were going to finish up with a brand-new song I'd written that my bandmates were going nuts over. Clint had to get special permission for us to add it to the list because it hadn't released yet, and the dancers were given the simple directive of grabbing a partner and dancing to the music.

Seeing the various components of the show in rehearsal had been exciting, but actually heading to the stage to put it all together on the field for the first time was an incredible feeling. Before heading out to begin, Ollie stopped me and handed me a snack. The little bag had grapes and string cheese in it along with bottle of water, and I flashed her an appreciative smile. "What would I do without you?"

"Wither away and die, baby cakes. Now, why don't you tell me what the hell is going on with you?"

My stomach dropped as I looked up at her. "What do you mean?"

"Something's got you in a twist."

"I can't stop thinking about Derek," I admitted.

She rolled her eyes. "You two are such idiots." I felt my face fill with red heat. "You're both miserable without each other but can't figure out how to get out of your own damned way. You'll figure it out eventually. And one day I'll be crazy Aunt Ollie to beautiful little Derek Marian babies."

Clearly she was trying to kill me.

I rolled my eyes at her. "Whatever," I muttered.

"Quick, eat. Here comes Clint," she said. "He probably wants to tell you to get this show on the road so he can get back to the hotel and sleep with your ex-girlfriend."

"What?" I snorted. "Please tell me that's a joke."

"Nope. Saw Jae sneaking out of his hotel room last night to get some ice. Clint's room is next to mine. It was ugly. I needed eye bleach after."

43

———

DEREK

I managed to get replaced on Jude's security detail for the Nashville trip, but Joel still let me stay on the case to keep an eye on social media chatter from anyone on our list of potential problem fans.

After Jude came out, I told Joel about the relationship history with Ari and the stalker named Martin. Of course, he'd already known about the stalker but not about the photographs and threat of media exposure. We had someone keeping his eye on Martin around the clock for the week.

Joel had reamed me out for not telling him sooner. I deserved the lecture but reminded him it was too little too late. He insisted on contacting the FBI to keep an eye on the guy for anything that may come in the future.

While helping prep the Nashville security plan, I had discovered Ari was part of a corporate group that had a VIP box at the game. Thank goodness it wasn't close to Jude's box. I notified Kevin to be aware of it and run interference with Ari if needed. The last thing Jude needed was to be blindsided by another sales pitch.

The week of the game, I ran queries through our database of fan correspondence to get any new hits or look for any recent comments on social media that could be a concern for Jude. The exposure of performing at the Super Bowl created a massive security challenge, and I wanted to ensure all bases were covered. I worked endless hours that week, double and triple-checking the smallest of details. My gut screamed at me that something was off. If I could just find it, I could help the team keep Jude safe.

On the day of the game I was in the office early again, when Joel came storming in.

"Get on a plane to Nashville," he snapped.

My blood ran cold. "What? Why?" I asked, almost not wanting to hear. "Is it Jude? Is he okay? Did something happen?"

"Not yet, but if you don't go tell that man you love him, I'm going to kick your ass."

I sat there staring at him. Joel and I had known each other for years. He'd been one of my instructors in the Marines before we ended up on missions together. We didn't talk about love.

"What?" I asked dumbly.

"You're making yourself sick. I don't know what the hell's the matter with you that you can't man-up and claim what's yours. That kid fucking worships you, and if you didn't feel the same way, you wouldn't be working twenty hour days to keep him safe when he's already covered by a four-man team."

"Listen, Joel, you don't know what you're talking ab—"

"Don't bullshit me, Wolfe. Just go out to Nashville and tell him. What's the worst that could happen? Your family disowns you? So what. Who would you rather have in your life? Jude, or your homophobic family? Because the way I see it, the worst that could happen is you missing out on a chance to be happy for once. And I don't see how giving up someone you love to keep the peace in your family is worth it."

Worth it.

Joel continued with a sigh. "Derek, think of Nate."

Now he was bringing out the big guns. Nate was one of our teammates who had been killed in the same attack that had messed up my hip. He'd died before he'd gotten up the nerve to propose to his girlfriend.

"What if he'd had another chance to be with Kelly? What would he tell you if he was here in your shoes? Jude deserves to be with the person he loves. Even if you don't think you deserve that, can't you admit that *he* does?"

WHEN I ENTERED THE STADIUM, my security pass gave me access to the sidelines during the performance. I'd arrived just in time to see Jude and the Saints take the stage. The crowd was riled up and ready for a great show, and I was excited for Jude and the rest of the band. What an incredible high they must have gotten from being in the middle of it all.

I took a spot on the edge of the turf between the field and the tunnel where I knew the band would exit after the performance. The stage was visible from where I stood, but Jude was too far away to make out any detail in his expressions as he sang. I had to rely on the images being broadcast to the large display screens overhead. His hair was down and his face was alight with energy. The sleeves of the shirt he wore were rolled up, exposing his forearms, and I noticed the leather bracelet I'd given him resting on one wrist.

God, he was breathtaking.

The band sang a familiar upbeat song for their intro and moved into a slower song I recognized. The dancers had these white sheet-type fabric pieces they danced with, like that parachute we all played with in gym class.

The next song was kick ass. It was from the new album and had the crowd going nuts in the stands. Everyone waved light wands in the air; the vibe in the stadium was magic.

When that song finished, Jude spoke for a minute to the crowd. I assumed the dancers or the band had to reposition themselves and he spoke to buy time. I mentally prepared myself for the familiar intro to "Bluebells," the song that taunted me even in my sleep. The earworm from hell and the song I'd gladly send overseas to be used in torture chambers. And I knew without a shadow of a doubt Jude agreed with me after six years of singing it during every performance.

"Ladies and gentlemen, this next song is a last-minute addition. I just wrote it a few weeks ago, so forgive us if it's not perfect yet. This one was never really meant to go public, but the band overheard me tinkering with it and insisted. I told them if I was going to play it, I owed it to someone to do a proper dedication."

My stomach flipped at the sound of his familiar voice speaking in the Super Bowl stadium during halftime, but when he prepared to dedicate the song to someone, my ears pricked up.

"This song is about regular old all-consuming love, just like any other country music song," he laughed. "But when it's your own love, there's nothing regular about it. One night someone asked me to dance in my kitchen. It was just a normal night. But when we danced, I fell head over heels in love. This song was inspired by that special person, who will always carry the biggest piece of my heart. It's called 'Dance With Me.' It's fast and fun, so please feel free to stand up and dance," he finished with a big grin to a crowd roaring with wolf whistles, *aww*s, and *whoop*s.

My throat burned and I felt my eyes prickle. He was so damned brave. The song was exactly the way he described it, lively and catchy. I knew as soon as the band started playing the song was going to be a smash hit. No wonder his bandmates went nuts over it.

> When the music blares and the drumbeats boom,
> Dance with me.
>
> Bodies facing
> Rhythm chasing
> Dance with me.
> Eyes are shining
> Stars aligning
> Dance with me.

When autumn night is dark and the campfire glows,
Sing with me.
When our bodies chill as the winter wind blows,
Sleep with me.
When the springtime comes and the flowers bloom,
Grow with me.

Bodies facing
Rhythm chasing
Dance with me.
Eyes are shining
Stars aligning
Dance with me.

If the summer comes and we're still in love,
Stay with me.

Bodies facing
Rhythm chasing
Dance with me.
Eyes are shining
Stars aligning
Promise me.

It all came slamming into me again like a two-by-four. Instead of standing by the person I loved while he bared his soul on national TV, I had sat in a room of homophobes and wallowed in self-pity.

Instead of claiming the most amazing man I'd ever known, I'd hidden in shadows and tried to be invisible. What was the fucking point? Why? So I could spend my life protecting strangers instead of protecting *him*?

That man had just stood on a stage in front of one hundred million people around the world and dedicated a love song to another man. And not just any man.

Me.

As the crowd in the stands roared, the field lights went out so the hundreds of dancers on the field could exit en masse as they'd been trained without the fans seeing behind the scenes. But they'd never trained alongside all the media and team support staff. The resulting crowd on the field was chaos.

I tried to make my way to Jude, to grab him and tell him how stupid I was. To tell him I loved him and would do anything to be with him, but I couldn't find him in the crowd. Picking up my pace to a run, I tried desperately to get eyes on him.

Finally I saw him. "Jude," I called out in a relieved rush.

His head came up at the sound of my voice and his face lit up like the sun. Had someone caught it on camera, they could have made millions.

"Derek?" he asked, incredulous. "What are you doing here?"

I couldn't wait to hold him, and my arms reached out to pull him in. God, there was no better place in the world than the arms of the person you loved most. I couldn't wait to inhale his smell and feel that wave of relief wash over me.

It all happened so fast. A hot pain sliced into my back just as I got to him, and I stumbled forward. My arms tightened around his body while I struggled to remain upright. Ringing sounds blared in my ears, and I realized my face felt numb. Another sharp pain landed, this time to the back of my arm.

What the hell was happening?

Jude.

I had to make sure Jude was covered. Without thinking, I quickly lowered us to the ground, bringing him down with me and curling into a protective shell around his body. It was the best I could do because I was losing my coordination.

"Kevin, Mike," I tried yelling. "Someone, get him out of here!"

A body landed on top of me and I could hear screaming. I turned my head to the side to see what was going on. There were cameras everywhere, zoom lenses bumping into people's backs, and journalists choosing to run toward the incident rather than away. The main lights on the field were still out, so it was hard to see details.

I felt Jude squirming in my arms and thought I heard him crying.

"It's okay baby, it's going to be okay. I love you." But I didn't know which one of us said it. Him or me.

44

JUDE

One minute I was riding the high of an incredible performance and the next I was being smashed into the sideline turf by Derek's giant body. I had been momentarily startled as I recognized Ari's wife, Britta Crowe in the crowd of dancers, but as soon as I saw Derek coming towards me for a hug, she fell from my mind.

Before I even had a chance to hug him back, Britta was on top of him. I wasn't sure if the attack was meant for me and Derek had just stepped in the way, or what. But he had obviously taken a blow. He stumbled and began to fall in some kind of controlled descent, landing both of us in a heap with him on top of me.

He screamed for someone to come get me, but I could hear raw pain in his voice.

"Derek, what happened? What's going on? Are you hurt?" I stammered, trying to twist around but discovering I was pinned down by his body weight.

"Baby, talk to me," I begged when he didn't answer. "Someone help!" I screamed as loudly as I could.

I couldn't see anything and could only feel the warm press of Derek's familiar body on mine. Frustrated tears poured out of my eyes as I struggled to find some way of getting loose so I could help him. "Goddammit, He-Man, just tell me you're okay," I begged.

Finally someone rolled him off of me and screamed about all of the blood he was losing. I didn't know where it was coming from, but the blood suddenly seemed to be everywhere.

"No!" I screamed when I saw how bad it was. Hands reached out to grab me, but I fought them off. I scrambled to cup his face and speak in his ear. My hands searched desperately for a way to stop the bleeding on his neck and shoulder. "It's okay, babe. You're going to be okay. I'm right here with you. I love you." I kissed the side of his face, his lips, his hair.

Hot tears fell from my face to splash onto the blood, and the rest of the world faded away.

There was only Derek.

Finally several medics swarmed us, taking over and shoving me out of the way. Kevin tried to shuttle me off the sidelines toward a tunnel, but I growled at him to back off.

When they loaded him in the ambulance, they let me ride along, but once we arrived at the hospital, I was forced to remain outside of the room.

I tried to insist on staying with him. Told them that he was my boyfriend and he needed me there. But rules were rules, they said. They couldn't let me in.

I wasn't family.

IT WAS Derek's father who finally let me in to see him two hours later. It took Derek waking up and demanding to see me before he agreed.

When I entered the room and saw him lying there in a hospital gown, messy hair sticking up and skin paler than I could have imagined, I felt my legs begin to buckle.

"Baby," Derek said in a hoarse voice, his face a mix of pain and relief.

I stumbled to his side and leaned over to hug him. His arms came around me and held on.

My tears made a puddle on his neck but I didn't dare pull away to wipe my eyes.

"Are you okay?" I whispered against his skin.

"I am now," he said into my ear. "Are you?"

I nodded. "Mm-hm. Just scared."

The hand without the IV came up to brush my hair out of my face. "Did they get the person who attacked you?"

I couldn't help but laugh and pull back to look at his face. "Attacked *me*? She attacked *you*. And, yes. They got her. It was Ari's wife, Britta. I guess Ari told her about our past after my interview aired, and she went crazy. I haven't really heard any other details yet."

Derek's hand kept smoothing the hair out of my face as his eyes searched me for any sign of injury or distress.

"What are you doing here?" I asked him.

"I was stabbed," he said with furrowed brows of confusion. I realized he was probably on some good pain meds. "A lot. I have stitches all over."

"No, I mean, what are you doing in Nashville? I thought you were still at home."

"I came to tell you I was an idiot," he said. The look on his face was so serious I couldn't help but laugh again.

"You could have told me that over the phone," I teased.

"Jude, I love you. Need you. I can't stand to live one minute longer without you by my side. The idea of not being with you makes me sick. I'm embarrassed and ashamed of myself for leaving you when you needed me the most. I should have been there when you did that interview. Should have told the world that you were mine. I'm so sorry." His last words finished in a hushed kind of croak.

I leaned down and kissed his lips gently. "It's about time." I let out a deep breath as I moved my hands up to cup his cheeks. "Honestly, if I couldn't get Joel to talk some sense into you, I was going to have to dedicate an original song to you during the Super Bowl halftime show. Can you even imagine?"

His eyes widened in surprise. "What?" he asked.

I laughed. "Derek, I didn't get where I am by waiting for good things to fall from the sky. If I want something badly enough, I work for it. Don't think for one minute you stood a chance at walking away from me. You're mine. End of discussion." I winked, causing his eyes to bug out.

I smirked and leaned closer to his face again. "Now kiss me some more before your dad comes in and kicks me out of your room," I whispered.

"You're not going anywhere," he grumbled, grabbing the back of my head and bringing me in for a kiss.

"Really?" I asked. It wasn't possible I was getting everything I wanted. It was just too good to be true.

"Really, Bluebell. I love you. You're it for me."

He leaned in again and kissed me. Oh god, his mouth was the best thing ever. Warm and familiar and home.

We kissed so long I thought his dad would barge in on us any minute and see the huge tent pitched under his blanket.

"Did the, ah, doctor say anything about restrictions from sex?" I asked him.

"If he did, do you think I'd admit it?" He smirked.

Hot damn.

I SPENT the rest of the day and night snuggled up against Derek's side in the hospital bed. We talked and dozed despite his father and brothers' obvious discomfort at seeing us together. Derek told me that he'd had a conversation with them before his dad let me in to the hospital room, and his family was understandably having a hard time with the news.

Finally, they left to head to the hotel and the airport, leaving us with just my dad, Pete and Ginger. Kevin and Mike hung around to keep an eye on us as well.

When Derek was released from the hospital, we exited the

building into a storm of reporters and cameras. I tried to shuttle him to the waiting town car, but he stopped to take questions before we got there. Derek Wolfe was voluntarily speaking to the press? I stared at him as if he were a stranger.

"Mr. Wolfe, are you the ex-boyfriend Jude has mentioned to the press?" the reporter asked.

Derek's eyes flashed and his mouth widened into a smile. "No, I'm not."

The reporter looked disappointed while he struggled to come up with another question. He didn't need to worry about it because Derek continued.

"I'm his current, and hopefully his always," he clarified, reaching for my hand and threading his fingers through mine. "I said once that someone would have to be an idiot to ever leave Jude, and I don't plan on being that idiot ever again."

The reporter wasn't finished. "Do you love him?"

Derek's smile got even bigger. "More than anything."

"Does he love you?"

"He'd better," he joked, turning to look at me. "Or I'm going to regret getting a tattoo of him and Walker, Texas Ranger on my ass."

I couldn't help but snort. "He's kidding," I told the reporters. Then I turned to him, "Wait, you're kidding, right?"

"You'll have to find out for yourself when we get home, babe." And then that fucker grabbed me and kissed me in front of the whole world like my mouth was a slot machine payout and his tongue was hungry for quarters.

EPILOGUE - DEREK
SIX MONTHS LATER

It was August and we were settling in at home after the craziness of the tour. We'd been back for two weeks and life was beginning to feel normal again. The tour had been both a personal and professional success. The album was doing well but the single of "Dance With Me" had gone outer limits, surpassing even the success of "Bluebells." On a personal note, I was doing double duty as Jude's personal bodyguard and very out and official boyfriend.

I worked directly for Jude now, no longer for Joel at On Your Six Security. That meant I basically got to be with him whenever I wanted, and he paid me a bodyguard's salary so I didn't have to refer to him as my sugar daddy. It didn't really matter since he'd put my name on all his bank accounts anyway, but it helped us keep a power balance that worked for us. We both knew I would never spend his money on myself despite his encouragement for me to do so. Maybe that would change one day but not anytime soon.

My parents had decided to take a break from speaking to me while I "took some time to think about life choices." I was trying to be okay with the break. The Marians had accepted me with open arms, and I realized life was too short to focus your love on people who couldn't accept you the way you were.

Jude had spoken to his bandmates about taking at least a year off from touring and they heartily agreed. Joey and Fiona had been secretly dating for a while now, and I had a suspicion they were thinking about making it official by starting a family.

I'd moved into Jude's house shortly after returning from the Super Bowl trip. He nursed me back to health which really meant he forced me to stay in bed and did naughty things to me while I was there. Oh, and I learned that changing the shape of a vegetable definitely did *not* improve its taste.

Halfway through the tour Ollie's grandmother had decided to sell her house and move to a retirement community. Ollie was back in the apartment over our garage, which made all three of us happy as could be. If not for Ollie, I'd never get to eat pizza or potato chips anymore, and I wouldn't laugh nearly as much.

It was Sunday, and we were at Jude's parents' for dinner. It was still a little strange for me to be a participating member of the family after standing quietly in the background for so long, but I was getting better.

Rebecca had helped me arrange a surprise for Jude, and I led him into the backyard with my hands over his eyes.

"If you throw me in the pool, I'll kick your ass," Jude warned.

"I'd like to see you try." I laughed. "Describe to me what that would look like exactly."

He laughed too. "Okay, fine, but if you throw me in the pool there will be a severe shortage of nookie in your future."

I laughed again. "Again, I'd like to see you try. You can't resist me, and we both know it."

"Okay, fine. But it will be nookie with *attitude*," he finished lamely

"Is that supposed to be a threat? Sounds more like a promise to me," I said.

We got to an area in the grass where Rebecca had put an open-topped dog pen filled with a mama dog and two of her fat puppies. I took my hands from his eyes and leaned in to kiss his cheek.

"Surprise, Bluebell. You get to pick a puppy. Your mom took in a stray at the clinic and she had puppies. They're not pugs, but that's only because you and I both know there can only be one pug in our family."

Jude's hands went to his mouth in surprise even while he shot me an evil glare for the pug reference. "Look at how fat and adorable they are," he said in a high-pitched oh-my-god-puppies voice. "Are you serious, Wolfe? You sure you're okay with us getting a puppy?"

I smiled at his thoughtfulness, realizing he thought of us as a unit. That still took some getting used to.

"Absolutely. The girls have been out here playing with them all afternoon, so they might be able to give you some insight into their personalities."

Just then Simone stormed through the kitchen door to the backyard yelling into her phone. Her face was dark like thunderclouds.

"I don't want your fucking flowers, *jackass*. Take them to that whore I saw you with or shove them up your ass," she snapped before poking the phone screen with an angry finger.

"Yeah, right his sister. His sister, my ass," she muttered under her breath. "*Son of a bitch*."

Rebecca interrupted the mutterings. "Simone, honey, language around the girls," she said, tilting her head in the direction of Pete and Ginger's almost eight-year-old daughters. As if those girls hadn't heard more swear words in their tender years than a veteran sailor.

"Fuck. Sorry, Mom," Simone said.

I laughed. "Well done."

She turned and glared before noticing the pen full of heaven on the ground in front of her. "Oh my god, the puppies are here!"

By the time we all cuddled them into a puppy slumber, we returned to the kitchen to help Thomas finish prepping dinner.

Jude announced he had selected not one but both puppies.

Five Marians, including Jude's mom, handed me twenty bucks each.

Jude's eyes widened. "What the hell?"

I put my arms around him and kissed his forehead. "You know I love you, but you really are a sucker. I mean a softie."

"Are you pissed I couldn't pick just one?"

Simone snorted. "He said you'd want all four, but you'd compromise on two to keep the peace. That's when Mom decided to only bring home two in the first place to save poor Derek from a house full of dog shit."

I snapped my head around with a shushing sound. "Zip it, sister."

Jude burst out laughing. "Four? Where are the other two? Does that mean we get to take home four puppies?"

"Oh fuck no," I said quickly.

"Derek, language," Rebecca said through a laugh.

"Sorry," I muttered.

"What the hell are you sorry for?" Aunt Tilly asked as she walked in and plunked down some kind of nasty-looking gelatin salad.

"Hiya, hot stuff," I said before kissing her on the cheek. My new tactic with Tilly was "if you can't beat 'em, join 'em." I'd decided to kill her with sexy talk. It gave Jude the heebie-jeebies, which made it ten times more fun.

"Wolfe, you're looking predatory as usual. I promised the girls you'd be wearing swim trunks at some point today. Don't make a liar out of me," she teased, referring to Granny and Irene. The three old ladies tittered with excitement.

"You first, darlin'," I cooed. "Show me what you got."

Jude groaned.

Next came Griffin and Dante, who usually rode together from the city. They were arguing about something in an "am not, are too" kind of way.

Jude interrupted. "What are you two arguing about?"

Griff grabbed Simone and tucked her under his chin in a hug. I caught a glimpse of a tattoo I'd never noticed on his upper arm. All I could see was something that looked like a spiked tail disappearing under his sleeve toward his shoulder.

"Remember that piece I was writing about using terms of endearments when picking up guys in the clubs?"

"Yeah," Jude said.

"Well, the whole thing got shelved when I took that ghostwriting job in February. Now that I'm done, I decided to take it up again."

"Tell them about the bartender," Dante interjected.

Griff flipped him the bird.

"So I've done the pick-up thing at several clubs already and only need a few more nights of experimenting before starting the article. The bartender at Harry Dicks keeps eying me like I'm doing something wrong, and last night he finally pulled me aside to accuse me of—"

Dante interrupted again. "Who gives a shit? Tell them about wanting to have his babies."

Griff blushed. "Anyway, long story short, now I want to see him naked."

Aunt Tilly sighed, resting her chin in her hand. "Tell us more about this stud muffin. Does he have a tight ass?"

Granny chimed in. "More to the point, when are you gonna fuck him?"

Pete and Ginger's daughters never stood a chance at growing up surrounded by clean language.

Griff melted into a red-faced puddle of mortification.

After dinner, Jude and I wandered back outside to check on the puppies. He looked at the sleeping pups before turning his gaze up to mine. His warm brown eyes shone with happiness and my heart felt like it would explode.

"What should we name them?" I asked, wrapping my arms around him. I could never keep my hands off the man.

"Well, for sure one of them needs to be called Kale. I was thinking the other one could be Tofu. Or maybe—"

"Fuck you. Take it back."

He laughed. "I think we should wait until we get them home and spend some more time getting to know them."

"That's probably a good idea, but the names have to sound right with Marian."

Jude looked at me strangely. "Why? They're not just mine, they're ours together."

"I know. I just thought it would be easier if their last name was

Marian so that when I become a Marian, it won't be confusing for our poor pups."

I was ready for his leap before it happened, so I caught him under his ass with ease. His legs wrapped around my waist and he planted a giant kiss on my lips.

His face lit up in the full-Jude smile that made me grin like a fool. "You'd better fucking mean it," he warned me.

"Just say when, Bluebell."

Up next is Grounding Griffin! *Follow Jude's brother Griff as he takes flirting with the bartender to the next level.*
Want to read a steamy short featuring Beck, Jude's drummer? Check out Made Marian Shorts, *a collection of four short stories set in the Made Marian world!*

INVISIBLE
BY JUDE MARIAN

You stand behind me — Invisible
But I see your shadow.

You run beside me — Invisible
But I hear your footsteps.

You watch me, all-seeing — Invisible
But I see all of you.

Always watch over me like you do,
But who watches over you?

Protection Perfection — I need you.
You stand tall and walk proud — I walk with you.
Your green eyes are sparkling — I laugh with you.
Our words have a rhythm — Please share with me.

Always watch over me like you do,
And I'll watch over you.

DANCE WITH ME
BY JUDE MARIAN

When the music blares and the drumbeats boom,
Dance with me.

Bodies facing
Rhythm chasing
Dance with me.
Eyes are shining
Stars aligning
Dance with me.

When the springtime comes and the flowers bloom,
Play with me.
When autumn night is dark and the campfire glows,
Camp with me.
When our bodies chill as the winter wind blows,
Stay with me.

Bodies facing
Rhythm chasing
Dance with me.

Eyes are shining
Stars aligning
Dance with me.

If the summer comes and we're still in love,
Marry me.

Bodies facing
Rhythm chasing
Dance with me.
Eyes are shining
Stars aligning
Promise me.

LETTER FROM LUCY

Dear Reader,

Thank you for reading *Jumping Jude*. Jude and Derek continue to hold a special place in my heart, and I can't wait for you to read about the rest of the Marian family.

In the next book, Jude's brother has a big mouth that gets him into trouble. *Grounding Griffin* and the rest of the Made Marian books are out now! All Lucy Lennox novels can be read on their own but are more fun as a series.

Please take a moment to write a review of *Jumping Jude* on the site where you found it as well as Goodreads. Reviews can make all of the difference in helping a book show up in book searches.

Feel free to stop by www.LucyLennox.com and drop me a line or visit me on social media. To see inspiration photographs for all of my novels, visit my Pinterest boards.

Finally, I have a fantastic reader group. Come join us for exclusive content, early cover reveals, hot pics, and a whole lotta fun. Lucy's Lair can be found on Facebook.

Happy reading!

Lucy

ABOUT THE AUTHOR

Lucy Lennox is a mother of three sarcastic kids. Born and raised in the southeast, she now resides outside of Atlanta finally putting good use to that English Lit degree.

Lucy enjoys naps, pizza, and procrastinating. She is married to someone who is better at math than romance but who makes her laugh every single day and is the best dancer in the history of ever.

She stays up way too late each night reading M/M romance because that shit is hot.

For more information and to stay updated about future releases, please sign up for Lucy's author newsletter here.

Connect with Lucy on social media:
www.LucyLennox.com
Lucy@LucyLennox.com

WANT MORE?

Join Lucy's Lair
Get Lucy's New Release Alerts
Like Lucy on Facebook
Follow Lucy on BookBub
Follow Lucy on Amazon
Follow Lucy on Instagram
Follow Lucy on Pinterest

Other books by Lucy:
Made Marian Series
Forever Wilde Series
Twist of Fate Series with Sloane Kennedy
After Oscar Series with Molly Maddox
Licking Thicket Series with May Archer
Virgin Flyer
Say You'll Be Nine

Visit Lucy's website at www.LucyLennox.com for a comprehensive list of titles, audio samples, freebies, suggested reading order, and more!

www.ingramcontent.com/pod-product-compliance
Lightning Source LLC
Chambersburg PA
CBHW021311190726
48288CB00003B/799